Alistair Lavers

TREASURE TROVE

The *Whitborough* Novels

Matador
9 Priory Business Park,
Wistow Road, Kibworth Beauchamp,
Leicestershire. LE8 0RX
Tel: 0116 279 2299
Email: books@troubador.co.uk
Web: www.troubador.co.uk/matador
Twitter: @matadorbooks

ISBN 978 1784624 989

British Library Cataloguing in Publication Data.
A catalogue record for this book is available from the British Library.

Printed and bound in the UK by TJ International, Padstow, Cornwall
Typeset in 11pt Aldine401 BT by Troubador Publishing Ltd, Leicester, UK

Matador is an imprint of Troubador Publishing Ltd

Dedicated to Barry Sheene

Precursors

Whitborough Castle, England. July 1645.

Christopher Millar, armourer for the Royalist garrison at
Whitborough Castle, stood in front of a stout oak door,
within a small antechamber built from dressed sandstone
blocks. He turned his shoulders towards the daylight
which streamed weakly through the rippled glass of a
narrow leaded window a few feet away, as he sought the
key for the magazine and powder room on the great ring
attached to the loops on his belt.

'Where must itt be?' he muttered, rejecting another
long iron rod with a curious square tooth at its end. 'A
match for my eye,' he murmured, turning over several
more rough casts whilst chastising himself, struggling to
keep his fingers in the light.

Suddenly, the door next to the window burst open,
the hinges protesting with a dry metallic shriek, and a
young man with a dirty face, wearing a helmet too large
for his head fell into the room, snagging the vent of his
sleeve on the black iron door handle.

'Begging thy pardon sir!' he spluttered, off balance
and poorly sounding. 'I am Isaac.'

'Gather thy person and arrange thy posture, boy,'
said Millar, trying to suppress a smile that was out of

character. 'Soe – Isaac, the Devil himself hath come att oure gates – is this the newes thy feet soe hotly bring?' he enquired, his one good eye still focused on the ring. 'Will thou speak now of the right granted thee to batter downe my door without the courtesy of sounding the knocker? It hath not fallen from its boss, in peril from thy charge I pray? Or is it knavery you practice, with breathless cheek?'

'The Devil! Oh no, sir! The door was stiff, butt then itt gave in wyth such suddainesse, I…' the boy replied, gasping for breath, 'I was…'

'State thy business!' said Millar, 'when thy lungs are able to feed thy tongue properly. I will await thee here in the interim.'

'Master Millar, Lord Fothergill requests all officers and aldermen of the garrison attende him in Chapel,' declared a sergeant, appearing in silhouette before the doorway beside a small company of men.

'Come inside if thou wilt, Sergeant. There is room enough for many more souls to safely converse within these walls, I am certain. Or have thou come to take me by force should I refuse this young man?'

'Lord Fothergill asks that all who are called by him come as soon as they are able, sir. And not to speak of itt – my Lord hath summoned thee to meet Surgeon Burns, Captain Kilminster and Captain Lett there also. I am not come to take thee anywhere by force, Master Millar, butt to safeguard the messenger.'

'I think t'would be better then if thou kept him within sight, and did not hide behind oure masonry, Sergeant. Though perhaps tis well that thou art here in our company anyways. The boy seems to have lost his tongue presentlie, or there is something in the manner of my bearing wch has rendered him mute perchance? I have not seen such a look of wide-eyed perplexity since the eclypse. Thou have come as I am about my rounds, to replenish oure guns. This cannot be delayed?'

'The boy was instructed to say the matter is both important and urgent.'

'Very well. Thou may tell my Lord Fothergill I will attende him as soon as I have started Merrick in my stead.'

Minutes later, Millar entered the nave of the old Norman chapel within the castle's inner bailey. He took his ease on the front pew, in front of the great Saxon font with the most senior men from their depleted regiment, Captain Lett, of the foot, culverin and battery, and Surgeon Burns, commander of the pike men, cavalry and engineers. After exchanging a few words of condolence with his fellow officers and enquiring of their health, he lifted the patch over his injured eye and gently touched the wound underneath with the tips of his fingers, feeling the swollen skin for any discharge. He wondered whether the sight of it uncovered was the cause of the young messenger's discomfort, then he drew out a small jar, containing a preparation of honey and comfrey, and dabbed some of the mixture over the cut. Moments later Lord Fothergill came swiftly into their midst, emerging from the chancel in fevered conversation with his second in command, Captain Kilminster, and moved summarily to address them without fanfare or ceremony.

'Sirs, I have convened this meeting of thee, my most

loyal officers of qualitie in haste. So I must first apologise for taking thee from thy duties, but this is a matter of importance. Events here may soon overcome us, but this taske which I ask of thee will be central to the survival of oure cause. The day of accounts draws nigh. When this last northern stronghold that was entrusted to us falls to the Parliamentarians, there will be no force despatched to reverse the defeat. No reliefe will come. Pontefract and Newark have succumbed, though Skipton still holds.' He muttered, almost as an aside. 'Oure original regiment of seven hundred are now soe depleted or lame we cannot meet the enemy without on any terms that do us credit – the besiegers will overwhelm us in dayes. Ye will know this in your hearts as well as I. The condition of the wells is also foremost in my mind. Tonight, thou will take the last of the siege monies and a strongbox, which is the King's property, into hiding at Caytonne Bay. Bury itt then att the place marked on the mappe layd down now, upon the bench before us. Then ride to Nottingham Shire to find the King's Court att Southwell. Deliver my articles of letter to the King's counsel and take thine orders thence. Colonel Rowbotham and I will make a sally after dusk to attack Meldrum and his battery att the church, to set a calamity in their midst; if we are fortunate, they will have no place left them to fire upon us, that we cannot see plainly to fire upon them. I pray oure good courage will aid thy flight.'

'How will we leave, my Lord? We are encircled here – itt is not possible.'

'There are still wayes out of oure predicament, Mr Burns. Thou wilt descend the cliffes beside the south eastern tower in darkness, by oure stores of rope and rigging. There is safe passage by tunnel beneath the walls, from a secret room within the grain cellars here of wch we have possession, leading into the undercroft beneath the old chapel. Therein shall ye find an old stone stairwell beneath the hearth. Ascend the steps, then push aside the stone under the fire basket. When ye have all emerged, replace the stone and grate then dust the joint with ash and soote to conceal itt. A boat from Queen Henrietta's supply will awaite thee neere by the pie stone on the rocks below, and take thee thence from our midst. The moon has stepped into its first quarter tonight and there is much cloud. Thy cloakes and hattes will assist to conceal thee. The mariners awaiting thee in oure service have orders to take thee past Fraser's Reef on the seaward side. Thou will not be observed from land in the outer waters, and from the laste tongues of rock itt is butt a short passage to the bay.'

'May we know now thy wishes concerning the monies, if we are captured, my Lord?' asked Captain Lett.

'Oure Astrologer Metcafle hath assured me the stars augur well for success, but itt is wise to discuss these thinges. Ye are all learned men. Should oure enterprise be challenged then we have been betrayed. Butt know this, the strongbox cannot fall into the grasp of the Republicans. Itt is the fortune – the bribe the Spanish called the Treasure of the Mar del Norte, rescued from the Armada ship La Ramblas, wrecked on Filey Brigg some seven and fifty years since. The greatest summe of the monies were meant to buy the support of English

Catholics against oure Queen Bess. Now itt is for the king to use as he may.'

'I heard a great treasure from the Armada was entrusted to Sir Henry Kettlewell's family my Lord, itt is the same?' asked the Surgeon.

'I would know the name of the source by wch you came to this knowledge, Mr Burns, in the natural course of events. I pray that thou have not exchanged this knowledge with your fellowes. That is all I shall say on the matter. When we declared for the king, Sir Henry, as thou whilst remember, came to oure colours. The treasure did not degrade in his keeping, his was already a rich house; I am sure the strongbox was never opened by the family. His death was tragic, but many more good men have followed him, have they not? I will stay here and see out oure end, though there are scarce fifty of us remaining who are able and whole. I must see oure soldiers are ministered to and afforded appropriate recompense then for theire service. I shall hope to see thee in better times, if God sees fit to spare my life. Return to thy posts until ten of the clocke, then make thy ways here. My steward Shepley will see to the arrangements and guide thee through the tunnels to the cliffe.'

Late after sunset, Lord Fothergill and four of his musketeers emerged from the door to the inner courtyard of Whitborough Castle, at the end of the processional way which led down to the keep. The first section of the castle, behind the main gate, had been built in the shape of a hunting horn, cleverly constructed to constrict and slow any attacking force entering the inner walls through the front arch. Halfway along its length, a crenulated bar with five crossbow embrasures and pitch gutters divided the bottleneck beneath into three narrow passages, each with its own portcullis. Beyond this the narrow killing ground flared out like the neck of a yard of ale, terminating before a high flat wall over a small doorway.

The five men had all washed from buckets drawn from the remaining well, dried into the wind with linen mops, then dressed in their best shirts and jackets and combed their long hair, which fell untied over their shoulders from under dark wide-brimmed hats. Their belts, bandoliers and short tuck swords were covered under long cloaks which brushed their ankles, rippling in the breeze like weighted sails. Walking quickly in the darkness and shadow below the high walls, they moved down the cobbled incline under the bar towards the keep, stopping at the head of a small force of thirty men, wearing dark smocks and pantaloons, who bowed proudly before their commander. Those that had them wore capes of felt, wool or linen, and most of the platoon had smeared their hands and faces in soot or wore scarves to conceal their features.

'Men,' announced Lord Fothergill, 'the end of oure resistance here is nigh. We have only dayes or houres before the besiegers finish us. I am not inclined to parley, or be broken, like a moth on a shutter by the iron fist of their mortars and cannon, buried and crushed under a fall of stones. Tonight may be the last favourable juncture, at wch we may reply in kind to the murderous bombardment of the Parliamentarians and theire Cannon

Royale. I have drawn forth what strength we could well make to send a sally tonight into the church under cover of darkness, to sett a match in theire powder and blow theire gunnes back into the bosom of hell from whence they came. Oure position is grave, but we can still strike oure foes while we may. I do not ask that thou follow me in this last adventure out of duty; ye may stay until we are forc'd to concede. Those of us who will come butt have matchlocks must exchange theire weapons for firelock muskittes, so no flame will betray oure approach. What saith thee now – will ye fight or nay?'

'Itt is not a slight thing that thou aske, my Lord. For if we destroy the church in this act, do we not make war against God also? No man here would covet the displeasure of almighty God afore the moment of his death, if we should die, my Lord,' said Matthew James, the garrison's carpenter, one of the walking wounded.

'All goode men here have all been firing into the nave, have they not?'

'Yes my Lord, but the act of bringing itt to ruine sits ill with us all.'

'I desire to know, Lord, whether we are to speak freely,' asked Gabriel Jugg, another of his veterans.

'The Church of St Mary ceased to be a house of God when Lord Fairfax and his army used it to shelter their ordnance, James. There will be none here amongst thee to ably prosecute an opposing argument for sound reasons – theires is the sin and the blasphemy. No such judgement or shame can be laid upon oure occupation. We will merely bring to an end the desecration of oure church, and one day – if we are spared – we may see the building of another on its foundacons. Tonight, four of oure distinguished men will break out and seek the King's Court. Oure attack will give them the spur they need to escape the district and ride south. I pray we shall destroy their gunnes and ensure they are not used on oure armyes in the south. If we are successful, – ye are free men. Escape how thou wilt after oure sally, may thou prosper whithersoever thou goest. I shall go into captivity to oversee the terms and the ministrations afforded oure wounded.'

The platoon made no protest, but nor did they give their consent in words, though the silence gave away their feelings for the church where many of them had been baptized and which had been worshipped in for generations. Lord Fothergill did not press them immediately, but met their gaze with stubborn conviction, reverently removing his hat, so his soldiers could look upon his face. One by one the men acquiesced, shook hands and said their goodbyes.

'Master Gray! Are the ladders assembled?'

'They are, my Lord, and hydden in the shadows, as you asked.'

'Then before we depart, let us say a prayer for oure deliverance, for oure fallen, oure crippled, and oure families.'

A lightning bolt flashed down from the dark fleece of cloud massing on the horizon, the first declaration of an approaching storm. The peal of thunder from its report rolled morbidly across the water, like the low baritone growl of an earthquake ratcheting up its power. It was soon followed by a second discharge, arcing over the dark waters of the bay.

From their elevated position on the south east corner of the headland, the four officers of the garrison, Lord Fothergill's steward and hand could see for miles in all directions under its light. All natural details within their sight were at once visible, before the panorama was swallowed up again by the night.

Another brace of interlinked flashes in the wound-purple foothills of a monstrous cumulo-nimbus cloud earthed simultaneously beneath the cliff. Each fresh thunderclap building upon the last, becoming one monstrous rumble, the molten silver lances of lightning becoming too numerous to count, dividing the sky into a cracked vision of ash grey shards, tinted with crimson fire.

Ambrose Shepley, Lord Fothergill's steward, looked out over the sea with anxious eyes, removing his cap to better gauge the strength of the wind, though not a drop of rain had fallen to his nervous face.

'We best convey thee to the ropes, sirs, afore the storm vents itts fury on our skulles.'

'We hold faste, until we heare the attack begin,' said Captain Lett in a stentorian tone.

'Aye, we muste wait yet,' added Master Millar.

'The matter of the lightning, sirs, the windes…'

'On the water we will not be soe easily glympsed.' mused Surgeon Burns, looking up at the sky and then again at the sea. 'The windes will aid us, Shepley,' he said, raising his voice above the gusts, addressing the steward but looking to the horizon. 'Itt blows strong and true from north to south. We shall have the wind astern. Twill add the power of four men to oure oars.'

Before Ambrose had the chance to protest, the sound of many muskets discharging in the distance reached their ears, signalling that the attack on St Mary's had begun.

'Gentlemen, please,' beseeched their guide. 'We must goe now, afore the storm is upon us. We have strong sacks to carry your muskittes, and swords laid out before the ropes. Tis a hard descent, weighed down by armes when the windes stir here. I entreat you to goe down the least encumbered by loose articles. Make haste sirs, we have butte a short interval.'

'We shall accept thy counsel in the spirit it is meant, Shepley,' replied Captain Kilminster. 'Let us go now with the steward, men.'

A sudden dramatic explosion on the far side of the curtain wall close to the Barbican gate checked their movement momentarily, before their party moved off. Master Millar crossed himself and looked to the steward.

'I pray oure Lord has spiked theire gunnes,' said Millar offering his hand. 'If you should meet with him agayne. Praise be to God if he survives, convey to him oure most fervent congratulations, Ambrose.'

'Oure blessings to thee, Master Millar. I will do that sir, be of no doubt.'

The party reached the ropes and began to uncouple their weapons. Captain Lett and Surgeon Burns knelt down on the damp grass and began testing the strength of the ropes which had been secured around the stout stones of an old window aperture inside the ruined Roman blockhouse near the cliff.

'The ropes are good for oure purpose?' asked Captain Kilminster, looking again to Shepley.

'Made by the best of hands sir, here in the port. There is a lattice of rigging tied to theire ends to aid thy purchase on the scree below, though the slopes are a smoother prospect than we would have to suffer on the north cliffe. I wish thee God's speed, Captain.'

'I muste thank thee for the service thy have done us, Shepley. If we do not meet again, do thy best for oure men. God sees thy works.'

'That I will sir, goodbye then. May the Almighty watch over thee also.'

In a minute the four officers had disappeared from view, leaving Ambrose and his young hand Daniel to tie up the sacks of pistols, swords and carbines, and weigh the two strong boxes, checking the strength of the knots before they lowered them down to the rocks after the escapees.

'Tis a bad omen, this storm, young Daniel,' he grumbled, clutching a bundle of arms to his chest. 'I wish I too was gone from this place and had my free libertie once more. There has been too great an effusion of good Christian blood here, the great tower is a ruine. What has been gain'd? Yea, itt will not do us good to ponder on it,' he grumbled bitterly. 'When the slight ropes are slackened, gather them up with the rigging and pack them into coils. We shall convey the heaviest of them last, then stow them in the undercroft at the chapel.'

The first droplets of rain began to fall over the shore, pattering upon the sandstone talus fields at the foot of the high cliffs behind Fraser's reef, where the Gryphon, a shallop of fifteen years, rode the churning currents mauling its hull, like a spirited horse struggling against its bridle, tethered to an enormous oak beam set in the rock. Only eight of her crew of twelve were aboard. Four remained at their oars whilst the others had scaled the straining nets lashed to the rock of their mooring to come ashore, spreading themselves out amongst the great rocks in the vicinity. Armed and alert, searching for the approach of the escapees. The pie stone, from which they had made land, lay at the front a huge outcrop of rock in the shape of a drum at the face of the headland. Unique amongst the other many shards and boulders surrounding it, for its smooth face and flat surface. Hidden from sight from the seaward side by the reef and inaccessible by land, it was used as a temporary mooring only by the most skilled local seamen, as the scouring rip tides funnelled between the reef and the shore made the landing treacherous to all but the most experienced.

Jacob Akin, owner of the Gryphon, watched the uneven progress of the four men he had agreed to transport on the edge of sight, weighed down by arms and two strongboxes under the lights of the storm. 'They are neare,' he called to the lookouts. 'Uncover thy lanterns and see them to the thwarts.'

Jacob turned his back on the high cliffs and returned to his boat, holding the folds of his cloak against the building wind and rain, hesitating briefly at the gunwale before making the leap from the rock onto the padded hemp mats laid down at the bottom of the keel to cushion their fall. Strong currents surged past the transom, relentlessly agitating the boat. The rain began to descend in great sweeps and the sky darkened as their party was ushered to the edge of the stone. Jacob took his own lantern from under his cloak and hung the light from a hook fixed to the mast and waited for the approach of his human cargo.

'Are there others to come?' he called to the black-cloaked strangers as they came into sight above him on the ledge.

'We are foure,' replied Captain Lett. 'Officers and Aldermen of the garrison.'

'I am Jacob. Thy may come down, butt thou must leap from the lip. We have mats below with wch to soften thy fall. Wait for the boat to rise upon the swell, then make thy leap. Twill shorten the drop.'

'We have boxes and sacks of armes, we cannot toss them downe. Are there nets or rope below?'

'I have a gutter for such work. My crew will send them downe after you are seated.'

'Two of us will see oure possessions are properly conveyed here, before we come aboard,' said Master Millar.

'I too will stay ashore to oversee,' said Captain Lett, determinedly.

'As ye wish,' replied Jacob. 'Stand away from the ledge, sirs, I am passing up the guttering. Summon my men to the edge to receive it if ye will.'

When the luggage had been stowed, and their guests were huddled grimly together behind the bow, a young man in a short blouson and wide pantaloons came forward to address them. 'Sirs, the sea is wrought and tempestuous against us this night; we may suffer more of the blows of ittes furys before we are landed,' explained Emile, who introduced himself as Jacob's son. 'I would counsel thee to remain seated and let us have the run of oure ship until we reach safe waters. If thou art close to an oar lock or any such projections within, on which thee can find a strong purchase whilst we are in the channel, then ye are welcome to employ them.'

'Does he imply that we may become wetter before we make land? I am a man, not a fish?' scowled Captain Lett smirking disdainfully. 'We may all be drown'd yet for want of a tail.'

'At least the air is warm, Daniel,' replied Millar, his voice flat and low, while his eyes passed over the fishermen.

'Look well now upon theire postures…' said Captain Kilminster quietly.

'The cudgels?' asked Millar, bringing his gloved hand up to his nose to muffle his voice.

'Ay, the boy revealed theire purpose in his clumsiness, when he upset the covered basket as we came aboard, a wholly unnatural reaction if theire concealment was of no consequence. They mean to overpower us, then toss us into the waters.'

'We wait then, til we are in a calmer locality. I propose we deplete theire numbers, before theire hands be upon us, then keep the rest on the point of our swords,' whispered Kilminster, drawing a finger across his throat.

'Agreed,' added Millar.

'Leave the master of the vessel to my blade,' whispered Captain Lett. 'I will subdue him first. With their captain bled, we can reduce the rest then to oure obedience.'

Jacob called his son to cut their ties to the rock with his falchion, then braced himself in the stern pulpit to guide the Gryphon through the channel. His crew bent hard to their oars with the current, flayed by the rain and spray as they ran with the wind, their taut lines humming like bowstrings, launched over the chop towards the broiling surf at the point of Fraser's reef.

'Come around beauty,' prayed Jacob, waving a square of bleached cloth aloft momentarily for the eyes of his crew, whilst struggling to hold the boat's rudder true as his crew reversed their oars on his signal. They slowed the boat sufficiently to make the turn onto the seaward side of the reef, before they were dashed against the rocks or funnelled past the breach in the reef to the leeward side.

'Over now!' shouted Emile, seeing his father fall on the rudder; driving men from the starboard oars to the outer planks on the port side, shifting their centre of mass and helping the boat make its turn, lowering the profile of the hull before they were blown proud of the water into the wind and capsized.

The port topside of the Shallop dove hard into the surf, her groaning planks trembling under the battering of the sea as the bow thrust and cleaved through the rough confluence of waters, almost inundating the foredeck before they caught the run of the current out to sea and the Gryphon righted herself.

'Emile – two to baile! To oars slow!' cried Jacob from the tiller, directing the crew to clear the bilges and take up a slow rhythm on their oars.

'I am disembowelled,' groaned Master Millar, raising

a pallid and sweaty face to the storm, looking as though he were about to vomit. 'If we should live through this, I sweare I shall never sett out into this cursed bay agayne.'

'Thou have matched my thoughts most eloquently Christopher. I fervently pledge to honour the sentiment,' added the surgeon, through pursed lips. 'I confess I am a breath from emptying my belly o'er the side of this wretch'd vessel.'

'A man to me – take steerage!' called Jacob from the stern.

'Be ready,' hissed Captain Lett, his hand going to the hilt of the tuck sword beneath his cloak.

'Not yet, Daniel. They will not move against us until they see us safe through the currents here, or we should all perish. Have patience, we will see what the traitor has to say and hide our hearts yet.'

'Michael will come, Papa, we are ankle deep at the beam,' called Emile, reassuring his father they now had a tolerable amount of water in their bilge for one man to break from bailing and go astern. Jacob waited for Michael to reach him at the tiller, then stood and exchanged positions, giving him his instructions. Then made his way forward over the boom and ballast lockers and into the company of his human cargo, huddled together under their cloaks.

'I am grateful for thy timely arrival, sirs,' said Jacob addressing his guests in his booming voice. Itt is not a place to waite on a night such as this, but we are on course outside the reef, one and a quarter leagues from thy deliverance. The sea is more gentle on our bowels from this point, but if you muste evacuate thyselves please convey thy swill to the waters and not defile oure bilges. I am certain we shall be in calm waters at Caytonne Bay within the houre. We will row ashore and meet thy horses on the flood tide, lest we are stranded on the sandbar. I pray we shall all be safely landed.'

'Oure thanks for thy good words, Jacob. Where will thou goest when we have made land?' asked Kilminster.

'We shall endeavour to make passage to Flamborough, then make shore if the storm does not worsen, if the cross sea does not trap us in the bay, gentlemen.'

'Who awaites us att oure journey's end, Jacob?' asked Millar, fighting his nausea. 'What was the arrangement?'

'A cousin of Lord Fothergill made the contract. His name was Drake. Hannibal Drake. We were tolde we would be paid an ingot of silver after thou were landed. Though I have misgivings about the arrangements, I must confess I did not like this fellow. He seemed to me no less trustworthy than a brigand, sirs. I can read a man well enough, thou must apprentice thy crew well to survive the sea. My feeling was the man would cut my throat for a pauper's purse, if we had met in Tuthill Vale and I was the stranger. I would not sign such a contract agayne so readily, my crew are God-fearing men, sir, butt the old superstitions die hard. They would not have set out on such a night as this, but we are contracted. I gave my word. They bade me fetch a basket of cudgels, butt I know not why, though I am glad of theire weight for this night season. It has helped us make the turn afore the reef.'

'Thou hath taken armes, as a Souldier?' asked Lett.

'I did, sir. One of the foote that marched proud from

Helmsley for Sir John Crossland. I protected oure battery of gunnes for three dayes and lost two fingers. Two of oure drakes we brought here on oure leaving. The castle was slighted for both sides after we had yielded, as part of the conditions for accepting the articles of truce and of the handover, to ensure it would not be held against the king. I desired to be in the garrison here with the hundred, but my hand is not fit for even the militia. I was not allwaies a souldier; the sea is my master agayne now sirs. I was a mariner before I took armes, this is my domain, my son's.'

Hannibal Drake reached into his old battered satchel and withdrew a balding ash-handled brush and a grimy bone comb from its stale depths. Deciding the comb was likely the better of the two articles for grooming, he returned the brush, which was now more of a keepsake, to his satchel, then proceeded to drag the comb's sullied teeth through the dark tangle of hair falling over his eyes, moving front to back, parting his thick mane of black hair, tucking the longest handfuls behind his ears while he looked carefully up and down the wide earth track of Cayton high street. Nearby, outside the Bell Inn, a row of dogs and mules waited for their masters, tethered to a long pole upon old stone pillars, polished with grease and soot. An old shire horse, some sixteen hands tall, stood patiently at the end of the line, seemingly asleep. Steam flared from its nostrils in great coils, like water vapour from the neck of a simmering jug.

Satisfied he was presentable, Hannibal pushed open the door of the inn. He removed the dung from his boots and stepped down onto the flagstones within. Immediately a cheer went up, accompanied by much laughter from the crowd arranged around the hearth inside, and the noise of many hands clapping the ale-stained bench tops.

Hannibal, who preferred to live in the shadows and was ill at ease in a crowd, set his face in a scowl and hurried past his tormentors to where he had arranged to meet his younger sibling, at the back of the inn in the stalls, behind a stack of large barrels which served to divide the public space at the front from the men's bar at the rear.

'Why is my presence the cause of such mirth, brother?' demanded Hannibal, finding his man, then looking into the neighbouring closets for any evidence of occupation. 'Why do I endure taunts and ridicules in my own hostelry – answer me!'

'Ridicule, brother? Itt should not be so, do they not celebrate your good fortune? Oure elevation?'

'Oure elevation? Good fortune! What say thee? Do not think thou may jest soe – explain thy riddles afore I smite thy petty mouth and gory locks.'

'I should not agree be struck for advancing oure prosperity! I have bought us the most magnificent horse in the district, for the same monies as a man may pay for donkey Hannibal.'

'The plough horse without?'

'He is called Hercules.'

'And I call thee dimwit… boy.'

'Thou mark me a dunce?'

'Thou have been a fool brother and have made me

the same by thine idiocy; tis no wonder I am jeered so bravely. When I instructed thee to purchase a beast of burden for oure enterprise, I did not mean thy should purchase the biggest mountain of horse-flesh in the parish. We are bound for Elvenhome ravine, not a meander across the fields of the Carrs behind plough and reins.'

'The smith said he is not only the equal of six mules, butt we may sell his dung at a proffit.'

'Ay, and thy shall be rich in dung to thy knees. I should not care if it soiled thy cods for a yeare each morn. Thou will walk oure leviathan back into the custodie of that scoundrel and demand he returne oure money now, or so help me I will beat thy braines out. If he refuses, you may warn him I will make sure to send notice to the magistrates, informing them he is hoarding stolen blades and has repayered the gates of Caytonne Hall with pig iron.'

'Now, Hannibal?'

'Now, Symon. This is thy small ale?' he asked, darkly, seizing the leather cup on the planks of their bench and throwing the brown liquid over the floor. 'Thou should have drunk it out. Be at the place we are due, with two mules of good stock, panniers and bridles and I will forget thy foolishness. I am done with wordes. Begone!'

'There is no moon to see theire boat by the headland, Samuel. Where are Hannibal and Symon?'

'Thou knowest as much as I, brother. We must pray they are neare with oure armes.'

'I care not for this place, itt is said devils slake theire

thirst in the brook, and conspire to muddle the minds of men.'

'Do not trust in all ye are tolde.'

'Tis true. The parson says Hannah Bramley was bewitch'd in its depths.'

'The parson tells all the little ones in the district itt is a place of satyrs, goblins and witches who wouldst afflict theire humours and enslave theire minds. Tis all nonsense. The parson is a man like ourselves, and uses scholarly deceit to protect his interests. A smugglers' ravine itt is, and shall be still. There are no night terrors in its clutches. Naught is convoyed here that is not controlled by affaires of men.'

'I should not be as certain.'

'Enough. Learn ye well how he tells his lies so prettily. I will have no more wordes from thee other than those wch concern our predicament. Think ye now of nothing else. We shall have oure fill of danger before the houre is done, and no room for melancholy fancies. We are four and they are six, itt gives me no comfort. If we have no surprise we shall surely die by these men. We must have oure mindes sett.'

'Hark… I hear a partee of horses below…'

'Ay, and we are still only two. It muste be the horses of the Kinges men.'

'If Hannibal and Symon are lost, what shall we do?'

'We go back to our hearths. Or go to the inn. I will have our monies, whether we are used or nay. I am doubtful those whoome we seek to robb can be seen. I cannot see the hands at the ends of my cuffs. Make safe thy pistoll, for the moment.'

Jacob steered the Gryphon deftly between the rocks and sandbanks to a stretch of calm water in the mouth of Cayton Bay, watching the hand signals from two of the elder men of his crew at the prow, who checked the waters and depth under their keel with weighted lines every few yards. A train of ten horses, led by four riders waiting at the edge of the surf, began to move out into the bay towards their boat, the men steadying the more nervous animals with soothing words and hands.

'Be ready to stand in the boat, sirs. Thy horses are neere in the surf.' said Jacob. 'We dare not drift further, or we may ground and be stranded. Emile! Sett a lamp to the cross beam. You are free to untye thine armes gentlemen. I wish thee Godes speed.'

Twenty minutes later, the Gryphon turned and began to track a course back into the open sea, whilst the four officers of the garrison rode off the sands at a gallop, chivvying their mounts onto the pebble-encrusted slopes and ruts of the clay escarpment, leading to Elvenhome ravine and the shelter of the woods. Then suddenly a gun discharged in the darkness. A horse stumbled heavily, and four pistols answered swiftly in exchange...

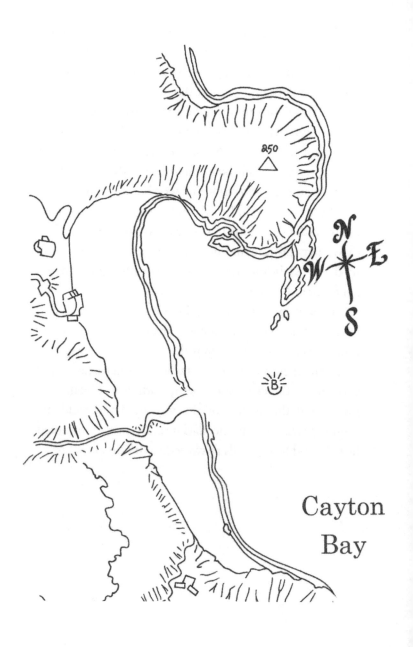

250

N
W E
S

B

Cayton

Bay

Chapter One

Monday

Dusk on the Yorkshire Coast. Three miles south of Landkey Island, 1983.

'I don't like this. I don't like this at all. It gives me the creeps, this place.'

'I know you don't wanna be 'ere, lad – but when you owe someone a favour, it's them that chooses how you pay 'em back; and stop bellyaching, you're starting ta mek me miserable an' all.'

'Sorry, Neil.'

'It wouldn't be my choice for a first date either, son, but we'll just have to grin and bear it, won't we? You can make friends with your feet again later. I did tell you to bring some wellies with you Robert, didn't I?'

'Couldn't you get a bigger boat?'

'This is the boat we've got.'

'It's bloody tiny. Are you sure we're gonna be safe in this?'

'Any bigger, we wouldn't be able to carry it. Or hide it. She's a Pevensey Angler. Lovely little thing she is. Like the skiffs I used to take you and your brother fishing in, on the Torridge. Remember?'

'Yeah, but it were a lot warmer than this place. I miss Polruan. I miss home…'

'If only your mother had learnt to be more discreet…'

'Yeah, well. Anyway, why am I doing all the rowing?'

'Because you're young – and I need to see where we're going. Try and cut your oars in on the blade edge like I showed you. You won't stir up the water so much. We need to be as quiet as possible. Invisible preferably. Noise carries a long way on the water, especially around here.'

'Looks quiet enough to me.'

'Always be vigilant, son. No Rudding's sat in court in four generations. Because?'

'Because we're smart?'

'Exactly.'

'Is *this* smart?'

'This is work. Now listen, enough of the backchat, in a few minutes we'll be in position, level with Camel's Hump,' he said, giving a nod to the dark outline of a huge mound of sandstone on the promontory to the north of the bay. 'Keep the hill on your left shoulder, and the buoy ahead in the middle of your chest. Don't let us drift and we'll be all right. There's a lot of jagged hard stuff under the surface. That means rocks… Hand me those glow sticks from that locker under yer backside.'

Traffic Policemen Clifford Dodds and Justin Deighton were relaxing in their patrol car, at the start of their shift on the long layby in front of Cayton Boatbuilders' workshop on Lower Gunstone, the main easterly route into Whitborough.

'Justin! Stir yourself, we're off traffic.'

'Huh! What? Did I nod off? Oh God…'

'There's a fire on the plateau beside Kenwith Woods,

2

above Cayton Bay. The Coastguard called in, and we're short stick. Did you check the maglites when you did the vehicle checks, Justin?'

'What's the big fuss? It'll just be kids. That lot from Beech Close and Southwold are always down there come spring. Making bloody mischief and chucking rocks at each other... God I'm so tired...'

'The torches, Justin?'

'Yeah, the mags are good.'

'The mags are *good*?'

'I mean the batteries are fine. They're fine!'

'Do you know their families, are they friends of yours?'

'I know a few of the parents. One of 'em told me they'd dug a pit trap last summer, because they'd seen one in some boy's comic, Warlord or something. Anyway, three ramblers were on the same track later that night and fell straight in the bloody thing. Two broken ankles, a broken wrist and fractured jaw. The little bastards were going back after school the next day to put stakes in the bottom.'

'What a wonderful story. The pictures would have made a lovely vignette for Orienteering Monthly. Have they ever started any bonfires?'

'The odd one or two – old rope and driftwood, paint cans, aerosols and pallets doused in lighter fuel. You know what kids are like.'

'Well, according to control this one is big. They must have been working on it for a while. A ring of fire. Johnny Cash, Justin.'

'Johnny Cash? Have we had him?'

'Johnny Cash is a giant of American music, Justin. Not some juvenile pyromaniac. Start the car.'

3

They came together slowly, in small groups and pairs from the patchy canopy of Kenwith Wood, onto the dark grassy plateau overlooking the sea. The Coven, formerly known as the Whitborough and district Isodora Duncan Free Dance Society, which was bright and gay no longer, but corrupted and damned, though they could still summon a very fine waltz.

The company of men and women, sinister and anonymous under dark hooded shrouds, formed themselves into a circle, within the ring of glowing embers in the centre of the plateau, spacing themselves around two figures, one tall and blond, the other short and rotund. The bright sickle of the waning moon shone down through the mountainous spring cloudbanks, tinting the landscape with a frost of white silver. In the trees, an owl cleared its throat, and a vixen watched its litter roll and tumble in the weeds and long grass on the verdant edge of the wood. It was a perfect, still spring evening.

'The hour is come,' remarked the Grand Wizard, Cornelius Agrippa, observing the position of the stars beyond the clouds. Derek Beautimann LLB, of Beautimann, Buerk and Trippe, was a complex and secretive man of many faces, solicitor, partisan squash player, occasional shoplifter and budgerigar murderer. Father to Samuel and Grace, partner of Sophie and ex-husband of Samantha. Lately elected Master of Ceremonies and Grand Wizard of the Black Hand Coven, a difficult and diverse group of individuals, whose collective conversion to the dark side had been long, bitter and much debated.

'Who's brought the cat?' he asked, looking to his deputy Mother Shipton for some signal or gesture, though she

4

dodged his eyes in a way which implied she had become an accomplice to mischief, or worse.

'We need to tie off the rope first, Derek,' she said, deflecting his question.

'Don't call me that. We're not at work, for God's sake!' hissed the Master of Ceremonies.

Two of their party, whose hearing was most acute, nudged each other knowingly. Very slowly, their heads began to shake.

'See to the fire there! And close the circle…' barked their leader, his dignity pricked, directing two of his other apostles to task.

'Who's brought the cat?' he repeated, more forcefully than before. But still there was no recognition or acknowledgement forthcoming from his audience, and the silence stretched out before them like a widening rift. The Grand Wizard drew back his disguise, revealing a frayed, though authoritative countenance, and a once handsome face, slowing losing the fight against age and gravity.

'Well, where is it?' he demanded, covering up the few lonely blonde hairs around his crown under a dull lead skull cap.

His deputy, Mother Shipton, wiggled her toes on the sandy grass and began to fidget nervously, tugging her hood further down over a guilty expression, as plain as the hairy mole on the side of her face. A nervous coughing broke out from the far side of the circle, although it did not appear to be the voice of rescue he was expecting. The Grand Wizard ignored his instincts and used the interruption to reassert his authority.

'You there! What ails you? Speak up…' he shouted.

'Look, we're not really going to bleed a cat are we?' came

5

a voice, which was female, coarse as sacking and backed up by a low rhythm of rebellious whispering.

'She's right she is! Good old Ann… Fighting talk.'

'Poor wee puss.'

'Bloodthirsty barstudds, wull nay stand forritt!' came another voice of dissent, from north of the border.

Caught off balance, the Master of Ceremonies stole another glance at his deputy, expecting an explanation. Though she was still staring intently at the ground, clearly ashamed by the revolt in their constituency, but too embarrassed to face the music.

'We all appreciate…' continued the voice, rising in volume and conviction, '…that you and Mauree…er Mother Shipton and certain others…' (there was an outbreak of hissing) '…want us to be as traditional as possible, and we understand that.' (More hissing). 'But this sort of thing,' she almost shouted, 'it's just not on! The majority of us here would like it to be known that we object to any sort of cruelty to animals… don't we, brothers?'

'And sisters!' snapped Madame Blavatsky.

'Now just a minute!' protested their leader.

'Here! Here!' vociferated the animal loving majority of the coven, save Gilles de Rais and Doctor Faustus, who were trying to persuade a short person dressed as Humpty Dumpty that they had come to the wrong fancy dress party. Emboldened by the effect of their protestations and the release of tension, the rebels took stock and awaited a conciliatory response from their leaders.

'Tonight,' began the Wizard with a tinge of trepidation, 'we invoke Tetarzepamdomestoz – demon lord of mines, caves and underground places – to obtain…'

6

'Must be a relative of that Marxist gobshite from the NUM,' quipped Casanova, to no one in particular.

'To obtain…' continued the Wizard, struggling over the chattering. 'The lost location of Sir Henry Kettlewell's civil war treasure trove, the famous lost gold hoard of the Spanish Armada!'

There was an audible gasp of admiration from one quarter and then more chattering, at which point the Master of Ceremonies took control and stretched out his arms, appealing for the attention of his rebellious underlings.

'For this, brothers and sisters, we require a blood sacrifice!'

'He's not giving up the butcher's block is he?' grumbled Nostradamus, as more whisperers joined the fray.

'I really miss our early days, Jamie,' sighed the Compte de St Germain, touching the cuff of his neighbour. 'The clever conjuring, the Latin incantations, the ceremonial wine…'

'Our bacchanalian nights? Or was it Benji's lime pickle?' added his friend, recalling their shared memories.

'Where did the love go? Where! Now it's blood, death and fire, every Tuesday and Friday! I can't stand it, Jamie. You stay, out of some misguided sense of loyalty and the hope that things might go back to the way they were. Is that deluded? Am I deluded? Now, after two years of scheming and trickery we're stood in a field watching some past-his-prime solicitor waving an ugly iron dagger about, like James Herriot's Jack the Ripper. It's just appalling.'

'Keep your chin up, Ron,' replied Thrice Great Hermes, controller of Beehive Taxis. 'I've got it on good authority that this useless bastard's time is up tonight. We're going to have ourselves a Scottish coup.'

'Really? Oh how Shakespearian!' he chortled. 'You're such a *naughty* boy! Who's to be Brutus?'

'That's enough!' shouted the Master of Ceremonies. 'This is not a debating society. We are the Black Hand Coven! The most feared satanic society in the north of England. You will show me due reverence…'

'In the north of this wood,' sniped Casanova.

'May I remind you all,' continued the Wizard, ignoring the chit chat, 'you have made an oath with your souls. We will not compromise the integrity and purpose of this gathering, to placate the soft sensibilities of those among us who would forget their obligations at the first mention of a little bloodletting,' he said, trying to browbeat his audience with his oratory.

'Oh what the feck's he on about,' groaned Alice Besant to Madame Blavatsky who was close enough to have her ear.

'I can't make out the whole of it dear, as he's a lawyer and they don't talk straight,' she said in her soft Devonshire accent. 'But it don't look like good noos for the cat.'

'Can we get on, now we've all had our say?' said Mother Shipton, who had suddenly decided to plant her flag and join the debate. 'I'm sure we all want to help the master and get things moving, don't we?'

'Thank you so much for your support,' sneered the Master of Ceremonies. 'It's so good to have you on side – at last,' he spat, with menacing sarcasm.

'I'm not sure if we want to *get on*, if we're going to be murdering cats,' said Witch Penrose, putting her arm around Humpty Dumpty. 'And if he ever touches one of my familiars I'll ram my broomstick up his arse,' she snapped, not bothering to modulate her voice. 'Ain't that right, sonny?'

she said, softly patting the pink paper maché dome of her new friend.

'Yes miss…'

'So this stuff we're picking up, is it gonna fit in here with us, in this boat?'

'Don't be rude about the boat, it's keeping your backside dry. As for the cargo, your Uncle Brian wouldn't say. Though I can guess. Some more of those black market giddy up tablets… Actually I do know, Robert, but I like to be mysterious. Antibiotic steroids or summat like that. He sells 'em to doormen – mostly. Personally I can't understand the attraction – it makes a bloke look like someone's stuck an airline up their arse and pulled the trigger.'

'So what do they do with these pills?'

'Well Robert, they take 'em… and they work out, and they get bigger. If they eat right.'

'Yeah, I know that, but…'

'Do they shove 'em up their backsides, do you mean son? Well, why waste a perfectly good mouth, albeit one that's probably got a chicken burger stuffed in it? Are you concentrating on where we are?'

'Justin, are you paying attention?'

'I'm all ears, Clifford.'

'Don't call me Clifford. Did you pack the radios?'

'In the holdall, with the maglites.'

'Get the black cap covers out too. I'll take the Brita handheld and the lens diffuser. We'll need some illumination, but not too much. Can't let the chickens see the fox, can we

9

now? Call in now and let them know we're leaving the car, to conserve the portables. Are you set?'

'Aye, I'm peachy.'

'Where's me sausage rolls?'

'There's the speedboat, Robert. We're in business. Put the fishing rod together and open the bait box though, just in case. I'll be glad to get back tonight. I've got a nice bottle of malt and a warm armchair to put down some roots into. They should have two black Mercury engines astern and a Sea Ray logo in-between, if it's our friends. And if all's well they'll have put a Roadrunner dog toy on the prow. If they've not been followed.'

'Don't you want the bin liners and the tie wraps yet?'

'Not yet son, oh – and by the way – you don't need to say anything. In fact, it'd be a good idea if you didn't. Just keep yer gob shut and keep us in position, and hopefully we'll stay off the reef on the way back.'

Back on the plateau, the warriors of Satan were beginning to split into factions.

'What about a vole, or a rabbit?' suggested Pythagoras, wading in for the carnivores, running his thumb down the edge of a bowie knife as long as his forearm.

'Or a guinea pig?' added Aleister Crowley.

'A guinea pig? Who's brought a bloody guinea pig!' spluttered MacBeth, trying to contain his laughter.

'Well, we're here to kill summat. Our Janice says cats kill more birds than all the bloody shotguns in Scotland, and she should know, she's in the RSPB. Am I right? Let's kill the cat and save some birds. I don't think that's unreasonable…' complained Aleister.

'I'm with Aleister, let's off the cat. Me, I'm a dog man anyway – my dog never pisses on our carpets,' said Doctor Dee, decisively.

'Hold on,' said Gilles de Rais. 'We could use our own bodily fluids, not just blood, other stuff, secretions... oh come on – wake up! Do I have to spell it out?' he implored, after an interval of confused silence trying to provoke a reaction.

'OH YEAH! – I love a bit of possession, me!' crowed Apollonius of Tyana, as the penny dropped.

'And lots of positions...' gushed Casanova.

'Has anyone got some protection?' enquired Lord Byron.

'Now just a minute!' protested the Grand Wizard, trying to halt the runaway train.

'What Cornelius was about to say – if you'd all be so good as to listen...' piped up Mother Shipton, 'was... we can spare the cat, if one of you gentlemen can spare his juices.'

'Oh was I indeed!' snapped their leader, then more quietly... 'Since you're my deputy, may I remind you that I make the decisions?' he hissed.

'Honestly Derek, you are blind sometimes,' she whispered. 'Things aren't going our way, in case you hadn't noticed. So let's compromise a little before we have an outbreak of anarchy, and keep our seats, shall we?'

'I can handle the bickering perfectly well on my own. I'll let you handle the ejaculations.'

'Oh that's charming, that is. Women's work, is it?'

'Here he comes, have you got your gloves on, Robert?'

'I could do with a break from these oars, Neil. My wrists are aching.'

'All right, but just a couple of minutes. It's calm, so we

11

shouldn't drift too much. When they pass the bags over, check the seals. One will be heavier than the other. Get 'em in the bin liners and put on the tie wraps, sharpish.'

A sleek black boat draws up beside their skiff, with three crew in black jumpers, trousers and balaclavas. Two clear plastic sacks full of small white boxes are passed from the launch to the skiff, and a small black antler attaché case is received in exchange. After a brief handshake, the launch disappears into the darkness in the direction of Landkey Island, leaving a fading white wake.

'Very stylish,' said Robert, watching the other boat disappear into the darkness.

'That was Anders and his sons Robert.'

'I didn't realise it could be so cool… smuggling.'

'Before you get any stupid ideas, nights like this don't pay for expensive boats. He's a bulb grower. This is just a little pocket money.'

'A bulb grower?'

'Right, grab those oars and get us back where we should be. We're going home, you'll be glad to hear. I'm gonna finish the rest of these blackjacks, unless you want some?'

'Can't stand 'em, Neil. You can't get your bloody teeth clean after scoffing 'em.'

'They're lovely with a Guinness. You don't know what you're missing, boy. They are a bit sticky though, I'll give you that.'

'Can I follow you with the holdall, Cliff?'

'Aye, it's probably best, looking at you. Until you've woken up.'

'Thanks.'

12

'Just try and keep your wits about you, and watch where you're putting your boots. Next time call in sick.'

'I've had two days already this month. It's the baby keeping us up. I can't be doing this all the time, if I want to get promoted. I'm going all the way, me. I want to be Chief Constable of North Yorkshire before I retire.'

'Chief Constable? You surprise me son. You don't seem to be one of life's natural bullshitters. You realise you'll have to get on the right side of all the wrong kinds of people don't you?'

'Dammit! The clouds just covered the moon. We're off course. Pull us over towards Camel's Hump, Robert.'

'Port or starboard?'

'Don't get clever. Let's just stick to left and right.'

'We're nearly half way, Justin. Are you bearing up?'

'As long as I can get a quick nap at the bottom, yeah.'

'Let's keep going then, get this round up over with. Do you want to give me the rest of the gear?'

'Thanks Cliff… hang on.'

'What?'

'I think I can see a glow down there. It's pretty faint. Do you see it, through the branches there?'

'Yeah, I can just make it out. We're not too far off then. Just keep going.'

'What the hell!' That wasn't there before!' cursed Neil, looking landward.

'What? What's going on?'

'Just keep rowing. There's light from a fire in front of the woods. A big fire. Shit! Shit! Where did this come from?'

'It's probably just kids…'

'I hope you're right.'

'They can't see us from up there, Neil. You've got to be right on the lip to see anything.'

'Well, we'll just have to pray they haven't looked over. I'm just worried about what other kinds of attention it's going to bring.'

'There's a high bank that skirts the plateau we can use on the way back. Plenty of good cover, it's a bit tricky in the dark. We can use that to get back to the car.'

'We don't have much choice now, do we? I wanted to go back through the wood. Shit, I think we've drifted off course again…'

'We're close. I can see the fire now, we should reach it in a few minutes. The path drops off these bluffs after the fallen sycamore over there. I'm switching the torch off, Justin. The moon's back out. We should have enough light.'

'Can I turn around now Miss?'

'No.'

'Miiisss…'

'And let me see those arms. I get very suspicious when I can't see a boy's arms. One can't see what their hands are doing.'

'I've got bogeys, Miss.'

'I can't help thinking Humpty, that you're in the wrong place. What are you doing here, boy? And don't wipe them on me.'

'My brother said unless I brought him some beer and vodkas to his beach party before I went to Cubs to the Alison

Wonderlands party, he'd tell Mum and she'd tell Dad I put glue in his Cortina doors and Dad would ground me and I'd get no pocket money for ages and ages and...'

'Slow down, slow down.'

'It's not fair!'

'Neither is putting superglue in your dad's car door lock.'

'I didn't mean it.'

'Calm down – here now, have a tissue,' she said, going into one of the deep pockets in her robe. 'Now where did your brother say you should go?'

'Nalgo Miss.'

'Well, this is Cayton Bay. You must have taken the wrong path. Where are all your bottles?'

'I lost them in the trees, Miss. What am I going to do?'

The two traffic constables had reached a vantage point overlooking the plateau.

'Well, well, well... What have we here? Dennis Wheatley's weekend warriors on parade... This is interesting, very very interesting. I think we'll stay out of sight, just for now. And observe. Call in and let them know we're at the scene. No mention of this little gathering just yet though, Justin.'

'Uh huh.'

'Why so quiet, Justin... Justin?'

'I think we're a bit out of our depth here, aren't we? Don't you think we should call in for back up? I mean there's a lot more of them than us, look at the fire...'

'Do you see any crimes being committed?'

'No, but we're outnumbered by weirdos.'

'We're outnumbered everywhere, son. That's the job.

How many of us do you think they can spare to play hide and seek in the woods? If they end up chasing us, rather than the other way around, then just shin up a tree. Or hide in the undergrowth. Does that make you feel better?'

'These aren't your average scumbags, Cliff.'

'As for the fire, I'd say it was under control, wouldn't you?'

'But…'

'Justin, if you're scared, we can turn around and go back to the car. But it's not going to do your promotion prospects any good, running away from a lot of comedians dressed in bathrobes. Is that what this is?'

'I'm not sacred! I'm just…'

'Well?'

'They give me the creeps, these people, if you want to know, all right?'

'Let me give you a bit of perspective, lad. Compared to breaking up a brawl in the Admiral's Glass, this is like babysitting a goldfish. The trouble with your generation, Justin, is you watch too many sick horror movies. You think anyone in strange clothes with funny stare is a fruit and nutcase with a sword tucked behind their back, just waiting to carve up the first poor beggar that comes their way. Sit down and keep your imagination under control. I need you running on all cylinders and thinking straight. Don't worry about this lot. I'll wake you up when they start doing something illegal. But don't start getting paranoid.'

In the dark span of Cayton Bay, the amateur smugglers were drifting into danger.

'We're going to hit the sandbar, Rob. I'm sorry, son, but you're going to get a whole lot wetter. Get a bag and hold on, we'll have to wade back from here. When we ground, get out as fast as you can.'

'What about the boat?'

'Forget the boat. The reef will take it. Here it comes now... brace yourself...'

'Our summonses are complete,' announced the Grand Wizard at the last strike of his gavel on their altar. 'We must remain now where we stand. The circle is sealed.'

'There's a gap over there, Miss.' whispered Humpty Dumpty.

'You're very sharp for a shorty,' said Witch Penrose, putting her hand on his shoulder. 'That, my boy, is the north station, which is always left open for klipthotic invocations. Which is a fancy way of saying we've left the door ajar for our guest. I'm afraid you're going to be stuck here with us a little longer, Humpty. But if anything scares you, you can shut your eyes' replied Witch Penrose, trying to sound kindly.

'Are there going to be any more men rubbing themselves, Miss?'

'I certainly hope not. There's enough of that at home.'

'Robert! Robert! Where are you lad?' called Neil in the darkness, over the roar of the surf on the rocks.

'Here!' his nephew yelled nearby. 'Here!' he called again. Neil could just make out the calls of his nephew over the crash of the surf, and staggered blindly over the slippery outcrops of slate and barnacle encrusted bedrock towards the voice, onto a great spear of weatherworn concrete, part of the side of an old wartime observation bunker, stained green with algae and overgrown with kelp.

'Oh my God Neil, you're bleeding…'

'I gashed my head getting out the boat, son. Can't see too well. Got blood in my eyes,' he gasped. 'What a bloody mess. I've still got this friggin' bag though,' he groaned.

'Are you okay?'

'Just cold, really cold, can't feel my toes.'

'Where's your bag?'

'It's there,' he said, flicking his thumb behind his shoulder.

'I must have swallowed a pint of friggin' seawater at least,' griped Neil, spitting, trying to retch.

'Let's get off this friggin' beach.'

'I've lost my wallet…'

'I'm sorry, lad.'

'My work's ID too, me friggin' Access card, ten quid. The shutter key for our unit … and me pumas.'

'I think we've got off lightly, considering. Let's get off this friggin beach and get home.'

'Hang on, Neil. You'd better wrap some of this seaweed around your head,' said Robert, starting to shiver. 'Then jam your hat on top. It'll help it heal, might help stop it bleeding. Mum says seaweed's full of iodine, good for cuts an' wounds and stuff…'

'All right. Just be quick.'

Thirty minutes later, in the trees overlooking the plateau, Constable Deighton awoke with a start.

'What's happening?' he gasped, trying to pretend he had not fallen asleep.'

'Nothing much. You've been snoring like a tramp for a good hour and a half, it's a wonder you haven't woken

18

up everything that walks, crawls or flies. Those two in the middle have been moving about a lot. The rest of 'em aren't moving at all. I'll tell you what, though. The tall one in the shiny cap is our scumbags favourite defence solicitor. Our Mr Beautimann, no less.'

'You're kidding!'

'Have a look for yourself,' said Cliff, passing his colleague a small pair of binoculars.

'Oh, this is too good!'

'Not so creepy now, eh Justin? Our little gathering?'

'This is as good as a birthday and a Christmas all in one.'

'He hasn't done anything wrong yet. But we can bide our time.'

'Not much happening the now, friend,' observed Scots Tony sarcastically, adjusting his testicles with a deep scoop of velvet.

'Silence!' snapped the Grand Wizard, watching the air inside the triangle of art.

'Sorry for any offence, ahm shure.'

'I think Casanova must be infertile,' announced Thrice Great Hermes.

A cry from higher ground put the coven on guard. It was soon followed by the noise of a body barrelling through undergrowth at great speed, racing toward their circle, scattering twigs, bark and stones.

'Close your eyes, boy,' said Witch Penrose.

The body of a man clad in dark clothing skidded through the open gap in the burning ring of embers and fell in a heap inside the triangle of art. For several minutes the prostrate figure struggled to move, then slowly turned over onto its knees and braced itself unsteadily on its palms, vomiting a long stream of shiny black spittle onto the ground. It followed up with an unrestrained stream of filthy curses and some very strongly expressed examples of the vilest language the company had ever heard.

Neil's family had often remarked upon his swarthy looks. His black curly hair, hawkish nose, grey eyes and strong jaw gave him a sinister charisma that some women found hard to resist, but made others blush and turn away. Many years spent working at sea in all weathers had accented his already striking features, and taken away any innocence and freshness he had briefly possessed. Presently, his face was streaked with blood, sticky black vomit and lumpy with nettle poison, muddy strips of torn seaweed hung down from the edge of his black woollen hat. His eyes, glittering with hate and pain, roamed slowly over the coven.

'What the hell are you creeps looking at…' he spat, glaring malevolently around the circle of strangers.

'It's got a Yorkshire accent!'

'Well, all demons come through fromt north though, dunt they?'

'Is that bladderwrack?'

'I command thee to remain!' commanded the Master of Ceremonies, grandly, moving closer to the demon, holding his hazel wand imperiously and pointing it rudely at his guest's bloody forehead. 'Until such time as I shall dismiss thee from our company, creature of Hades, be at my…' The Grand Wizard got no further. His nemesis reached up, snatched the chain of his kabbalistic talisman, pulled hard and head-butted him, felling Mother Shipton with an unintentional jab from his elbow.

'Bastard!' snapped the demon, getting to his feet and cracking his host's ribs on his knee.

The coven were speechless and frozen, unable to comprehend what was happening, as one of Satan's minor franchisees snapped Mr Beautimann's hazel wand over his thigh and kicked him coldly between the legs, as he lay groaning pathetically, before striding off into the darkness.

'What the hell's going on!' asked Aleister Crowley.

'What the hell is going on!' added Gilles de Rais, in tandem, finishing him off.

'It can't do this,' whimpered the Master of Ceremonies, gasping in agony. 'There are rules! Rules!'

High over the heads of the coven, something terrible began to move between worlds. A glittering, luminous fog began to issue from the tear in time and space opened by the ritual, accompanied by the smell of rancid Brie and music festival toilets.

'What the hell just happened?'

'Just sit tight, Justin. I'm not exactly sure, but it appears the human sacrifice has just kicked Mr Beautimann in the bollocks and run off. I'm beginning to enjoy this delicate little drama. The air's getting a bit ripe around here though, have you dropped one?'

'Have I dropped one? What d'you mean, have I dropped one! Why does your arse get the get out of jail free card?'

'Calm down.'

'You cheeky bastard, you're the one who's been stuffing his face.'

'God, what *is* that smell…' groaned the Grand Wizard with real disgust, still clutching his groin, wiping tears of agony from the corners of his eyes.

'Don't you dare!' snapped Witch Penrose, scowling. 'I'll have you know, mine only smell of roses!'

'Aye. Rows o'shite,' smirked Scots Tony, scratching his backside.

'It's getting worse, Cliff… What are you staring at?' asked Justin, looking over to his colleague, who was gazing up into the sky.

'I've not seen anything like that before. No fog or sea fret I ever saw moved like that. It keeps spreading…' he said, transfixed.

'Do you think we should call in?'

'What? No,' said Cliff, lowering his gaze. 'Let's get that ponce in cuffs first.'

'Yeah, absolutely,' he said uneasily, drawing his baton and finding his torch before taking another glance heavenward. 'OH SHITTINGHELL!'

Beneath the small outbreaks of petty squabbling and heated arguments, a new mood of collective foreboding began to take hold over the coven, an unconscious detection of a forgotten guest, jolting awake some very stale sixth senses, like a school bell exploding over a hibernating bear. Very slowly, one by one, their eyes began to tilt towards the stars.

A gigantic black globe of simmering ectoplasm hung rotating over the circle, filled with darting lights and fantastic shadows, surrounded by a huge swarm of emerald green blowflies that rushed around its cankerous circumference in a frenzy of demented excitement. Its leathery surface heaved with the blackened bas-reliefs of innumerable screaming death masks, rising and falling back into a luminous lucent sea of filth and corruption.

Their speed of emergence seemed to increase at first, as if the demon were searching for a face which best matched the rictus expression of terror and panic on the face of the Grand Wizard, who was peeing on the ground beneath his skirts. Their ghastly visitant appeared to run out of patience and settled on the unlovely countenance of one Ethel Bere, a prostitute and murderess it had snatched at a disastrous conjuring in a room above the Heavitree Arms in Bideford a hundred years before.

'NICE NIGHT FOR IT,' hissed the demon, trying to provoke its hosts, through the pox scarred lips of an old English tart.

'CAT GOT YOUR TONGUE?'

'We never touched it! Truly!' wailed Mother Shipton, before passing out in a heap.

The Grand Wizard, gripped by a rigour mortis-like terror tried to squeak, but his words evaporated before they were born, though amongst their older veterans, help was at hand…

'Are yee gonnae ask ett sumthen the now, eh?' called Scots Tony, completely unmoved by the horrific entity blocking out the stars. 'An hurry yuz up, we've got wa vidyo narstay tae watch the neet at hame.'

'Aye, we've got the Evull Dayd on vidyo,' crowed Mrs Tony, chipping in.

'Hey! We're round tae yours hen,' piped Ann McCloud.

'Shut up, Shut UP, SHUT UP!' pleaded their leader,

wondering where he'd left his Observer's Book of Things that go Bump in the Night, and wondering why he'd never read it.

'Aye, yer wellcum hinny, anyone eylse?'

A dozen pairs of bloodshot eyes surfaced on the pellucid ectoplasm of the demon, and began to study the Master of Ceremonies, in the way a tiger admires a goat.

'Yeats! Get the chalice!' yelped the Grand Wizard, finding some small kernels of courage as the last mouthfuls of the espresso filtered by his kidneys trickled over his shoes.

William Butler Yeats, or Brett from Crown Garage, shuffled unhurriedly towards his master, bearing a silver-plated drinking goblet engraved with the shield of the St John's Ambulance Brigade, defaced by a Chiquita banana sticker.

'WHAT IS THIS? AND WHAT'S IT HOLDING?' boomed the demon. 'I DON'T KNOW WHAT SORT OF BOOKS YOU'VE BEEN READING. WHERE'S MY BRANDY AND GINGER? AND IT HAD BETTER BE SCHWEPPES, NONE OF THIS OWN LABEL SUPERMARKET SHITE.'

'We ain't got no brandy, Mr Beautimann. We ain't got no mixers eever,' he sniffed lamely.

'Give it something… anything, you imbecile,' gulped the Grand Wizard, trying to control the panic in his voice.

'I only got…' he mumbled, going into his pockets. 'I only got a squashed Mars bar…'

'A Mars bar!'

'CORRRTOSSITOVERERETHEN!' barked the demon, re-absorbing its eyeballs and materialising a brace of stinking mouths, packed with rotting teeth and ulcerated gums.

'That thing needs a proper bath. Proper,' sighed Madame Blavatsky, casting on. 'I don't care much for the flies either. Just so long as they stays off my wool.'

Mother Shipton, forever destined to be one of life's number twos, had regained herself and was adding up the pros and cons of returning to duty, though her present circumstances were not affording her much comfort – quite the reverse. From the top of her sand-caked fish crate, she had a perfect view of what remained of the triangle of art, and was now trying to alert the Master of Ceremonies to the danger, with a series of short sharp tugs to his hem. Though she stopped abruptly, after realising it was wet and sniffing her fingers.

'What's that pillock up to now?' complained Thrice Great Hermes, Controller of Beehive Taxis.

'I know,' sighed the Compte de St Germain, in sympathy.

'I've got two new virgin drivers on tonight! Get yer arse in gear! No bloody sense of urgency…' he complained loudly.

'Derek! The wotsit's breached!' hissed Mother Shipton.

'WHERE'S MY SHORT, FOUR EYES?'

'I demand…' began the Wizard, his voice shaking. 'I demand you tell us…'

'YESSSSS?'

'The lo… location, of Henry Kettle… Kettlewell's treasure…'

'UNDER THE FAT COW ON THE CRATE,' said the demon, matter-of-factly.

'Derek, the triangle! It's broken..!'

'Where's that lad gone?' asked Witch Penrose to herself, looking about for Humpty Dumpty, who had seen enough and was sprinting off towards the trees, still wearing his egg. Denzel Pearce and Mitch 'Mouse' Hogg, a pair of shore fishermen from Bridlington, were returning home from Whitborough harbour after quiz night at the Newcastle Packet on Foreshore Rd. Making ten knots on a calm sea, chatting in the forward wheelhouse of their Coble, and approaching the headland between Nalgo and Cayton Bay.

'D'ya go out list neet Den?' enquired Mitch of his friend, over the burble of their engine.

'Aye. Had a few int Keys wee Jim. Game o' darts. Nowt exciting.'

'I 'eard you'd 'ad some bother getting indoors after hours.'

'Oh you 'eard an' all did ya? Easy mistake when you've 'ad a few. Front door same as ours. I thought she were a funny shape. It were only when she grabbed me that I realised it weren't our Freya. Starts tearing off me shett – barmy as a sex mad ram she wa. If I'd not 'ad that big rustay crocodile clip fromt boat's odd battery, I'd 'ave been a goner. I'll not mek that mistake again. Mad bitch…'

The demon, alert to the conversation between the Master of Ceremonies and his Deputy Mother Shipton, flushed its outer epidermis with a blinding light and focussed on the scrubbed out remains of the triangle of art, the last barrier to freedom between itself and the outside world.

The coven shielded their eyes and dropped to the ground, but their master, exposed to the full glare, fell backwards onto his deputy, crushing their makeshift altar. Several large blowflies settled on the territory of his shoulder and began to drool.

'Stone the crows! There's a bloody UFO over there, Mitch!' called Denzel to his mate walking aft as they cleared the headland. 'Look at that! It's a friggin flying saucer!'

26

'Is that for real! Look – there's a load o' bloody monks running about look, underneath it… Where's the bloody camera…'

The two traffic patrolmen had seen enough and had started to retreat, their instincts for self-preservation overcoming their sense of duty and public service.

'Did we just see what I thought I just saw?'

'I'm not sure if I saw what you thought you just saw. I thought I was seeing things. There's nothing wrong with my eyes – but I'm seeing things I shouldn't be seeing…'

'Things that you don't want to see?'

'Exactly. Cliff…?'

'Just give me a minute son. I need a minute…'

'Cliff, if you don't say something I think I'm going to go mad.'

'Pull yourself together. You're on duty. You can go mad in your own time. Right now we need to keep it together. And you're not helping.'

'I don't…'

'You don't what? – Look, a man may see some terrible sights in his lifetime… Cat shit in yer slippers. Brush painted caravans. Val Doonican, on that friggin stool…' said Cliff, his speech tailing off as he contemplated another horrible cardigan.

'Who the hell is Val Doo..?'

'All I'm saying, Justin, is that this is one of those things we're going to try not to think about. So stop thinking about it. This never happened… What are you looking at me like that for?'

'You've got a really really big wasp on your chin. Don't move whatever you do…'

'Eh!'

'That thing's just turned black – or disappeared. Where'd it go?' said Denzel, throttling back their engine. 'Where's the camera, did you find it?'

Tetarzepamdomestoz turned off its glaring lights and suddenly exploded. Thousands of gallons of concentrated evil spewed out over the woodland canopy, releasing hundreds of glowing orbs which sped away over the treetops into the distance as the coven took flight like woodlice, sprinting to shelter from under an upturned stone. Only Mother Shipton and her master remained, two forlorn figures in a heap, drenched by a toxic punch of snake venom, pus and rancid saliva, abandoned and unmissed, coughing and spluttering.

'I don't think this will be a night I'll remember with any fondness,' sniffed Mother Shipton, pulling off her tainted robes and fumbling for a packet of tissues. 'Here, take a couple of these, Derek…' she said, offering her companion some relief. 'For your face,' she murmured. 'I take this to mean we're not going to Nostell Priory on Friday.'

The Grand Wizard wiped his nose and forehead, then looked at the tissue in disgust. 'I have the knowledge we came for,' he muttered. 'How good it is to have the loyalty of friends,' he added sarcastically, looking at the empty circle. 'I had everything, everything under control until that…'

'Oh yes! Everything!' said Mother Shipton.

'Are you being sarcastic?'

'Me Derek? Am I being sarcastic? Oh no. Perish the thought I might dare to suggest our little gathering tonight was anything less than a brilliant success. How would you describe it?'

'Is it my fault we had an interloper? No! I followed every

detail. Every observance Nothing was missed, nothing left to chance! How were any of us to know that some thug would arrive out of nowhere and screw everything up?'

'Derek, that thing is out there… It's free. Who are they going to blame? This is going to come back to haunt us…'

'Is it my fault that the triangle was scrubbed out? Is it? We had no time, Maureen. No time to make a repair. It was too late. I was incapacitated. You were unconscious, or pretending to be, as I recall.'

'That wasn't my fault.'

'Neither of us were culpable. That's my point.'

'I just think you could have handled things with a bit more confidence earlier on.'

'Confidence, well thank you for that. I'd just become victim of a vicious psychopath, while trying to control a company of adults that act like six year olds, and a demon the size of half a football pitch. Do you expect me to hold everything together in those circumstances?'

'Well if you want an honest answer – yes.'

'It's gone Den. Whatever it was. I can't see owt. Just them queer lights fading off. D'ya think we should tell someone?'

'Report it? No way. We'd be a laughing stock. Best keep quiet about it, I reckon. I think we should have a brew.'

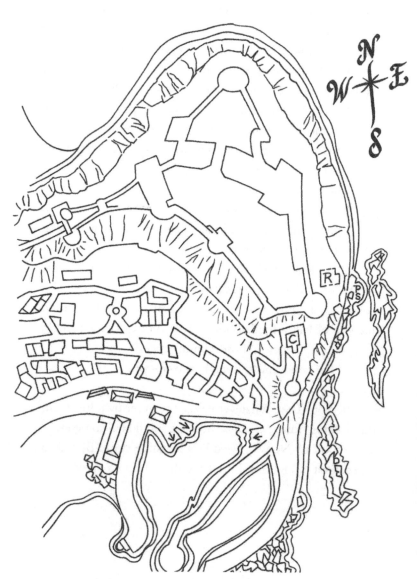

Whitborough on Sea Old Town and Harbour, 1983

Chapter Two

Tuesday

The pale sickly light of early morning breached the far horizon of the North Sea, and spread its faint watercolours across the sky, like an artist with invisible speed. Under the drifting clouds, rolling grey green breakers rushed ashore to their destruction on the smooth beds of pebbles and pea grit stones that carpeted the long sweeping crescent of Victoria Bay, casting forth showers of tiny wet diamonds that caught the light once before dying out forever. A cold spring breeze ran ashore, stirring the trees with fingers of silk and the tang of salt, and draping a cloak of cold mist over the landscape.

High up, over the sleeping town of Whitborough on Sea, England's first resort, untidy gangs of seagulls, fulmars and guillemots dipped and soared on the rollercoaster winds, up draughts and thermals rising from the cliffs and bluffs around the bay. They traced bizarre elliptical circuits over the lichen-stained slates of houses and workshops below, for no particular reason and with no particular care.

Seen from above, the town spread itself handsomely between two beautiful bays, extending in a south-westerly direction towards the wolds in a perfect template of old Regency grandeur. Its elegant borders augmented by layers of fine gothic renaissance architecture, domestic and civic.

Further developments in the early years of the twentieth century saw the town enlarged to the north and south, with the addition of numerous Edwardian redbrick terraces and town houses.

Despite its long Christian heritage, and the establishment of the Abbey at Whitby, there were no places of worship of any great age at its centre, but many fair examples in the settlements around it. One of the best stands beside the main lane through the village of Folkton Gifford, a small hamlet which winds upwards along the face of the moraine beside the flat glacial valley of Cayton Carrs, whose residents look across the wide green expanse of fields and culverts to Bickering Heights. From the tower of the church there, one is able to see the great spine of Oliver's Mount curving towards Victoria Bay and the spire of Filey church, six miles to the south. The bell tower's tiny steps twist tightly and steeply upwards in semidarkness, boxing in the visitor so snugly about the shoulders that one is easily marked by the dust of the ages which lies thick upon its stones, until one emerges into sunlight and the panorama across the valley floor, seen from the small patio at the highest point of the roof. The church was built around a pair of Roman pillars supporting a great arch, into which Saxon stonemasons added their own decorative bands and glyphs. The main structure, including the tower, was constructed after the Conquest.

Another fine church worthy of note lies to the west of Great Norton on the road to Pickering, in the village of Aveyou Nympton. It has two fine old yews with stone seats beneath them, which must have been old when the Tudor dynasty was born. On its south wall is fixed a sundial of great age. The tower and chancel are early fourteenth century. A carved stone screen of tall slim gothic arches with decorative ivy tracery survives from the same period. It encloses the front of the nave, which has an old wagon roof from the choir and the tombs of two Lords of the Manor, who fought in the Crusades, returning to live out the remainder of their years in the parish.

The town had first become famous for its spa waters and because it was such an attractive stage for the new fashion for sea bathing, which had become immensely popular in the country in the years after the Napoleonic Wars. But Whitborough had since dazzled its visitors with a series of ornamental parks and gardens, after the success of its arboretum, which was to prove even more wondrous than the natural amenities from which it first drew prominence, with each new addition more exotic and ambitious than the last, inspiring travelogues and recollections from the lands of Empire in which one could linger, imagining other cultures and adventures, situations and romances.

Peaholm Mere, the last and most extensive, was a homage to the most beautiful water gardens of Japan, a tree walk of wonder under a necklace of lanterns and weeping willows, past temples, pools, sculptures and streams. It surrounded an island of waterfalls, trees and exotic flora and fauna from the far east. A hotel, which to all but the most pedantic connoisseurs of Japanese architecture was the mirror image of Osaka castle, bestrode the island's summit, though the cultural identity of its interior, designed by a committee of prominent political incompetents was much less certain. If a team of skilled construction engineers, blessed with a deep and sympathetic knowledge of Japanese art and architecture had conceived the form and the setting, a company of chimpanzees masquerading as local officials and councillors had dressed its interior. The end result was a migraine for the eyes. Across the ceilings, the eyes of its guests and visitors were drawn to a great sweep of bloodthirsty murals depicting the famous battles of Trafalgar, Waterloo and Agincourt in varying degrees of skill. They were imprisoned by heavy lengths of intricately patterned Victorian coving abutting a series of Greco Roman plaster friezes, which in turn pressed pitilessly against a run of Scots Baronial wainscoting and marquetry above the gothic revival skirting's, without space, breath or intervention. Persian carpets and Venetian rugs broke up the form of art deco parquet floors. Across the walls, heavy gilt picture frames enclosing scenes of Arthurian legends and looming stags' heads bumped against dangerous overhanging knots of ceremonial weapons, fighting for attention among the kind of busily embroidered silk wall panels, curtains and table lamps one might expect to find in a low rent Chinese takeaway. The overall effect on the constitution of anyone with even a rudimentary appreciation of the visual arts was to instil a queasiness which could only be relieved by staring at a blank sheet of paper for several minutes, to coax their racing pulses back to earth.

About these magnificent parks, large Georgian villas and terraces, relics of a more confident age stared out over wide carriageways, bordered by orderly sequences of tall sycamores, gaslights and tethering posts, and in rank between neat model plazas in the Italian style, enclosed and protected by three sided porticos, where bowls were played on firm green lawns, kept smart by mowers, nail scissors and the cut of whispered gossip.

Architecturally speaking, the twentieth century had made

little impact in her districts, thanks to a strong and proper disdain for modernity and some deliberately draconian planning regulations, designed to deny the vulgarian urges of the few champions of twentieth century housing and construction.

Only the sudden and dramatic extinction of property and persons under a surprise bombardment from the German Navy in December 1914 had altered what man had built, or reduced to ruin. Their introductory volleys fell from the sky just before breakfast, shattering the peace, as one local grocer later remarked, with the sound of charging locomotives.

The African Queen, on Abbotsham Road, took its last delivery at 7am before passing into history, together with Derrigans butchers and Walter's for Buttons, just three of many personal tragedies to befall the town on that dreadful day. Most other buildings and businesses avoided the same fate and escaped with minor damage, but nothing remained to mourn of George Rudkin's fine Fish and Chip Restaurant, smashed to smithereens and burnt to ashes, the destination of a four-gun broadside intended for the ballroom of the Grand Hotel.

Although these losses caused great outpourings of grief and outrage in the country as a whole, causing a rush of men to recruiting offices, demanding Lee Enfields and directions to the coast, there was an unspoken acceptance among the older families in the district that this sort of thing had been going on for centuries, though in a far less spectacular way.

Evidence of Whitborough's earliest origins, unearthed during excavations at the site of the main castle dyke in the 1950s, suggested the town had begun life as a busy fishing and trading settlement. Evidence also suggested it had been a popular destination for a race now known as the Vikings, who had given the town its name, Whitvik, from an old Norse word thought to mean 'fantastic blaze'. Their modern descendants, now Swedes, Danes and Norwegians still came to visit, though instead of inflicting random acts of rape, murder and amputation on the local population, they bought hundreds of heavy metal albums and ate ice cream until they were sick.

As the last milk float trundled lazily back to Whitborough Dairy, the first paperboy of the morning, James Trippe of Long Acre, lit up, fell off and tried again. Notes for the Milkman in Whitborough made very interesting reading, but requests for two pints of gold top and a ginjelly were not unfamiliar to the delivery drivers of the dairy. To give their business an edge, against the increasing threat of the supermarkets and the shrinking of their market share, the dairy's owners, the Wilkie Hocklings family, had started to sell alcohol-infused jellies and cream cakes as 'pick me ups,' on the doorstep, which were proving to be a huge hit, in addition to their other activities. The council and local police force had long turned a blind eye, justifying in private their unofficial support of smuggling as an important local tradition, if not a useful public service, that should be protected from the assault of modernist thinking and specifically modern law, by people who were uniquely placed to best understand its values and historic cultural importance.

Inside number 32 Long Acre, Mrs Joanna Trippe lay awake beside her husband, staring at their fixed rate ceiling, after bullying her pillows into a stepped arrangement, and attempting a testing sip of her earl grey tea.

'Last night Miles, I heard a commotion and voices next door,' she announced imperiously, using her words like a stick with which to liberate her husband from his gentle slumber.

'My first name is Trevor, Joanna, as you must know. When you wish to engage me in conversation, using my first name would be the correct form of address.'

'Miles has more gravitas,' she continued, unmoved. 'People would take you more seriously if you used your middle name.'

'Trevor is a perfectly good name, and has been, for forty years. If you think I'm going to change it now, so you can bask in some tenuous imagined sense of reflected superiority because you believe it gives you passage by association to the world of the upper middle classes, you had better think again. Did you notice I was asleep?'

'You're changing the subject.'

'I'm sure we're both capable of covering two topics at once, darling.'

'Noise, Miles. Noise. That's how we began this conversation.'

'It's a favourite tactic of yours, isn't it Joanna, changing the subject when others are getting the better of you.'

'The noises next door…'

'What noises?'

'The noises I heard last night! Doors banging. Furniture being dragged around in the bedrooms. Didn't you hear any of it?'

'But the Bealeys are away on holiday, aren't they?'

'Congratulations Trevor, welcome to our conversation.'

'Well, I'm glad I've got my name back.'

'Don't be superior, Trevor…'

'Have they got a house-sitter?'

'What kind of house-sitter rearranges someone's furniture in the middle of the night?'

'What this has got to do with us, I fail to see. Or is that just me?'

'Don't be so evasive.'

'I'm trying to be asleep, when you're ready to get to the point.'

'I'm being serious.'

Mr F folded his arms and shut his eyes.

'Thank you, Trevor. Now I've got your fullest attention, I distinctly remember hearing a commotion next door last night in the early hours.'

'A comm…'

'Let me finish please…'

'Did you hear voices?'

'No. More of a retching, or someone being strangled, quite possibly. I want you to check their windows this morning, before you leave for practice. But be discreet – it could be somebody we know with a spare key.'

'Of course, dear. I always relish the chance to stare through our neighbours' windows at close quarters on behalf of my wife.'

'There's something else.'

'For God's sake, Joanna.'

'Have you noticed something odd about James, recently?'

'James has started to smoke. I know. I imagine he thinks the breeze will take the smell out of his clothes when he's cycling. Just make sure he doesn't discover your little secret dear, or he'll never look at his mother through the same rose-tinted blinkers ever again.'

Just next door to the Trippe's, inside number 34 lay the snoring corpse of Dean Beadle, senior sales assistant at Clash City Records, still wearing the leather jacket, leather jeans and Doc Martens of the night before. A large, uncapped bottle of gin lay beside him, propped up amongst some pillows, discarding its contents intermittently in large slops as the bed moved about under the weight of a large punk squatter.

It had been a little over two weeks since the event which had temporarily altered his sleeping arrangements. The house party he had arranged in his parents' absence had been a soar-away success. For his guests, it had been a night of beautiful excess. There were only two dissenters, who had arrived back at their property just as the excitement had peaked.

Dean's Mother Dorothy, modestly Methodist and nervous of vice, would forever avoid revisiting the memories of bacchanalian carnage which marked their homecoming and carpets that warm spring evening. For what had occurred inside number 32 Cooks Row Cottages could only be described as a sex maniac's last stand, a pervert's Rorke's Drift, fuelled by gigantic quantities of alcohol, baby oil and bubble wrap, and pursued with all the gusto and energy of youth.

Her first thought had been to call the hospital, the police and the army, but as shock and mental disorientation had disabled her ability to think properly, she was overcome by the extent of the desecration. She collapsed in a faint after examining the jobbing end of a Tallboy, a battery-operated sex aid of giant proportions, marked by terrifying contours and veinous ridges named after the blockbuster bomb used by the RAF during WW2, which had fallen into the valley of the ferns beneath the enchanted castle, and lain in ambush inside her fish tank, ready to pounce on their dainty Black Moors.

Dean senior, a man to whom sin was a distant memory, began to reclaim their home by propping up his wife and boy, prior to assisting the departure of the guests his son's appetites had not already done for. Heartened in his labours by the harrying barks of Penny, the family's West Highland Terrier, the canary yellow survivor of a hideous hair-colour mixing experiment and many puddles of snakebite.

Dean's disgrace had been compounded the morning after, when his father had eaten some small sweets from the coffee-table bowl in the mistaken belief they were something made by Rowntrees. It soon became apparent to him what they were not – after stepping into his bath, he had plunged into a terrible hallucinogenic voyage, wrestling the lovesick tentacles of a giant octopus, brandishing a set of sheepskin decorator's rollers upon the barnacle-encrusted deck boards of a U-Boat in a wild Atlantic storm.

He was later accosted by chance, by his mother's sister Primrose near their old house, and had been made to stand mutely as she assaulted him with a vocal dressing down, akin to being assaulted by a bare knuckle boxer. Through a ten minute verbal onslaught, from her A-Zs, through her Ps and Qs, and Fs and Offs, as she explained in loud detail the intricacies of incontinence, and the mood of the family as they had waited for several pints of dilute radox to gallop through his digestive system, while he blocked and parried the cuts and swipes of eight adoring tentacles.

'I should think he'll be laughin' about it, – in another ten years, son. Course, me – well you, I'd keep me 'ead down low for a while. An' it wunt 'urtya… ta get a decent 'aircut sometime soon. Tamorra frinstance. You look like one o' them parrots off Animal Magic.'

A tiny ceramic clock beside the bolster pillows began to chirrup, filling Dean's inner ear with the sound of recorded birdsong. Very slowly, his shell-shocked consciousness began to creep back into the warm space from where it was so brutally ejected each Friday night. A swaying arm, beautified with carp, leopards and take-away dragons reguardant crashed down on the pretty china alarm clock.

An hour and twenty minutes later, he descended the smart staircase of his new home, moving unsteadily across the Byzantine tiles and into the sunny rectangle behind the front door. He kicked aside the post and cleared the steps to the old cobbles and flagstones on the street, still gripping the front door handle. The brutal slam caused a nesting guillemot to lose its footing on the guano-stained portico above and tumble down the lead flashing into the gutter, as the neighbours prepared to observe the ritual of motor mechanical heresy and cold revving which signalled the departure of the 8am Ford Mexico to Market Square.

Clash City Records, without doubt North Yorkshire's most hair-raising retail experience, looked out over the careworn cobbles and mucky running gutters of Market Square, out of place and out of time, like a stale school bully forced to tea with Grandma.

Its precincts marked the end of Whitborough's main commercial district and the crooked dog's-leg borders of the old town. An eccentric press of small Georgian and early

Victorian villas and terraces, fishermen's cottages and tall Hanoverian blocks jemmied between the ancient shoulders of timber framed homes and outbuildings converted into expensive mews homes, like a blending of old Edinburgh and Burford. The division of this eclectic jumble of elderly dwellings was further complicated by the maze-like collection of random passages, cuttings, lanes and ginnels which completely disorientated all but the most determined map readers.

The shop occupied the basement and ground floor levels of a large late Georgian townhouse, formerly a country butcher's, vaunting a single low-braced, bay-windowed frontage, guard railings and matching horse troughs given over to planting, though often used as urinals, depending on the time of day. For five noisy years, it had attracted music lovers from every northern county, but not all music lovers, due to the singularly foreboding qualities of its interior.

The proprietors, two young entrepreneurial brothers, Brian and David Drake, had not had an easy start in the music business, after discovering that the initial brief for the transformation of the old meat and game counters, had guillotined all previously friendly communication between themselves and the shop fitters they had approached for advice. So they decided to visit a friend in Leeds, who ran an ecclesiastical reclamation yard called Heaven Can Wait, whilst pondering their next move. Later returning from their trip with the names of two former stage carpenters for Hammer Films, who according to their references were the only joiners in England who could make a dovetail joint look frightening, in addition to their rare and peculiar talents. The elder, Mr Upround, had perfected a method of casting in plaster the most nightmarish characters from literature and folklore, so rich in form and detail they could make a guard dog incontinent.

After the commission was agreed and the shop fitting completed, the finished suite of rooms passed into the hands of a mad society decorator from Tetbury, an occasional advertiser in the trades section of County Life magazine, whose passion for the more macabre elements of gothic renaissance and the sequential consumption of calvados and port, found the ideal canvas for his oeuvre.

What emerged from the frenzy of rag rolling, airbrushing and baleful trompe l'oeil was an interior which screamed charnel house revisited. It was as if a cutting from the gatehouse at Highgate cemetery had been used for the artificial insemination of the Tower of London, to sire an interior which guaranteed the voluntary self-ejection of anyone who shopped inside the top twenty. Though just to make sure, a leering waxwork of Rasputin stood guard inside the vestibule, clutching a Luger and a bottle of ouzo.

The staff, chosen for their appearance as much as their knowledge of the rock and alternative music scene, had become almost as notorious as the business itself. Amie van der Kop, an amputee and former dog handler for the South African Police, the most recent. She had come upon their premises by chance, during a spell of gardening leave which her superiors intended to make permanent. In part due to the consequences of using a tampered leash during a disastrous parade ground ceremony, when her Doberman Boet had run amok and clamped its jaws over the testicles of the trombone and tuba. Nicknamed 'Stainless', because of her blade-shaped prosthetic lower right leg, chosen to replace the original, mauled by a Bull shark whose eyes she had plucked with her engagement ring.

Michael, the assistant manager, a former illustrator and graphic artist, walked the streets as his hero Peter Cushing in the uniform of a Victorian gentleman, thanks to a large inheritance, in connivance with his girlfriend Fenella a fan of corsets, music hall and 'the Good Old Days', though this did not include doing cartwheels on horseback.

Brian and his brother were making their way to work in his black Saab 900 turbo, from their home on the Neastsfield estate on the southern outskirts of Whitborough, listening to the local radio station Yorkshire Coastal FM.

'Good morning to all our listeners on a fine spring day on the beautiful Yorkshire coast from Yorkshire Coastal FM. Here is Steve Marshall with the news and weather.'

'Thanks Darren, an accident involving a Police vehicle and a minicab from Beehive Taxis during the early hours of Wednesday morning, has led to the closure of Lower Gunstone in both directions from Wheatcroft. Residents have been diverted through Cornelian Drive and Lime Grove. Accident investigators are still at the scene gathering evidence and conducting house-to-house enquiries for witnesses to help determine the cause of the crash. The drivers and passengers of both vehicles have been detained in Whitborough hospital. A spokesman for the hospital has issued a statement this morning denying speculation that the police officers were seriously ill at the time of the accident, although unofficial sources inside the hospital have told Yorkshire Coastal FM that the officers involved have been placed in the isolation unit within the ICU department. Diversion signs are now in place, and drivers are advised to use Higher Gunstone until Lower Gunstone is open to traffic. We will keep you informed during our regular traffic reports.

Local doctors' surgeries have been treating large numbers of local people and holiday-makers for insect bites this morning. Victims of the painful rash-like sores are reporting unusual symptoms from fever and euphoria to vomiting and hallucinations. Doctors are advising anyone suffering from the bites not to drive or use machinery.

Entries are now being taken for the third annual coal hump race from the Strand Cinema to the Corner Cafe, following the success of the two previous events. Entrant forms are available from the Whitborough Gazette Offices, the Council's Tourist and Leisure Offices on Chingswell St and our own offices in Hawker Hurricane Square. The weather will be warm today with temperatures between 18 and 20 degrees Celsius, with cloud dispersing throughout the day. Now we're over to Darren Richmond for the morning request show and our first request from Phil Miller at Northam tyres and autos, it's Blondie and Heart of Glass.'

'Heart of Glass, my ar…' said Brian, cutting off the volume.

'Hey leave it on' said Dave, 'it's a great song.'

'I meant him, Darren dipstick.'

'Who? The DJ?'

'I had the great misfortune to spend three hours with that plonker in the judges' booth at the Battle of the Bands last year. Horrible mullet, shirt like a fruit salad. He thought he was a pop star, instead of a gob with a bad haircut and a giant ego. Put some dumbbells in his trousers and he'd be the ideal anchor for someone's boat.'

'Did Neil call last night?'

No. But he doesn't always. Something about some whisky. I'll call him tonight if he hasn't rung me first. It's all paid for now anyway. Michael's volunteered to cover if we need to take time out for the distribution this week.'

'How's Fenella?'

'Still looks like she's been dragged through a graveyard backwards. She's started fencing, y'know.'

'Fencing? What, gardens?'

'Swords, Dave… can you imagine her mixing cement with a sack of Postfix? So avoid getting near the hat pins. Are you getting us some tea while I get the grille off and open up?'

In the clement centre of a large, comfortably furnished vaulted cellar, hung with tapestries and diaphanous drapes, lies what appears to be a large rectangular wardrobe, heavy of oak and ornately carved, studded with four pairs of robust pierced silver handles , resting on six marble pad stones. A reddening fire of orange embers burns brightly inside a large fireplace nearby, throwing dancing patterns of light across the lime washed walls and ceilings. One of the doors begins to move, in the manner of a lid, betraying the object's true function. A nineteenth century resting place for the deceased, with room for two.

'What time is it, my wickedness?' asked a muffled male voice, affecting a lordly confidence and quiet superiority.

'Time you had risen, my darling,' replied another. 'Ah, I see that you already have.'

46

'Your touch is most pleasing, my sweet, but we may not have time. The Triton awaits. But first I shall need to make my toilet, and thence take breakfast. I am contemplating either a stock knot, or the four in hand to stay my collar. My boldest cravat knot is not, I regretfully concede, firm enough to keep its smartness in the wind. I shall wear my black breeches with the jet buttons and the Prussian blue waistcoat. My black double-breasted overcoat and half cape over.'

'Yes, my darling. Shall I warm your riding boots and gloves also?'

'And the pudding basin.'

'Good morning, reception, Whitborough hospital, Janet speaking, how may I help?'

'Doctor Rowbotham, please. ICU.'

'And your name sir, please?'

'Inspector Marshall. Whitborough Police. I'm calling to find out more about two of our officers who were detained in the early hours this morning after a traffic accident. PC Justin Deighton and PC Clifford Dodds. I was given Doctor Rowbotham as a point of contact.'

'Putting you on hold, Inspector…'

Twenty minutes later… 'Doctor Rowbotham speaking… hello? Hello? Inspector Marshall?'

'Yes? This is he. I've been on hold nearly half an hour.'

'My sincere apologies, Inspector. We were in the middle of our scheduled post-operative outcomes meeting. I had no idea you were holding. I'm so sorry. Had I known, I would have had the appointments desk arrange a callback. Consultants are always fought over…'

'Can we get back to the subject of my men?'

'Certainly, er...'

'I am rather busy myself. To borrow your expression, which is even more pertinent to our officers, who are quite literally fought over on a daily basis.'

' Yes, quite.'

'My men?'

'Ahh, PCs Deighton and Dodds. An intriguing case for us. It appears your officers were seriously ill before they were injured, if that makes sense. Have either of them visited any countries in the equatorial regions very recently?'

'Portmadoc. And Instow.'

'No, I don't think that's the answer I was...'

'Can we stop beating about the bush?'

'Certainly. Before the road traffic accident, we believe your men were incubating what we think is a virus called Huartaneccapox. It's a common virus passed from primates to primates and on occasions to humans in contact with primates, by the exchange of bodily fluids. It could be blood, saliva or.., well – I'm sure I don't have to paint you a picture. There aren't many cases outside of South East Asia, according to my colleagues in London, though their bloods were examined in Leeds at the toxicology unit initially. We were lucky that they had have a specialist in malaria and tropical diseases with them at the moment, as part of an exchange. We would have been somewhat out of our depth otherwise.'

'I don't understand...'

'And there we are in one mind, Inspector.'

'How the hell does someone catch a monkey virus from Asia in Yorkshire; and how long is it going to be before I can send someone to interview them?'

'Perhaps they had visited a zoo very recently and handled some primates? There would need to be – shall I say a degree of contact, of the intimate kind. In answer to your other question we are keeping them in isolation for forty-eight hours while we assess the effectiveness of their treatment.'

'I'm not sure I like where this is going.'

'Has anyone else at the station fallen ill, or failed to report to work today?'

'I called you to enquire about their state of health, not to listen to insinuations that are, quite frankly, beyond the pale. I suggest you re-examine your test results, before I suffer any more of your smutty allegations – goodbye.'

'Extraordinary man…' mumbled Doctor Rowbotham, replacing the receiver. 'One would have hoped for better from a public servant in such a position.'

'Bloody pervert,' spat Inspector Marshall. 'A degree of contact of the intimate kind,' he said, mimicking the consultant. 'Condescending twerp. If this gets into the papers we'll be a bloody laughing stock…' he grumbled, reaching for the intercom. 'Get me someone from the press office at Northallerton on the line asap, Delia,' he said to his secretary, 'and ask George to come up to my office would you. Thank you.'

'Yes, sir. It may take me an hour or so to locate someone at headquarters, the refurbishment is quite advanced and they're all in different wings and temporary buildings. The press office has had to be moved twice already, and the telecoms aren't where they should be yet. But I'll try. I can get the front desk to find Ray.'

'Thank you Delia, do your best.'

Brian Drake sat on the old brass doorstep plate of number 9 Market Square, and smiled as the heat from the sun-kissed metal spread through his black jeans to the skin beneath. Resting his top lip gingerly on the edge of an old chipped mug of tea, to test the heat of the strong brown liquid within, as he watched the passage of friends and neighbours across the flagstones and cobbles. On the other side of the square stood Fantorini's Tuscan Restaurant, the Stage Door pub and the Old Eastern Spice Paradise Curry House.

A few doors away to his right, at the shadowy edge of their bohemian terrace, stood a cold close corridor named Bleake Passage, a gloomy crepuscular cutting between Market Hall and the rough brick flanks of the King's Arms. Uneven with alcoves, bowers and subterranean shops, it endured as an obstacle course of clapperboard signs and strange jutting architectural anomalies, as an impediment to the fleet of foot, for the convenience of pickpockets and desperate sexual adventurers.

Halfway down its dusty length stood Corfe's café, or Toxic Feaneys, as it was known to those working locally in the medical profession. The proprietor, Eilis Feaney, a strawberry blonde lady of no fixed dimensions, scatty and overflowing with grievances, had learnt her cookery skills, such as they were, in very unusual circumstances. As second 'chef' aboard a merchantman called Racketeer, during the Battle of the Atlantic, under a careless rogue from Horns Cross called Harry Piers. There were no real chefs in the Merchant Navy, only cooks, and even then they were only reheating tins for most of the time. It was a bad war if you were pernickety.

Beady in one eye and short sighted in the other, Eilis was the Bonnie to his Clyde, the ketchup to his flame. Together they had survived seven passages on several ships, leaving Racketeer after a mutiny off Birkenhead, before returning to port to blight the health and appetites of the Marisco, the Domicillia and the Kyle of Lochalsh. Strafed during their last convoy by a Focke Wulf Condor, which claimed the left foot of Montgomery Charles, the Kyle's adopted gull, eleven panes of Liverpool safety glass and a tureen of oxtail soup, still hot. But which was probably best left untouched anyway. She was still poisoning into her sixth decade.

Brian set down his mug on the warm flagstones by the front doorstep, inclining his ear toward a new noise, a rumble of thunder increasing in strength from the west. Michael, the shop's assistant manager was on his way to work, playing a brutal operatic aria through the hot chrome exhaust pipes of his 650 Triton, carving his way through the streets, spreading waves of uncomfortably close-spaced vibrations that loosened dentures and window panes alike. His approach was joined by a new cacophony to the north, a low roar from the tuned engine of a speeding car.

'Dave! Put the dog in its basket. The delinquents are coming,' shouted Brian, getting to his feet and retreating into the vestibule.

'Robbie love… I'm off, I'll see you tonight. Have a nice day off!' yelled Glenys Rudding as her son lay snoring under his quilts in the dormer bedroom of their home on Osgodby Lane. 'I'll put the black bag out…' she added less stridently, before tottering down their drive in her white heels to meet the red Whitborough and District 102 to town.

Michael untied the chinstrap on his black and white Davida helmet and shook out his long hair, then unfastened his gauntlets and pushed them inside, dismounting in the sunshine beside the war memorial in the centre of the square, as Brian approached with two mugs and a small white box under his armpit.

'Is that mine? How kind…'

'The tea. Not the paracetamol. Unless you're in need? It's part of Dean's birthday present.'

'I expect he'll grow up to be a fine young man, one day,' replied Michael, smiling broadly.

'And when are you going to grow up and put a quieter exhaust on that thing?' asked Brian, nodding towards the Triton's peashooter mufflers.

'They make it what it is, Brian. Strangling its bark would be like putting baffles in the whistle of the Flying Scotsman. Or strangling a Spitfire engine. Only a philistine would even…'

'I apologise,' said Brian. 'Could you help Dave inside, asap.'

'Certainly, Brian. Thank you for the drink. Most thoughtful,' he said, smirking.

'How's Fenella?'

'Quite gothic, thank you.'

A bright orange Ford Escort Mexico skidded onto the northern junction of the square from Pastry Lane just as Brian and Michael separated, its engine howling and tyres squealing, just missing the open doors of Humphreys grocers van. Then regained itself and ran onto the parking spaces under the shadow of the war memorial, scattering a party of portly pigeons.

'Well I'll say this much…' began Dave, inside the safety of the shop. 'He certainly is making the most of that car while it's in one piece. I just hope I'm not crossing the road when that mad bastard's driving it.'

Brian walked around the rear of the Ford, taking in the rally sponsor stickers, and knocked on the split rally-style window panel above the driver's door, pressing the front of the small box against the thin perspex.

'It's your lucky day, son!' he mouthed at the driver.

Dean looked up and smiled sarcastically, squinting in the sun.

'Don't you want 'em then?' asked Brian.

'Paracetamol! You bought me paracetamol for my birthday – you tight arse, Brian!'

'Don't be stupid, you can have a few albums, at cost…'

'Cost!'

'I'm pulling your leg.'

'I get a card then, do I?'

'Of course you do.'

'Gimmie a couple of those though will you Bri, I'm a bit shit. Overdid it a bit last night…'

'Thirty pence,' said Brian, deadpan. Dean shot him a filthy look.

'Just kidding!' said Brian, spreading his hands in mock surrender. 'Here – have some tea. You can keep the packet and I'll have what's left later. I'll see you inside in a few minutes. When your car recovers you'll probably be able to lock it.'

'It was made for thrashing – it's a Mexico,' Dean protested.

'And this is a market place. Full of other cars and vans, mums with prams and old people…' grumbled Brian. 'I'd remember that too, if I were you.'

'Beautimann, Buerk and Trippe. Good morning, you're speaking to Shirley, can I ask who…'

'Shirley – it's Mr Beautimann, is Maureen in today?'

'No sir, she rang in sick, said she had a fever. Are you enjoying your holiday, sir?'

'Yes, yes. If Mrs Marshall calls, could you ask her to let me have her instructions following the survey she arranged for the property we're handling the conveyancing for. I wrote to her nearly ten days ago, but she has not got back to me yet. Hold my mail too, thank you.'

'Yes sir, can I give Maureen your regards?'

'Don't disturb her on my account if she's ill. Would you send her a card from the partners? Charge it to petty cash, but mail it out on our address here with the DX number.'

'We could just leave it on her desk, sir?'

'It's better for the business that it goes out and comes back, Shirley.'

'Just as you say, Mr Beautimann.'

'Dave, the phone's ringing,' said Brian as he came into the shop.

'I thought you'd want to take it?'

'Okay, pass it over – Clash City Records.'

'Brian, its Neil. Meet me at the war memorial at ten thirty,' Neil said, coughing harshly.

'Are you all right?'

'No, not really.'

'Everything go smoothly?'

'I'll see you later,' said Neil, hanging up abruptly.

'Any news?' asked Dave uninterestedly, looking out at the traffic.

Brian rolled his eyes, then looked thoughtful momentarily, letting the phone drop down onto its cradle.

Dean stomped wearily down the flagstone steps to the record department in the cellar, pausing to duck under the oak beam above the half landing, then took the last three half-steps in one stride and found the light switch on the wall. Squeezing between the wall and the till at the far end of the basement, he shuffled through the masterbags underneath the singles counter and took out a copy of No sleep 'til Hammersmith. By the time the second track had played out, what little dust had settled on the upper shelving had fled to the carpet, ready for the hoover. Sitting on his stool, he picked up the intercom and pressed the talk button.

'Cellar to bridge – need tea. Urgent, over.'

Derek Beautimann steered the long bonnet of his blue Jaguar XJS into the customer parking bay of MacKenzie Dye Building supplies, slipped off his cap and checked his face in the vanity mirror. The mottling on his forehead was beginning to lose its redness, though the skin was starting to peel, and the backs of his hands still looked hot and pink. He pulled his driving gloves back on and replaced his cap, opened the door and swung his legs out, locked the car then walked over towards the showroom doors, checking either side for attacking fork lift trucks, though the yard was still empty.

'Ere's a fish out of water,' groaned Nev Churchill, looking up from the payments processing desk behind the counter.

'You better go and see what he wants then, Neville,' said Barbara.

'Where's Andy?'

'He went to the warehouse to do the audit.'

'So what are you doing?' he asked without shame.

'I'm strictly kitchens and bathrooms, aren't I,' she smirked sarcastically.

'Bitch,' he mumbled under his breath, dropping a box of invoices into the desk drawer.

Derek was standing at the counter, trying to catch the eye of one of the staff.

'Shop!'

Neville stood up and ambled towards the counter, carrying his stapler. He hated having to deal with the general public. They always seemed to think he had nothing better to do than waste half an hour showing them lots of power tools they had no experience of using and had no intention of buying, then left abruptly, without so much as a thank you, to wander around the yard looking lost and getting in the way.

'I want a spade…' announced Derek flatly, 'and a pickaxe.'

'Soil, aggregate, sand, edging or posthole spades sir? Or is it a shovel you need? Pickaxes – we got sharp end, broad head and breaking axes. Alloy or ash handles. We don't stock mattocks, though.'

'I just want them for digging,' replied Derek, slightly irritated.

'What kind of spoil are you moving sir?'

'Spoil?'

'Whatever material or materials you plan to dig out, sir,' said Neville, making a huge effort not to yawn.

'Soil, of course.'

'We just want to make sure you have the right tools for your project, sir.'

'Of course. I'm not trying to be awkward. What's a mattock?'

'Sharp end or broadhead?'

'I beg your pardon?'

'Pickaxes, sir. Or if you're breaking up rubble we have another type specifically for that with rubber grips.'

'I'm excavating soil. There's no rubble involved.'

'I'd recommend a general purpose spade and a broadhead pickaxe in that case, sir. Is it sandy or clay soil? Clay is heavier, so we'd steer you towards a spade with a narrower blade. Makes the going a bit easier for a gentleman like yourself. Gloves?'

'I'd better have one for clay…'

'The broadhead pickaxes have alloy shafts with plastic grips, so they're tough on the hands. Suede or textile?'

'Ahhh…'

'For tough jobs suede is best. Most of the lads prefer them.'

'Suede then.'

'Is it on account sir?'

'Cash.'

Neville pulled open a drawer below the counter, slapped a grubby calculator on the countertop, then punched in the figures for Mr Beautimann's order whilst he stood awkwardly between the point of sale displays for their Velux windows and a stack of tile adhesive tubs. 'Twenty-nine pounds sixty-five sir, excluding VAT.'

'Can I have a bag for these?'

'We don't have bags for foo – tools, sir,' said Neville hurriedly, correcting himself.

'I beg your pardon!'

'I can carry them to your car sir, if you'd like?'

'Yes, do that would you. It's the blue XJS.'

Brian Drake picked up the phone beneath the counter for the fifth time since his second cup of coffee.

'Brian? It's Phil. When canna packup ma gear?'

'Phil – you're speaking to me *on the phone.*'

'Aye, right enough. It's certainly a phone Brian, eh. Not a walkie talkie, right anuff?'

'No. You're speaking to me *on the phone. On the phone!*'

'Oh shite… Aye, weyll ahl bee queck, the theng is Brian…'

'Speak to me – *in person.*'

'That's the theng. Ah cannae find ye in person, when 'ayr ah cum doon you're no there!'

'Perhaps it's just a happy coincidence? Tomorrow, one o'clock. The benches at the top of Coldharbour. Is that soon enough?'

'Aye, that'll do by the way. Ya daynt haff tae bee funny, Brian.'

'See you later.'

'Later, aye.'

'Oh, and no company. Come on your own.'

'Aye okay.'

'Patience threshold problem?' observed Dave, drily as his older brother slammed the phone onto its cradle. 'Not a good idea, him calling us here.'

'The next time I'll just hang up. Bloody gym junkies. He hasn't got enough patience to have a threshold. All those bloody steroids have pickled his brain.'

58

'Not everyone goes badly on 'em, Brian. Ian's still sound. Good lad is Ian.'

'Oh no, not everyone. Just the ones that bother me.'

'Well, you know the answer to that, don't you. Give it up.'

'I can't. We still need the money.'

'No we don't, Brian. You do. And don't tell me you don't get a vicarious thrill from being Dr Jekyll. They'll turn on you eventually, I'd hate to get on the wrong side of that lot.'

'What time is it? I'm meeting Neil at ten.'

'Plenty of time. That black cane you bought Michael for his birthday? He says it rattles when you shake it.'

'It's a swordstick, not a cane.'

'What!'

'It's a swordstick. He's a smart lad. He'll figure it out.'

'You didn't tell 'im?'

'And spoil the surprise?'

'You bloody nutcase – he's walking around like some Victorian ghoul with a three foot long kebab spike inside a walking stick.'

'A proper Percy.'

'Eh?'

'Percy Blakeney. The Scarlet Pimpernel. The James Bond of the French Revolution. He had several sword canes. Pistols disguised as snuff boxes, lapel knives. Miniature grenades made to look like shoe buckle pommels. The man was a walking arsenal of tricks. Fascinating character.'

'Brian, what if he gets stopped by a copper?'

'If you were a copper, would you go anywhere near him? In those clothes? Come on, most of 'em think he's an extra from Poldark.'

59

'You might 'ave a point. But…'

'It wouldn't even enter their heads. Swordsticks! Nobody knows what they are, they've passed from living memory. I've never seen another in any antique shop in England. Besides, you can't draw it until you figure out the mechanism. It's a special kind of disc and pin release.'

'Oh well. That's all right then. That'll stand up in court. "Yes your honour, – I was carrying an offensive weapon, though at no time did it pose a threat to anyone because it has a secret safety catch that only someone who was intimately familiar with it could trigger." Case dismissed. There's a shifty looking bloke with a shemagh wrapped round his head waving at you from the memorial, by the way. Doesn't look too 'appy.'

'Why are you so sure it's me he's waving at?'

'Well no one I know looks like Yasser Arafat.'

'It must be Neil, come to say he's leaving for Palestine then. Mind the phone, I'll be back soon,' said Brian, opening the door. He walked out into the morning air, and zigzagged between the traffic queuing to turn out of the square and reached the bicycle racks, closing in on the stranger, wondering who was going to speak first, though the man pulled the head scarf closer around his face. Brian broke the silence first, sensing some tension, but not wanting to waste time.

'What's with the sand scarf, Neil?'

'I fell 'ead first in some nettles – and I've cut me head open. So don't tekk the piss. I'm not in the mood.'

'Sorry to hear that, mate.'

'What's pissing me off is I can't even go to A&E and get it sewn up, because of all the heat we had getting your gear last night. There were a queue like a conga outside the doctor's an all. Claire had to patch me up at home with some steri strips and some superglue.'

'Is me stuff safe?'

'Yeah I'm fine, thanks for asking Brian. Robert's fine as well.'

'Where's the stuff, Neil?'

'One of your bags is at Roberts. The other I 'ad to leave under the back of the surfers' hut behind the boards. Are you deaf Brian, or just an asshole? I'll send Rob your thanks, shall I – for a job well done?'

'My bags are under the old cafe?'

'Just shut yer cake 'ole an open yer ears. We had trouble, the boat hit a sandbar and we capsized, and afterwards it got worse – we had company.'

'In Cayton Bay?'

'In Cayton Bay. Not the quiet little place people seem to think it is. Ever seen Race with the Devil Brian? Two couples on vacation in a big RV?'

'In Whitborough? You're 'aving me on!'

'Well, they'd love your shop, wouldn't they. And yer Black Sabbath t-shirts.'

'It's just fashion for heavy metal kids. They're about as satanic as the Army Cadets.'

'Well, there were a group of bloody Satanists on the plateau last night. And two coppers in the woods, though we missed them I think. I think they kicked a wasp's nest, so they were a bit pre-occupied.'

'So what about the other lot?'

'I decked a couple of the bastards. Seemed to put 'em on the back foot so we could get away. They seemed to be expecting me – haven't figured that out yet. Didn't stick around too long though. Bad manners when you've just kicked someone in the bollocks, Brian.'

'One bag's no good. I need them both – you'll…'

'I'll what?' growled Neil, taking a defiant step forwards.

'Look, there's no need to…' stuttered Brian, suddenly on the defensive.

'You're cruising…'

'No, no – you've been through too much, I can see that. I was only going to ask if…'

'Let's get one thing straight. I came here to let you know where your stuff is. My part in your little enterprise is over. X marks the spot,' he snapped, thrusting a piece of paper at his brother-in-law's stomach. 'And you can stick it,' he added, looking at Brian then striding away from the memorial.

'The Arab delegation has stormed off. Very complex people the Arabs. I think Brian and I might need a minute alone, D,' said Dave.

'Sure. I'll move some dust around.'

Sonja Knowles flew into the attic bedroom of the dormer bungalow she shared with her husband Mark and two boys, on Osgodby lane, as he was one leg into his trousers, and burst into tears, fidgeting with her rings and tugging at her bracelets.

'Sonja, what is it?'

'Oliver's not in his room, Mark! He's gone!'

'He went to cubs last night though, didn't he? Didn't he stay with George's family?'

'No. I don't think so, nobodies rung. His bed's not been slept in…'

'Wake Connor up, ask Connor,' said Mark, pulling on his socks. 'Connor!'

'Connor! Connor! Where's Oliver?' she shouted, barging into her eldest's room, interrogating a lumpen mound under a Yamaha duvet cover.

'UHHH. What!'

'Connor, listen…'

'Mum, stop shouting.'

'Did you see Oliver come home last night?'

'No. Can you shut my door, Mum?'

'Get the phone book out and call George's parents, Sonja,' yelled her husband. 'If they don't pick up then call the police,' he shouted, pulling on a shirt. 'I'll check with the neighbours. Can you call work and let them know I might be late.'

Twenty minutes later, underneath the enormous quilt on Connor's bed, his girlfriend began to speak. 'Conn? Conn, wake up babe. It's gone eight.'

'What?'

'I've got to go.'

'Not now Jess, please. They'll see you. Me mum's on one. Just stay under the quilt until she goes.'

'I can't. Look – I'll sneak out through the conny. I've got to get home before college to get some other clothes. Mum and Dad are taking me out for a Chinese before our finals. I can't miss it, Conn.'

'Oh God…'

'Where are my knickers?'

'Over there, on the Death Star.'

'Where?'

'The black thing. In front of the Christopher Walken poster.'

'Where's my bra?'

'On the Messerschimdt.'

'Conn!'

'The plane with the yellow nose…'

'Point!'

'There…'

'You can call me later. I'm going to Viv and Tereasa's after the meal for a catch up before Easter weekend. Shelley split up with Gary and I want to find out what happened.'

'They were together at the beach party.'

'Oh she was putting on a show, they just had a snog – because. It's over. How come your Oliver never arrived? You don't think he and his friends had some of our beer? I was so embarrassed, us turning up empty handed.'

'Ollie's only nine, Jess. I doubt he's got a taste for it yet. Nobody noticed we brought nowt anyway.'

'Oh yes they did! That bitch Sarah Fenton was trying to milk it, until she sat in that puddle of tar or creosote or whatever it was. I nearly lost it. Marie and Jane were in fits.'

'He was supposed to be coming down with George and Matthew. The three of them were carrying our drink straight from Cubs. Did you know he glued up the locks on Dad's new Cortina? Dad thought it was the Coleman's kid. He had a stand-up slagging match with 'em on their doorstep. He'll be bloody furious if he finds out it was Ollie.'

'Oh no!'

'Jess, stop giggling!'

Back at Market Square, the Drake brothers were in conference.

'So what happened?'

'He left it. Left it under the surfers' hut. But he gave me a map. A friggin map!'

'Well, can't you ask 'im to go get it. Why did he leave it there anyways?'

'He fell ovver and gashed his head. The boat capsized. There were two coppers sneaking around there too.'

'Oh great! That's just fantastic! What a balls up!'

'Well, I have to go and get it myself.'

'Did you have an argument?'

'What makes you think we had a bust-up?'

'A bust-up, was it?'

'Dave, we didn't have an argument, okay?'

'It didn't look too friendly from where I was sitting.'

'Dave, I've got to figure out how to get our gear out of there. That's my biggest problem right now. So can we change the subject, please.'

'It may be *our* gear, but it's your mess.'

'How would you go about getting to it without suspicion, in the daytime. Without being seen?'

'You won't probably. The thing is, you'd need to look like you belong in the landscape. You need to blend into the surroundings.'

'You want me to dress up like a bloody Druid? Or a crusty?'

'No no no. What I mean is, you need people to accept you're there for a reason. You need to have a purpose… you can't go down there in your leather, you'll stick out a mile.'

'Sorry, am I being thick? Because I'm just not catching your train of thought at all?

'Get some walking gear, a backpack, a pair of walking boots. You'll need a big rucksack for the bags, something with a frame. A sleeping bag rolled up underneath.'

'Dave, you're a genius.'

'It's not hard Brian. Better get second hand gear though; it'll make you look more authentic, the more scuffs and knocks the better. Nothing new or shiny.'

'Who do we know I could borrow from? What about your old gear? You did that Duke of Edinburgh's thing,'

'The Duke of Edinburgh's Award scheme – I only did the bronze; I don't even know if I kept any of my stuff. I can't remember.'

'Dean went to Glastonbury, didn't he?

'In his car.'

'Shit.'

'You could try the charity shops in town and the Army and Navy store. Boyes is good too, for outdoor gear. Won't cost you much…'

'Sonja, what did George and Matthew's parents say, hun?'

'They said Ollie went down the path to Kenwith woods with their boys just after getting to Cubs. They say they got separated and lost him in the woods. He said he'd found a new bunker and wanted to show them.'

'I don't believe that for a minute. Those boys know those woods well enough, they've been in and out of them for years. If you really get lost, then you shout. The other possibility is he's fallen and knocked himself out. Did you call the police?'

'What did the neighbours say, Mark?'

'No, nothing.'

'Well I called the police station and they're sending somebody to take a statement from us.'

'What, this morning?'

'Yes, in an hour or two. God Mark, I'm so worried.'

'Is Connor out of his pit yet?'

'He was in the bathroom last time I heard. Then I heard him go out the conservatory, when I was on the phone. But the shower's still running up there.'

'Sonja, did you order a taxi?'

'No.'

'Well there's a Beehive taxi pulling onto our drive, there's a boy in the back... It's Oliver!'

'So no one is allowed access to them?' fumed Superintendent D'Ascoyne.'

'Not even the relatives, sir. For forty-eight hours at least, they said.'

'You did emphasise the importance of us speaking to them, I trust? I've no report. No logbooks. Nothing. We've no idea what happened to them since their last radio call on Tuesday night.'

'Dr Rowbotham insisted they needed forty-eight hours at least to assess their condition.'

'Did he give any hint at all about when they were going to come round?'

'Only that they were in the isolation wing in separate rooms, sir.'

'Well, we'll just have to hope that the Chief Constable doesn't ask me for an explanation – for the damage report and repair requests in the next two days. That's all, Ray.'

'Yes sir.'

'Oh – Ray?'

'Yes sir?'

'Until these doctors report their findings, I don't want

to have any unsubstantiated rumours circulating. Do I make myself clear?'

'Absolutely clear, sir.'

'Ask Sergeant Moyne to come up, would you? And if you hear anybody speculating, you're to report to me.'

'Yes sir.'

'Well Moyne, when did the SIO hand over to Highways?'

'Just after 7.30am, sir, though Highways were still clearing up at 9. The on-call investigator is sending us his report this afternoon.'

'Have we organised cover for Dodds and Deighton?'

'Derek, do I look like I do a lot of walking? I'm built for comfort, not marching through the bloody wilderness. I'd look ridiculous in hiking gear. Desperate actually.'

'Maureen, we're only going back to the plateau.'

'So why do I have to wear hiking boots and a bloody nylon safari jacket?'

'Well, we can't go in our ordinary clothes – we'll look suspicious. It's only for tonight. If you're afraid someone you know is going to see you out of your heels, then you've no cause to worry have you? You're not going to see them on the Pennine Way. Besides, there are lots of faa…er fuller…'

'You were going to say fat, weren't you, Derek?'

'No…'

'Don't bother trying to sugar it. Just come right out and say it.'

'I was going to say lots of fuller-figured people enjoy outdoor pursuits.'

'I've been sitting here just waiting for you to call and

insult me, then drag me off on some wild goose chase, when all I want to do is sit in comfort and eat a couple of cream cakes. I need a little treat to mend my nerves. Quite frankly, after last night's fiasco, I'm amazed you're even considering going back there; I think we both need a night of peace and quiet. What's so important that it can't wait until tomorrow night?'

'The treasure I found isn't under your sofa.'

'Treasure you found?'

'Maureen, I…'

'Treasure you found?'

'I found a small chest…'

'Derek, are we talking treasure as in gold and jewels?

'I found some gold coins in a small chest last December.'

'Don't let me stop you Derek. You just keep going.'

'The location was marked on a map, inside the secret compartment of a linen chest I bought at auction last year. I was sure from the markings, engravings and the quality of the construction that the chest had once belonged to Henry Kettlewell and was contemporary with the disappearance of his fortune in the summer of 1645. The Royalist garrison at the castle was besieged by the Parliamentarians and surrendered in July of that year, if my history is correct, by which time his fortune had disappeared. He was recorded as having been killed, but the garrison's commander ordered some of their officers to take it to safety and bury it temporarily nearby, to prevent it falling into the hands of the Roundheads, who looked as though they were going to overwhelm the defenders at the castle.'

'Keep talking…'

'His fortune was never found – even the Crown never

knew how much was lost. Much of it was gold coin from an Armada ship that foundered off Filey Brigg in a storm. They called it the Treasure of the Mar del Norte. The Spanish were going to use it to buy English mercenaries to bring down Elizabeth I, if the invasion was successful. Of course it never happened. It was a disaster.'

'And you've got some of this gold?'

'I took it home.'

'How much have you got, Derek?'

'There's a lot more nearby. But that part of the map had crumbled away, I needed the last piece of the jigsaw. Hence the ritual.'

'The fiasco.'

It wasn't a complete waste of time Maureen.'

'It was a bloody disaster Derek, let's be honest. But you're too proud to admit it – God only knows where that thing is. It'll come back to haunt us, I'm telling you now. But I'll forget about that for the moment. I want to hear about this gold you've found, so keep talking.'

'The point is, I know where the rest of the treasure is. But I need your help. That's why I'm calling you.'

'I want to see some of it, before I even agree to move off this settee, Derek. Until I see some of it with my own eyes I'm staying put right here.'

'So you'll help?'

'I want to see it, Derek.'

'Well, stay where you are, I'll be round within the hour. Don't move.'

'I just said I wasn't going anywhere, I'll leave the door off the latch and put Bert in the conservatory.'

'Right Oliver, we're not going to get angry with you son, but we want to know where you've been all night. Now we want the truth. We know you went down to the woods with George and Matthew, instead of going to cubs,' said Mark Knowles, looking to his wife as they sat around the kitchen table.

'Oliver, you must tell us where you've been' said Mrs Knowles, sounding tense.

'I found a new bunker – from the war, Dad. I took them down to see it, but we got lost in the dark we did. We got split and I was in my egg, but I couldn't see. I got lost and…'

'What were you carrying in those bags?' asked his father.

'Bags, Dad?'

'The carrier bags. Matthew and George said they were…'

'Drinks, Dad. They were drinks for the tuck shop.'

'Then why didn't you leave them at Cubs?'

'I heard some of the other boys saying they were going to steal them off us, so we left before they could get us. We was going to hide them in the woods, for them to be safe. We could get them back later.'

'You took those bags all the way down to the woods?' asked his father, trying not to sound like an interrogator.

'You're upsetting him, Mark,' said his wife.

'I just want to be clear on the bags,' he said determinedly.

'I don't give a damn about the bags,' she countered. 'I'm just glad he's home.'

'I got lost Mum, it was dark.'

'He's tired, Mark. He needs to sleep. Ollie, go outside and shake your head over the lawn. You've got bits of paper mache stuck in your hair. Make sure you give it a good rub or it'll be all over the carpets. Then go to bed and get some sleep.'

'We'll talk again later,' added his father ominously, as he went into the hall to let himself outside. As the door closed, Mr Knowles let rip. 'You do realise, you've just let him off the hook, what were you thinking, Sonja? We were just getting to the truth, and you give him a reprieve. It's very nice to have him home, but aren't you at all concerned about where he's been and what he's been up to?'

'Of course I am!'

'Then back me up! Don't send him off to bed and give him time to cook up a story.'

'I'll ask him to come back...'

'Not now. It's too late; if we get him back down now he'll just clam up. We'll have to wait a few hours – and before he has any food, Sonja. If he's hungry it'll help us get to the truth. Matthew's dad told me he'd seen a Vodka bottle label through one of the bags.'

'Vodka! Is he sure?'

'That's why I was pressing him – I doubt they were drinking it themselves. So who was it for? I think he's cooked up this old bunker story; no one's found a new one in decades. I think our son and his friends were going to a beach party...'

'Connor!'

'Oh my God Derek, it's beautiful! No Bert! Down! Get down...' snapped Maureen , turning over the heavy gold coin in her fingers.

'Down! This must be that King Philip of Spain,' she whispered, her eyes widening.

'I thought you were going to put him in the conservatory?'

'What's that, Derek?'

'The dog... Get off! OFF!' he snapped, pushing her

72

rough-haired tan and white terrier off his clean socks. The dog looked up at him, stopping momentarily, then carried on assaulting his ankle with its private parts even more vigorously than before.

'Who's a Daddy's boy then?' she cooed, enjoying Derek's discomfort, biting into another jaffa cake. 'He likes you,' she grinned.

'If you won't put this dog somewhere, I swear I'll…'

'What, Derek?'

'Will you please just put it in another room,' he pleaded. 'Please, so we can talk sensibly.'

'BERT!' The terrier stopped again. Maureen rolled up her TV Times magazine and hit the dog on its hindquarters. But Bert whirled around and bit the magazine – and her finger.

'AHHH, YOU LITTLE BUGGER!' she yelped.

'Perhaps he'd like a jaffa cake?' asked Derek, trying to bring his facial muscles under control.

Brian picked his way through the Tuesday afternoon crowds on Long Acre, Whitborough's main street, carrying two large bulging carrier bags and a tatty second hand rucksack which he used like buffers to move through the of tourists and locals crowding the streets. The early spring sunshine was drawing large numbers of people from York, Leeds and Newcastle to the seaside towns along the coast.

Reaching the shop doorway, he hurried inside and dropped his bags behind the counter. 'Michael, can you manage here for ten minutes? Dave and I need to talk upstairs – Dave?'

'Got some outdoor kit, have we?' said Dave.

'A few bits.'

'I think I shall manage,' sighed Michael theatrically, pretending to brush some imaginary fluff from his elaborate cuffs. 'I shall send out for some teas.'

'Two brandy coffees.'

'David is a fervent supporter of the view that compact discs will be the format of choice for all recorded music by the end of the decade, Brian. I myself am in the opposite camp. One cannot compare what looks like a camping shaving mirror, with the feeling one gets holding a Bakelite album and all its accompanying paraphernalia, posters, lyric sheets and so on…'

'Really.'

'He read it – in Sounds.'

'Must be right then…'

The two brothers went toward the rear of the shop and opened the door to the old staircase, walking up the bare wooden boards into the derelict first floor rooms.

'Right, mekk it quick. I don't like being up here, even in daylight,' said Dave, speaking first.

'I need you to help me to get the bags,' said Brian.

'What – tonight?'

'It won't tekk long. I know you were going to the pub – but we won't be longer than a couple of hours, I promise… I got you a pair of walking trousers while I was out.'

'It's Wednesday night, Brian. I was going out for an Indian with Luce.'

'We can go as soon as we close – we'll be back home for seven or eight.'

'I still need to have a shower and get changed.'

'Please – just this once. There's no one else I can ask, I'm stuck.'

'A couple of hours?'

'I just can't leave the stuff another night. It's too risky.'

'We park as close as we can to the trail?'

'Yeah, absolutely. We can change in here as soon as we close, it'll save time – then go straight there.'

'Well, we'd better not be more than two hours. You owe me, Brian…'

'Yeah, yeah.'

'What did ya get?'

'A second hand rucksack with a frame for a tenner, from Help The Aged, some trousers and a lightweight jacket from the camping store and some walking shoes. You're a 32 waist, aren't ya?'

'I'm a 30 waist, but they'll be right. You need a bit o' slack in your outdoor gear.'

'I saw our traffic warden, when I was coming down Long Acre.'

'Who was he ticketing?'

'He was in his civvies, I nearly didn't recognise him, his face was all blotchy and puffed up. He was with that guy from Beehive taxis – they looked like a pair of plague victims, everyone was giving them a wide berth.'

'Nice.'

'It's not funny, Derek. So you can wipe that smirk off your face.'

'Maureen, I'm not smirking.'

'Oh yes you are. You'd better show some sympathy or you'll be going alone.'

'Honestly Maureen, I'm not smirking.'

'Go upstairs into the bathroom. There's a bottle of TCP

and a box of plasters in the bathroom cabinet on the top shelf,' she said irritably, holding her hand under the cold tap over the kitchen sink. 'You little sod!' she snapped, frowning at Bert behind the conservatory door as he stood on the arm of her cane chair, trying to look appealing.

'We'll need to set off fairly soon, Maureen,' said Derek, examining the base of a classical figurine from his host's formica display cabinet.

'Put the coin on my mantelpiece – I'll be ten minutes upstairs and then we can go.'

Robert Rudding woke late and stood up gingerly, stumbling forwards and nearly tripping over his clothes. He hobbled into the bathroom and turned on the bath taps, walking past the clock in the hall without registering the time, then sat on the toilet and tested the temperature with his fingers while the bath filled. Pouring four large capfuls of Radox into the hot water, he climbed in nervously after the water had reached two thirds full. He bit his lip as the water turned his clammy skin pink. Alone in the house he took his time, then dressed slowly before walking downstairs into the kitchen. He took out a bottle of milk from the fridge to pour on his cereal, then suddenly noticed the black bin liner he had left beside the shoe rack the night before was no longer there.

Robert flew into a panic, dimly recalling the voice of his mother many hours earlier. He flung open the back door, looking up and down the drive. Just as he about to run down to the kerb, his neighbour emerged from the adjoining bungalow and nodded as to him he walked over to his car.

'Morning Robert. Are you all right, lad? You look a bit off colour,' he asked, stopping suddenly.

'There was a bag in our kitchen, Roy. Did you see me mum put it out this morning?' he asked, sounding jittery. 'A black bin liner, did the bin men take it?'

'She missed them, Robert. I took it for you.'

'You took it!' he almost shouted. 'Where?'

'Is something the matter?' he said, taken aback.

'Sorry Roy. Me mum put it out by mistake – it was mine. There was some of my stuff in it.'

'Oh lad, I am sorry. What there something valuable in it?'

'Yeah, really valuable, it's really important. Where did you take it?'

'I didn't take it to the tip lad, I just pushed it in one of the bins on the precinct, outside the fish shop. I should think it'll still be there if you… Well I suppose I could take you down there and…'

'Can we go now?'

'Are you going to put some shoes on?'

'Give me a second – you can start the car, I'll be two minutes.'

'Are we going in my car or yours, Derek?'

'Yours – if that's all right. It's less conspicuous. Shall I drive?'

'You're not insured. But thank you for offering.'

'I'll just get the pickaxe and shovel out of my boot.'

'Are they clean, Derek?'

'Yes of course, they've never been used. They're wrapped up in a holdall.'

'Well, there's some of my court shoes and wedges in there, so be careful where you put them. Don't just go chucking it in.'

'I thought we could park on Golf Links Road, close to the car park, then walk across the field to the stile. It'll save us some time.'

'Is that the only bag you're taking?'

'Yes, but it's expandable. Anyway, I'd planned to leave the tools behind if we find something, and come back for them later.'

'I don't wish to be nosy, Derek, but what does your wife think you're doing, going out with a spade and a pickaxe in that huge bag.'

'We don't stalk each other when we're apart, Maureen. We have our own sets of friends and our own interests. We have a healthy balance of time together and time apart.'

'But you must have an alibi…'

'Why must I have an alibi?'

'Well – what do you tell her when we have one of our "meetings." Surely you don't tell her what goes on?'

'Of course I don't. It's none of her business.'

'Oh. Sorry for asking…'

My private life and personal arrangements have got nothing to do with you. So can we just concentrate on the here and now?'

'I was only asking.'

'Well, don't.'

Chapter Three

Tuesday Evening

The cold cloak of late afternoon shadows swept down upon the sparse wilderness of Langdale End, smothering the vibrant green colours of spring under its steady advance into the valleys and hollows within the landscape, turning purples to monochrome and greens to shades of grey and charcoal. The last rays of the setting sun stuttered across the untidy contours of lumpen fields, broken walls and borders, towards the low box huddle of mossy stone cottages at Cloughton village.

Here on the widest part of the high street, inside the lounge bar of the Shirestones Hotel, stood Lindsay Boldwood, polishing his optics and glasses in the manner of someone with time on their hands. Unaware he was soon to become the only active werewolf in North Yorkshire for nearly four hundred years, infected by a strange trick of biology through an exchange of paperbacks during a visit to the County Council's mobile library.

It could have been Jacques Cousteau's Undersea World, Born Free or Frederick Forsyth's The Dogs of War, for she had sneezed on all three. But it was probably Mrs Comery's staple gun and the small drop of blood it had drawn from her thumb that had sealed his fate. It was about to make his night-time strolls around the district more interesting than he could possibly imagine. Only his companion cat Bagshott had thus far sensed the danger. Shunning the warmth of his ample lap for the safety of the high pelmets around the hotel's windows and the carved oak fence around the top of the old welsh dresser, hissing with all the venom a sedentary old cat could muster each time he approached with her milk and dried biscuits.

The only other clues that things were not all as they should be became apparent after he experienced a rush of blood and sudden feeling of euphoria passing the cold meats counter at Costcutter, and an overpowering desire on his sporadic walks to scratch and take the air at each and every lamp post and gate.

At the pool table behind the bar, Mr Boldwood's nephew Graham and his friend Ben were working on the last page of the accident statement for Graham's latest insurance claim, sharing creative writing duties and composing a simple illustrative account of the events prior to his taking flight over a boundary wall beside the B1076 and breaching a corrugated asbestos sheep shed with his Barry Sheene replica helmet.

Graham was trying to flatter his friend into continuing their collaboration.

'Are you okay doing the drawings? I'm bloody hopeless at stuff like that, Ben. I can't draw for shit. I really can't.'

'It's your handwriting though – I'm not doing the whole thing for ya.'

'No – yeah – I'll write it up, I'd just make a balls up of the drawing.'

'Right. Well let's get it over with. So let's get this straight – you were tekking the first bend just before the national speed limit signs, on the road out the village to Heyburn Dyke, right?'

'Aye.'

'So – if I draw the curve of the road here, in the middle of the box and put an "X" on the middle of the curve, to mark where you high-sided; that'll leave plenny o' space to get the other stuff they want inside the margins, the road numbers and the walls and the pavements and gives us enough room to put in the sheep pen.'

'Don't forget to put the shit in. It was the friggin cowpats that made me highside.'

'I don't get to draw much shit at A-Level. But our Art Lecturer Rommel says, if I do a degree I can paint as much shite as I like and call it art. As long as I can justify it in an intellectual sense he says, keeping a straight face of course. You was inside the white lines on your side were ya – about halfway round when you lost it, right?'

'Then the bike hit into the wall that I cleared. What d'you mean, in an intellectual sense?'

'I'll tell you later, let's get on with this bloody form of yours first and leave the art world bullshit for later. What they wanna know is where the bike got out of shape, and started to skid and stuff.'

'The middle of the road … in the shitpats.'

'Your side?'

'Sorta.'

'We'd better not put you anywhere else. They'd kick out the claim.'

'My side then.'

'The cowshit was on your side wasn't it?'

'It was all ovver – and the cows had walked through it. I can still smell the bloody stuff now.'

'Boys! Are you having another?' called his uncle through the serving hatch at the bar.

'Two more pints of lager Unc, thanks.'

'Why'd they call 'im Rommel? This bloke, your teacher.'

'He went out to Tobruk in the sixties after Uni on some hippie ticket. Got hooked on the desert and the food. Used to wear sand goggles and an Afrika Korps pith helmet he bought at one of the markets in Tobruk during the day. Then at night he'd get pissed on schnapps and this weird local hooch. There's a picture of him sat on an old Panzer in the desert, in the darkroom at college. How many rounds is that?'

'I think this is the fourth.'

'It says, "what was your estimated speed at the time of the incident." Any idea?'

'Forty, fifty maybe, I dunno, but I was braking when I saw the shit-slick.'

'But you were still in the thirty limit…'

'Thirty – put thirty.'

'Let's put twenty-five. It's a tightish bend after all. Just to be on the safe side, Gray.'

'Okay, twenty-five then.'

'Just out of interest, how long have you got to wear that thing?' said Ben, looking at Graham's plaster collar.

'Two more weeks. It itches like mad most of the time. I've got a fully grown beard going on underneath the friggin thing. I can't even have a piss standing up, coz I can't see where I'm going.'

'How'd you sleep wee it?'

'Not well at all, it's a right pain. I need to prop me sen up with loads of pillows and sleep half sat up. I can't wait to get the friggin thing off.'

'Have you got any change for the jukebox?'

'Have a look in me denim, top left hand pocket I think.

There's a few fifties and some tens in there. What we having on?'

'Thought I'd stick some DC on, an' some Blue Oyster Cult, UFO, Zepp.'

'There's that track called Complete Control on it too, stick that on, it's ace.'

'That's punk innit? The Clash?'

'Yeah but the guitar is awesome, my brother's into stuff like that. And the Damned. It's brilliant. Stick it on.'

'All right, it's your coin.'

Brian and Dave were preparing to leave their home in their Saab.

'We can go down Cornelian Drive or Golf Links Rd. Golfers is a bit quieter,' said Brian.

'Go to the end of Golf Links, where the car park is. It's dark there and there's hardly any traffic after six.'

'Have you still got Neil's map?'

'Map? If you know where the surf hut is it's a waste of paper.'

'Yeah, it probably was, but he needed to show me which side of the hut he stowed the gear under.'

'Suppose so. You know where now, do you?'

'Yeah – behind the boards under the outside tap at the back.'

'Was there just the one bag, Brian? I want to be in and out quick.'

'Yeah, only one.'

Lindsay Boldwood had been looking forward to a few peaceful minutes alone with his newspaper and a chance to try out the Slendertone belt he had ordered from Grattans Catalogue a month before, shut away in the privacy of the toilet block at the back of the inn.

Unfortunately, the lychanthrope virus, which had lain dormant in his hypothalamus since his infection, now began to replicate, secreting gigantic amounts of corrupted hormones into his pituitary gland, kick-starting a very inconvenient and violent metamorphosis, which the rapid electrical pulses from his new toning belt only exacerbated.

The migraine, which had begun to build behind his eyes as he took his seat with the celebrity news pages of the Daily Mail, was going to cost somebody an arm and a leg by the end of the night. Or at least the equivalent in damages.

The sudden and forceful erection of his dormant sexual organ caused him to yelp in agony, when the tender end of his manhood thudded against the cold porcelain of the toilet bowl at the same moment his toenails ripped through the seams of his loafers.

Coarse hairs poured forth from the darkening skin on his back, chest, arms and legs as the runaway transformation accelerated with grim momentum. He struggled to his feet, on paws, reaching out for support, wrenching the toilet roll dispenser away from the tiles, as a massive abdominal spasm expelled his breakfast with a percussive splatter, before he tripped over his fallen trousers and smashed down the door, howling in pain when the door closer slider retaliated and ripped a clump of pubic hair from his groin.

'Did you 'ear that?' said Ben, struggling to communicate above the noise of the jukebox.

Graham squinted and squeezed his eyebrows together, making a face.

'Did you 'ear that bang?' called Ben, shouting over the fade out to "Rock and roll damnation."

'What?'

'Did you 'ear the bang out back...'

..'It's probably Unc changing a barrel. Go ask him if we can help ourselves to another.'

'Where's the cellar room?'

'The hatch is in the yard, you can get there through the bogs.'

Lindsay Boldwood could accurately state that no one had ever left his pub on all fours, under a cloud; it had never crossed his mind he might be the first exception. Panting in the doorway of the toilet block he surveyed the beer garden, such as it was, with its huge potted palms and layers of decking, and cocked his leg on a large hosta, reading the scents drifting in the air. But the overpowering aroma of freshly made Bolognese cooling in the pump room eclipsed them all. He started to run, straight towards the ramp leading down to cellar, bounding towards the scent of the meat.

'Mr Boldwood?'

The sudden arrival of a powerful new odour made the hairs on his coat prickle. A delicious mixture of sweat, urine on leather and young blood assaulted his senses, but it was too late. His run had carried him to the very lip of the ramp, and he plunged down the slippery galvanised sheet steel of the keg slide, landing in a heap on the woven nylon sacks used to cushion the force of a full barrel after its roll.

Ben arrived at the toilet block exit, just in time to see an enormous animal hurtle across the yard and disappear into the basement, glancing briefly back towards him for a split second before it fell out of sight. Without conscious thought, he slammed the door and pushed the top and bottom bolts home trembling, then dashed back into the main building.

Four miles away in Cayton Bay, another evil was stirring. The greater part of the mine demon Tetarzapamdomestoz had left the bay and arrived in the town to infiltrate the water tanks and kitchens of Whitborough's Grand Duchess Hotel and the adjoining Gay Cavalier Theatre, but had left enough of its essence behind to leave a significant legacy of harm on the plateau. The grass had come to life again as a carnivorous carpet, each stalk working with its neighbour to sniff out beetles and insects. Buttercups closed on flies and bees, whilst nettles dripped poisonous sap on small mammals and ladder ferns grew sharp fibrous thorns. Hedgehogs ambushed foxes. Nature was turning on its head.

Ben Wilson ran back into the pool room of the Shirestones hotel, kicked the door shut and pulled a pool cue from the rack, unscrewing it quickly with fierce concentration, before ramming the thinner front end into the gap between the bottom of the door and the carpet and kicking it home with the steel toe of his motorcycle boot. Then he grabbed another cue and wrenched out the plug for the jukebox.

Graham watched, open mouthed with fascination as he tore down a thin tapestry from the chimney breast and wound it tightly around the end of the cue, knotting it off then soaking it with brandy from behind the bar.

'Gimmie your lighter Gray, quick…'

'Ben, what the hell d'ya think ya doing!'

'Give us yer the lighter…' said Ben, sounding petrified.

'Mate, are you all right? You're as white as a bloody snowball…'

'I need the friggin lighter now, Graham, give it 'ere…'

'Are you gonna set fire to that?'

'You bet your arse I am. I want some friggin protection when that bloody thing in the yard gets in here.'

'Thing – what thing? What you jabbering about? Gray, hey, no – not the matches, don't light that… I'm serious, mate.'

'So am I – there's a friggin wolf loose in the back yard!' shouted Ben, shaking a pile of loose matches over a beer towel, 'It's bloody huge – it's just scared the shit out of me. I think it got your uncle, mate. I'm sorry. There's blood and bits of skin all over the floors and the wall in the toilet block. It ran into the cellar. But it saw me, Gray. It's the most evil looking thing I've ever seen. It's in here! In the friggin hotel.'

'You're kidding me aren't ya!'

'No. No way am I making it up. I was going for a piss, until I saw all the gore. I had to walk through puddles of it to get a look into the yard. The bog's wrecked, door smashed up. I'm scared shitless.'

'You've got a wet patch on your jeans – down to your knee, mate,' said Graham, trying not to sound judgmental. 'Look mate, – you're scaring me, but I need to see. You can't expect me to believe my uncle's been…'

'There's no way I'm staying here if you open that door, Gray. No way on earth I'm staying in this place. I mean it.

I'm telling you straight. I'm leaving here right now – with or without you.'

Just at that moment both young men heard a loud deep growl under the floor. Then they looked at each other – the colour draining from their faces.

'Is..?'

'Yeah. Yeah, I think so… Go!' hissed Ben, pointing to the front doors.

Suddenly the floor hatch behind the bar flew open and Ian Dermott – the pub's part-time second chef leapt up, slamming the hatch lid back down.

'If you've seen what I just saw, then get the hell out now,' he warned. 'The door to the stairs isn't gonna hold it for long. Get out of here, lads. I'll be right behind you.'

Ian had been scrubbing, peeling and slicing up the vegetables for lunch, when he heard a dull thud and a flurry of scratching sounds from inside the pump room next door. He dropped the potato he was skinning in the gritty brown water of the sink bowl and laid down his peeler between the taps, then rinsed his hands and dried them, grumbling to himself, then stood still and listened. He heard loud slurping and panting noises beyond the door, like a large dog out of breath.

'Bloody fox hounds!' he spat, grabbing the wooden shaft of the floor mop with one hand and seizing the door handle with the other, pulling the door open.

Stepping down into the cold air of the scullery, it took his eyes a few seconds to comprehend what he was looking at. Sprawled over the stack of pallets in the corner of the cellar, where he left food to cool, was something about the size of a Great Dane, as stocky as a bear – in the shape of a wolf. He could only see the back of it. But at the same time he was also extremely relieved he couldn't see its head, which was deep inside the stew pan of paprika and black pepper seasoned Bolognese. He closed his eyes and opened them again, being very careful not to make any sort of movement. But the thing was still there, gulping down the last remnants of five kilos of best mince. What he couldn't understand was how it had come to be wearing Mr Boldwood's Royal Navy tie and a strange kind of money belt. It was probably the most bizarre and unnerving picture he had ever seen. He also knew he didn't want to spend a moment longer with it at any price. As quietly as possible he stepped back up in the scullery and pulled the door softly back into its frame. There was a faint click as the bolt slid home, then a growl and a burp. Snatching the biggest Sabatier knife from the draining board, he grabbed the keys and dashed towards the wooden steps leading up to the bar.

Derek Beautimann and Maureen Moment moved carefully through Nalgo woods towards the cliffs and the sea, convincingly attired as a couple enjoying a walking weekend along the coastal heritage path, though to the more experienced walker, it would have seemed like an odd time of day to be looking for a place to camp.

'How deep was that first box you found, Derek?'

'It was about two feet under the surface. It took me a couple of hours to pry it out of the ground though. The top layer is mostly sand and soil, then it got a lot harder, mostly clay – very tough and clingy. It was a constant battle to keep the spade clean. The box was tangled up in a root ball too, so it was doubly hard. When I'd managed to free it, the bottom fell out. I certainly hope it won't be as difficult this time.'

'We could have brought some WD40 and sprayed the tools every few minutes. It stops the soil sticking.'

'How did you know that?'

'Oh it's just one of the things I've picked up over the years.'

Derek stopped for a moment, looking through the trees along the path at the sea.

'I hope you realise I haven't come along to stick my arms in a hole up to my elbows, Derek.'

'Yes, yes. But I hope you'll be able to help when the time comes to move the coins, Maureen. I'd be grateful if you could be more than just a lookout.'

'Well, I don't want my nails ruined. I know we've got gloves, but it's not the same.'

'Not the same as what?'

'Not putting them in a hole. I'm proud of my nails. I certainly won't be turning up to work looking like I've been digging a trench.'

'We haven't got too far to go,' said Derek, stopping again. 'Besides, if we find some more of these coins you'll have enough money for manicures for the rest of your life.'

'Okay, here we are, Dave. Can you help me get the rucksack on?'

'Is it in the boot?'

'Yeah, it's open. There's a torch in there an' all, in the red bucket with the sponge.'

'I thought you said we were only gonna be a couple of hours?'

'Well – yeah. But we can still take it with us. You never know…'

'I'm not carrying it, I've got nowhere to put it.'

'Stick it in the rucksack then.'

"I'm not gonna get stuck down there on curry night when it starts getting dark, Brian.'

'Just relax, we've got plenty of time.'

'I'll relax when I'm in the bar, necking some Carlsberg.'

In the Accident and Emergency admissions department at Whitborough Hospital, the consequences of the Black Hand Coven's disastrous encounter with other worldly entities the night before were beginning to show up in the general population.

'I'm sorry Madam, but if you have the symptoms described on the poster here we cannot admit you at the moment. We've run out of isolation units at this time. York and Malton Hospitals do still have some capacity.'

'You mean you don't have enough toilets, isn't that right? Am I right?'

'I'm so sorry, Mrs Halliday. But the doctors say that you must use the temporary toilets outside for the time being. We can't let you use the ones in the department because we would be breaching infection control guidelines. The doctors are recommending that anyone with the symptoms that you describe stay in their hotel and see their own GP as soon as they feel well enough to travel.'

'I'm on holiday, love. My GP's in Batley – the Duchess is like a bloody sick bay. Everyone's being sick or they're stuck on the toilet. I didn't pay good money to stay in a hotel full of sick people. I need some antibiotics and I want to see a doctor now.'

'Mrs Halliday, we can't admit you. If you need to use the toilet before you go, there are toilets outside.'

'I'm not going to use a prefab, young woman. I'm not going to lower myself to that, how dare you!'

'There is no other alternative, I'm sorry.'

'What am I supposed to do – shit in my drawers?' she hissed. 'Is that what it's going to take for me to be able to see someone here? Humiliate myself! For everyone to know my business?'

'Mrs Halliday, please don't use that kind of language.'

'There's no more bloody room for anyone else's business,' grumbled another lady, just within earshot.

Mrs Halliday glanced over her shoulder briefly, looking for source of the remark, then attacked the receptionist again.

'So what am I supposed to do? Where am I supposed to go?'

'Any chemist can help you…'

'A chemist! I don't believe I'm hearing this…'

'The doctors are recommending people go to their nearest pharmacy for treatment.'

'I heard enough. I can assure you you'll be hearing from my husband – and my GP. When I get back home from this rotten town,' she shouted intemperately, storming out through the sliding glass doors. 'The place is a shithouse!'

'Tighter.'

'How's that?'

'More on the right strap.'

'Right … now?'

'That's it.'

'You don't want it too tight, Brian, it'll chafe when you

92

start to walk. You don't want to cut off the blood to your arms.'

'It feels okay. How's it look?'

'You'll pass – right, let's get going, do that loose belt up too, over your gut. It's got a few scuffs and scrapes, but you want some wear and tear showing, you won't look so much like a virgin.'

Derek and Maureen reached the end of the woodland part of the trail, emerging from cover onto a bluff carpeted in tall grasses and thistles above the beach leading down to the plateau.

'The grass down there looks an odd colour, Derek.'

'Nature is very resilient, Maureen. I'm sure it's only a temporary effect – a few natural toxins,' he replied, unconvincingly.

'Sure of a lot of things, aren't you? Everything looks as though it's been scorched…'

'Most woods do after a fire.'

'Yes, but there hasn't been one, has there? Oh dear God, Derek, what have we done? This is all our fault.'

'It wasn't anyone's fault. It was an accident – look, we're wasting time.'

'If we find anything tonight, you're going to make a donation to the conservation volunteers to make amends,' warned Maureen, following her companion in crime.

Derek looked briefly around and found the place where he had been standing the night before, where all his careful preparations had been ruined by an extraordinary occurrence of bad luck and then a brief act of violence. He wriggled out of the straps on his holdall, then dropped it carelessly on the grass. There was a faint rustling noise underneath.

'Did your hear that?'

'What? I didn't hear anything,' said Maureen, looking at the ground with a puzzled expression.'

'I must have dropped the holdall on something.'

'Lift it up and see.'

'Nothing … I can't see a thing.'

'Well, don't kill anything else tonight. I think we've done quite enough damage, don't you?'

Albert 'Incapability' Barnes, Brian's gardener, awoke suddenly from his alcohol-assisted slumber, jolted back from oblivion by one of his own rattling snores. Then wiped away a wet cord of drool from his chin with his sleeve, moistened his lips and checked his teeth with his stale tongue.

Pip, his adoring canine companion, lifted her tail and squeezed out another green cloud. Manoeuvring her head inside the trough of Albert's lap she stretched and yawned, bracing her legs against the posts on the surf hut veranda overlooking Cayton Bay.

'I think we'll stay here tonight, old girl. As soon as it gets dark, I'll pick the lock, or jemmy that door open and we can go inside and sleep off the ice cream. Is that all right with you?' His Labrador sighed and closed her eyes, letting go another weather balloon's worth of methane.

'Had you thought about what you're going to say, should someone come along while you're up to your shins in clay, Derek?'

'I shall say that I am digging a latrine. That should bring an abrupt end to any further conversation.'

'Well I certainly won't be testing it, that's for sure.'

'I'm going to start digging, Maureen. Find a spot nearby where you can see along both ends of the path and keep eye on the trail,' said Derek, tapping the ground under the spade.

Robert Rudding's nerves were getting closer to the margin between controlled panic and a seizure. Finding all three of the bins on Westfield High Street empty, he was wondering how much more bad luck he could stand before his life returned to the blissful state of steady boredom he was more used to coping with. Then he saw the dustcart.

'Gotcha,' grinned Albert, kissing his lock picks before slipping them back into his pocket. 'A warm night indoors, Pip. And a nice soft bed, and you old girl can have the other… Now, let's have a look in this kitchen.'

The old Sea Cadet and Scout hut was almost a hundred and twenty feet long and nearly twenty feet wide, more of a barrack than a hut, timber-framed with wooden joists and rafters mounted on concrete pad stones, and protected by red cedar shiplap cladding and a tarred roof. After the war it had been bought by Whitborough Corporation who had connected it to mains services and installed showers and a new septic tank, then leased it to the Mainwaring family, who had run it as a cafe until the mid 1970s when they relinquished the lease before its renewal. After another refit it was mothballed after budget cuts and remained unoccupied until the surf club raised enough money to buy the lease.

At Clash City Records, Dean and Michael were preparing to leave after cashing up for the day.

'A Grimshaw moon,' observed Michael, buttoning his coachman's overcoat and half cape. 'I do find these after-hours stock takes are a burden on the constitution…'

'You out tonight?' asked Dean, looking closely into the shadows inside his wallet. 'I'm meeting Mouse, John, Darren, Chris and Ade in the Stage Door at 9 if you fancy a beer. I think we're off to Mystery City after last orders, if you want to come along.'

'I've a mind to take Fenella to the King's Arms, old chap – after we've walked Fangoria and Biter. But we may well get to the Stage Door later, before you all leave. Will Miss Brahms and Mr Lucas be with you?'

Yeah, and Rumbold.'

'Until this evening then,' said Michael, buckling his gauntlets and fastening his helmet.

Graham and Ben collided again, bashing shoulders on the steps in the exit then tumbling outside onto the forecourt of the Shirestones Hotel through the pub's offset double doors, clutching their helmets and gloves and still off-balance from too much alcohol. Ian the chef came swiftly behind them, still in his grubby whites and Nehru hat, a hunted expression still fixed on his face.

'Have you seen that friggin thing in there?' he asked, beads of sweat breaking out on his forehead.

'I did,' said Ben, still on edge. 'I don't want to talk about it. I just want to get as far away as possible, Ian.'

'Damn right, lad. I just need to call the police from Charlie's next door, and then I'm gone. Best of luck, Graham.

I don't know where your uncle is. I haven't seen him since I starting prepping.'

'He was in the toilets.'

'Maybe he's hiding.' Len looked at Graham, then down at his feet.

'Lads?'

'Len says the toilets were covered in blood, all smashed up.'

'Oh Jesus – I'm sorry son, I really am. He was a top bloke – but if he's still alive we can't help him. I've gotta call the police. Then I'll call an ambulance. If we go back in there there's no chance we'll make it out alive, if that thing's there. We've got to save ourselves, lads.'

'I can't take it in…'

'Neither can I.'

'What is it?'

'You've seen it – I've seen it. Do you want to put a name to it?'

Ben was silent.

Forty portions of best mince had not satisfied Lindsay Boldwood. Nor had chipping the planks from the pallets beneath the casserole dish, especially when you were a werewolf used to chewing bones instead of wooden slats full of nails and rusted staples. Only the hot bloody bones of something still living or recently deceased were going to appease the ache in his jaws and the churning hunger which was still burning in his belly. The scent trail which hung in the air around the scullery entrance promised to lead him to something much more satisfying; and so he began to work on the door, raking his claws down the tongue and groove plank where the wood was at its weakest, before making a breach and feeling the other side through the gash he had made punching through the thin slats, for a key or a bolt or a latch.

'There! Did you hear that?' said Derek, throwing down his spade and lying flat on his belly to reach down into the muddy trench.

'Have you found it?'

'Come over if it's clear, Maureen, I've hit something hollow, I think it's the chest.'

'Listen,' he said, when she made the lip of the trench, holding the spade and dropping it on a small patch of mud-smeared wood; there was a dull hollow boom from the object still held in the grip of the earth. 'There's something inside, I'm sure. Quick, hand me that bar.' he said, stepping back into the trench. Maureen peered down past the layers of topsoil and clay beneath the turf, reaching into the tool bag.

'This thing?'

'Thank you,' he said, receiving the wrecking bar.

'I can smell liquorice…'

'There is definitely an essence of something similar nearby, very odd.'

'It's the soil, the soil smells of liquorice. Perhaps we conjured up Bertie Bassett as well; after everything else I wouldn't be in the least bit surprised.'

'That's not funny, Maureen. I'm going to need some help getting it out I think, after it's uncovered,' he said, breathing steadily, scraping tea loaf sized clods of earth from the box.

'I can see the top of it,' said Maureen, getting as close as she dared to the edge of the hole. A muddy box-like shape began to emerge as Derek continued to scrape and clean, exposing the proportions of a stout chest made from thick oak plank and metal strap-work, covered in fine cast square studs around an eighth of an inch in diameter.

'Oh my God! I've found it! I've found it!'

'Oh thank God!' gushed Robert Rudding, shaking off pizza crusts, coleslaw, chip scraps and litter from the bin liner he thought he'd lost forever; furtively replacing the lid on the ownerless bin cart. He crept away, carefully observing the locals as they passed him by, as though someone were going to snatch it from him at any moment. At the back of Follifoot's supermarket, he set down the bag and lit a cigarette to calm his nerves, then stopped briefly behind the butchers, to wash the bag down under the outside tap.

Brian followed his brother through the tight undergrowth, into the tunnel of trees skirting the cliffs, until the path opened out into the woods and they could walk shoulder to shoulder on the wide trails of compacted soil, leading down to the old bunkers and the gun battery above the beach hut.

'Making good time so far.'

'We're doing all right,' replied Dave, without stopping.

'I tell you what, I'm overheating – I'm starting to sweat.'

'It's the padding on the back of the rucksack Brian, I forgot to warn you about that,' said Dave, chuckling. 'We're almost there, you can cool down in a sec. Here's the first bunker,' warned Dave. 'Watch where you're putting your feet on these concrete steps, they're covered in moss, and there's a few chunks missing on the way down past the Bren gun embrasures.'

'Can you move it, Derek? Is it heavy? Is it still stuck?'

'Maureen, when I need you, I'll ask. Now will you please go back and watch the trail, please. The last thing I need right now is someone coming up behind me and taking me by surprise.'

'Please yourself,' she mumbled, flouncing off.

The ledged and braced door between the pump room and the scullery, below the bar of the Shirestones hotel finally gave way, and Lindsay Boldwood smashed down what was left of its carcass, ran past the sinks to the staircase leading to the hatch and leapt onto the stairs.

'The friggin thing won't start!' groaned Ben, stabbing the electric start on the right handlebar of his Suzuki X7.

'Use the choke!' yelled Graham.

'It's on already!'

'Use the kick-start.'

'All right! All right!'

'Come on mate!'

Ben kicked hard twice and the engine finally burst into life, making clouds of blue smoke from its expansion chambers.

'Okay she's fine, jump on – let's go!' he shouted, whipping up the throttle. Graham climbed onto the pillion and slapped Ben on the back. The bike shot forwards with a raucous shriek and flew off the kerb, its front wheel climbing fast until Ben dabbed the brake pedal under his foot and brought the front tyre back down to earth, changing up through the gears. Two more bikes, a pair of RD250s drew up as he tore away.

'That was Wilko – friggin idiot,' shouted the first rider

on the white and red machine to his friend on the silver bike. 'He's gonna get nicked for sure going that fast in Cloughton – where's he off to?'

'What the hell's that behind the door!' cried Kirsty Brakes on the back of the second RD. 'Is that a frigging bear or what?'

The new arrivals gaped at the creature trapped behind the glass doors in the vestibule, as it stared back, unblinking, swallowing the last few inches of Mr Boldwood's cat.

'Sergeant Moyne, Whitborough Police, hello?'

'Me name's Ian Dermott, I'm a chef, one of the chefs at the Shirestones Hotel in Cloughton.'

'Yes sir – how can we help?'

'There's a wild animal – a wolf loose in the pub. I think it's killed the landlord.'

'Did I hear you correctly, sir? You did say a wolf?'

'I don't know what to do.'

'Sir, is it someone's pet?'

'Someone's pet? Are you out of your friggin mind! This thing is bigger than a Great Dane with teeth like a friggin dinosaur – would you want summat like that as a pet?'

'Sounds like you've got the Hound of the Baskervilles in there, Mr Dermott. May I ask if you've been drinking, sir?'

'No I 'aven't bin bloody drinking. Are you gonna get someone round 'ere and shoot it or just tekk the piss, because I can assure you it will kill someone else soon if you don't stop wasting time and get some of your lot out 'ere with some rifles. Is this call being recorded?'

'You'd like us to send someone to shoot it, Mr Dermott? Is that the reason for your call?'

'Dint you 'ear what I just said?'

'There was some background noise just then sir, some motorbikes I think.'

'Well, if you send 'em 'ere unarmed, I'll be watching from the 'ouse next door so I can see your toytown cop plod mates getting eaten alive. An' you won't be able to say I didn't warn you.'

'Calm down, Mr Dermott.'

'I'll calm down when I know it's dead, ya dopey bastard. Don't you tell me to calm down, just get someone over 'ere now – packing,' said Ian at the top of his voice, slamming his neighbour's phone back into its cradle.

'Mr Dermott, I would like you to leave my house. I refuse to have people using bad language inside my house,' said Mr Fothergill.

'I'm not going anywhere, Charlie. You haven't seen what I've seen, and there's no way on earth I'm getting caught outside with that thing in the pub.'

Mr Fothergill straightened his tie and tank top, left his lounge and returned holding a Lee Enfield .303 sniper's rifle, a beloved memento of his, kept from the Korean War. Drawing back the bolt he pushed a clip of bullets down through the breech, pushed the bolt forward then drew it back again in one quick movement, forcing a cartridge into the breech tray, then he pushed the bolt home.

'It's loaded,' he said, pointing it at Ian.

'Don't point that thing at me mate, I'm not in the mood. I've had enough excitement to last me the week.'

'I want you to leave my house, Mr Dermott.'

'I'm not leaving till the police arrive – so you can tell them why you've shot me instead of that wolf next door that's killed Lindsay.'

'Wolf? What wolf?'

'Dint you 'ear me ont phone a minute ago?'

'No, I was in the kitchen. I don't eavesdrop on people's telephone conversations. It's not proper.'

'There's a bloody wolf next door in the pub. I think it killed Lindsay.'

'Oh my word! I am so sorry. Please forgive my rudeness Ian, I completely understand – are you sure it's a wolf? In Cloughton!'

'If you wanna check, then be my guest.'

'You've seen it?'

'It's wolf-like, but bigger and nastier. Any road, I don't wanna talk about it. It's gonna give me nightmares for the rest of me days. Does that thing work?' he asked, looking at Mr Fothergill's rifle.

'It should do. I've never fired it since Imjin in Korea, but she's well looked after. There are seventy-eight less Godless communists in Korea, thanks to my precious Eloise. She saved my life more times than I could tell you. How in God's name did you come to have a wolf in your hotel? I thought he only had a cat, Mr Boldwood.'

'Can I borrow that? It's a No. 4 Mk2, isn't it?'

'Yes it is… How do you know that? You want to borrow her? Are you mad?'

'Do I look like I'm friggin joking? I used one o' those a few times at the range at Normandy Barracks in Driffield a few year ago. When I were in t'Air Cadets. Got me RAF marksman's badge wee it. Five shots inside a 2p piece at twenty-five yards. I know 'ow to use it.'

'Keep your eyes peeled, Maureen, I'm going to try and break open the lid,' said Derek, taking a few quick breaths as he took a practice swing with his pick axe.

Ian Dermott and his neighbour Mr Fothergill ran to the bay window of the lounge when they heard the noise of glass breaking and wood splintering next door. Then he saw something he had never imagined in all his nightmares, and fervently hoped he would never encounter again, shaking its fur and sniffing the air between the picnic benches.

'As I live and breathe...' he half whispered. 'Are there really such things in the world? I see it, son – but I can scarce believe my own bloody eyes. God save us and help us,' he said, crossing himself. 'I think we'd better have a whisky...'

Dave and Brian stood a few yards away from the rear of the surfers' hut, checking the perimeter for any litter or other signs of recent visitors and listening out for any noise.

'Sounds quiet enough,' whispered Dave, coming back to his brother at the far corner of the plot.

'Help me get this thing off Dave,' asked Brian, struggling to free himself from his rucksack. 'I don't think I've got the strength.'

'You wanted it tight.'

Brian grimaced and managed to squeeze one shoulder free, groaning with the effort.

'Oh thank God, that's better,' he sighed, flexing his shoulders, then sat down on a fallen tree trunk to get his breath back, whilst his brother peered through the wooden barge boards at the bottom of the hut, looking for the bin liner.

Ian gripped the rifle, lining up the front and rear sights on his target as his neighbour gulped down a third slug of Famous Grouse, covering his ears with two settee cushions; then he let off the safety catch and curled his finger around the trigger. Taking a deep breath he expelled the air slowly from his lungs, feeling his body relax as he hugged the rifle to his shoulder, then he gently squeezed the trigger. The rifle bucked and the brass butt plate slammed back into his shoulder as the muzzle kicked up and slightly to the right. Then Ian drew back the bolt as fast as he could and chambered another round, his ears ringing with the volume of the report, firing a second and third time as the stink of cordite filled his nostrils.

'The friggin thing's coming! There's only two more in the clip! Have you got a bayonet for this thing?' he shouted to Charlie, kneeling on his footstool with the rifle pushed through the small windowpane they had broken out.

'I've got another sixty or seventy rounds in clips, in the Martin Ware teapot on the mantelpiece.'

'Empty 'em ont sill then, quick! Come on Charlie! Hurry up! Hurry!'

The pickaxe smashed through the lid of the chest and cleaved in a palm sized portion of oak panelling from the centre, making a metallic crunch as it buried its tip in a pile of coins and jewels.

'Damn! Damn it!'

'What's the matter, Derek? Are you all right?'

'Yes, I'm fine. The thing went straight through, I just hope I've not broken something. I didn't expect it to breach the wood so easily, that's all.'

'Well pull it out then…'

'Just give me a minute. Are you watching that trail?'

'There's nobody near.'

'Just go back and keep looking.'

Ian's first shots had struck Mr Boldwood squarely between the eyes, rocking him backwards and fracturing his skull, which began to heal again almost immediately. Though the pain was extremely acute, the werewolf roared in fury and charged at Mr Fothergill's bay window, its teeth bared and the tail of the cat flying between the gaps in his incisors like a limp dressing gown cord.

'Shoot it!' yelled Mr Fothergill, clapping his hands over his ears again, forgetting he had just picked up the hook ended poker from the iron boy on the hearth.

'Shut it!' hissed Ian, snatching the trigger accidentally. The rifle fired again, making his neighbour's glass figurines reverberate, but his shot went high, ploughing a bloody furrow down the spine of the monster before it crashed into masonry below the bay window and fell back into his lavender.

Albert clicked his tongue and put down the binoculars he'd been using to watch the two ramblers.

'It's no good girl, I need a Jimmy,' he said to Pip, who was snoring again on a large beach rug. He stood up and ambled along the corridor linking the communal lounge areas, to the toilet and showers at the far end of the hut, then opened the toilet door and found his zip, positioned himself under the old high level cistern and waited for his problematic prostate gland to relax enough to empty his bladder. As he started to flow, the peace was suddenly shattered by the piercing screech of rust scarred nails being wrenched from dry shiplap. Albert unscrewed the window bolt with his free hand, forcing up the small sash window beside the cistern pipe and looked out into the gloom, resting his chin on the staff bead as he finished his business. Pip started growling and barking.

'I'll set me dogs on yer!' he shouted, feeling for his zip, and trying to sound younger and larger.

Dave stopped abruptly, looking back at his brother. Brian stubbed out his cigarette on his boot, looking back at Dave.

'Albert? – Is that you Albert? It's Brian...' said Brian, suddenly recognising the voice.

'And Dave,' said Dave. 'Dave Drake. Hi, Albert.'

'Albert, what are you doing in there?' asked Brian, after letting out a sigh of relief, seeing the creased, ravaged face of his gardener. 'You gevvus a right start, you old bugger.'

'Well at the moment lads, I'm taking a piss,' Albert said, speaking through the lower portion of the window frame. 'Not that it's any of your business. Come around to the front doors, I'm not talking to you through this blummin window.'

'Brian, I can see the bag,' said Dave quietly as Brian walked towards him and Albert closed the window. 'One good tug on these boards and I can get it. How the hell Neil squeezed it through, I don't know.'

'He'll have crushed the packets, that's how, then pushed it through with his boot. We can't just tekk it and leave now,' he grumbled, the frustration showing on his face. 'I'm trying to think about what we're gonna tell that old fool as a reason for us being 'ere. At the moment, he's probably scratching his head, trying to figure out why we've come down here, so let's keep him off balance until I can think of an excuse for us being here and pulling the hut apart. Just keep the pressure on, then we can sneak off in our own time.'

'You could say we were pinching a bit of wood to break up for kindling, to make a fire – he's probably a bit pissed anyway. Be quick, but be nice. I'm not here to pass the bloody time of day, remember. We can catch up another time.'

'Perfect – that's what we'll tell 'im then, we came out to do a bit of walking and decided to have a campfire for old time's sake; I would say go now, but he's gonna be suspicious if you disappear.'

A minute later the brothers found themselves face to face with their old gardener as he pushed open the half-glazed doors onto the old veranda.

'So this is the secret you've been keeping from us, Albert,' said Brian searchingly, slapping his shoulder as he stepped inside without waiting to be asked.

'Secret, what secret! I ain't got no secrets…' he grumbled unconvincingly.

'Don't be modest, Albert, I think it's fantastic what you're doing.'

'Eh?'

'Getting yourself a new hobby at your age. I wouldn't have thought you were so adventurous. Would you, Dave?'

'Yeah, it's great, Albert. I wouldn't have put you down as a swimmer.'

'A swimmer? Oh no – I don't swim. I can't.'

'Well if you've joined the club, you can't be that bad. Have you bought yourself a longboard?'

'Club, what club? What do I want an *ironing board* for?'

'Albert – you're in the surf club hut.'

'I know, but I'm just here for the night. That's all,' he said sheepishly.

'You broke in?'

'Ay, I've not broken nowt. I just picked the lock – I haven't stolen owt. I was only gonna sleep here with Pip tonight. I just couldn't face the walk home tonight lads. Honestly…'

'Albert, we won't tell anybody.'

'Oh, thanks lads,' he said, relieved. 'That's good of yer. I'll leave everything tidy, honestly they won't know I've bin here.'

'Except for the dog hair.'

'Poor old girl, she does shed a bit. Mebbee no one'll notice, eh?'

'Did you walk all the way from town to get 'ere Albert? It's a bit of a trek from Whitborough to Cayton Bay.'

'I got a lift from me old mates, Wiggy and Armin. They was off to the Rifleman's Arms in Cayton. Said I'd come, so I could take Pip to the beach. Then I had a nap here and woke up a bit later than I should. I'd missed me bus,' he mumbled, trailing off.

'Wiggy?'

'Wiggy. Dean's Grandad.'

'Ludwig?'

'Aye, Wiggy, no one calls him that no more – that's his old name. Anyway – what you doing here, pulling this place to pieces?'

'All cars, we've had a report from the chef at the Shirestones Hotel, a Mr Ian Dermott, saying a large dog or a wolf-like animal, may or may not have attacked the landlord inside the premises. The chef was calling from a neighbour's house, in a very nervous state. Use caution when entering the premises. No other persons remain inside, according to Mr Dermott. Over.'

'Eleven at Cross Lane. Received and understood. Our ETA is twelve minutes. Over.'

'Ambulance has been despatched, ETA ten minutes. Crew will wait for you to survey the premises before entering, to assess risks. Over.'

'We thought we'd have a wander down to the beach after work to get some fresh air, get away from the crowds, before the Bank Holiday weekend, didn't we Dave?' joked Brian. 'Then we thought – let's 'ave a camp fire. But all the twigs and branches in the woods are too damp. To tell you the truth, Albert, we just thought we'd pinch a bit of wood to use for kindling. Stupid really. It's a pretty good view through here, isn't it?' continued Brian, walking towards the glass doors on the side of the hut overlooking the cliffs.

'I saw a pile of old barge boards under the veranda here this afternoon, son. Take some of those to burn if you want.'

'Well, since we're here, thanks Albert. Are those your binoculars?' asked Brian.

'Oh no, I was just watching that pair down there,' he said, nodding towards the windows. 'Something not right about them two, they came with a tent, laid it out and then just left it on the ground all limp like, didn't even put the poles together. The bloke keeps hacking away, digging, but she just sits on her arse looking up the trail. Then every so often she goes back to him, looks in the hole but he waves his arms and shoos her away,' he mumbled, trailing off. 'Do you want a brew, lads?' he asked, wandering back towards the kitchen area.

'Brian! Tell him we've got to go,' hissed Dave.

'Hang about..,' said Brian, picking up the binoculars and bringing them up onto his nose, adjusting the focussing wheel. 'This looks odd … Albert? Have you put any lights on? You might have stumbled onto something here, old fella.' said Brian, staring ahead.

'He can't hear you, he's gone to the kitchen,' said Dave, impatiently. 'We haven't got time for this.'

'Dave, just come over and have a butcher's at these two,' whispered Brian. 'Quick.'

Dave marched forwards and grabbed the binoculars, muttering. 'How long is it gonna take him to make us a brew and get three mugs back here – we're wasting time.'

'Can you see any other holes around 'em? Near where they're digging.'

'Why? What's that got to do with anything? Will you just get to the point.'

'The point is – they already knew where to dig, dint they? There's no other holes I can see; they came with a tent, laid it out like they were going to put it up – then just left it.'

'So?'

'They never intended to use it. It's only been unfurled to disguise the real reason they're there. Whatever's in that hole.'

'So? Just a minute. You're saying there's something valuable down there…'

'Well look at him – he's up to his gonads nearly, it's a bit deep just for a hole to crap in.'

'He's kneeling down now and pulling at something…'

'It's pretty heavy,' gasped Derek, tugging at a tangled maw of knotted roots to free the last corner of the mud-smeared box from the clay. Then clasping the wood to his chest he struggled to his feet, dropping the chest onto the edge of the trench with one almighty heave.

111

'Yuck!' said Maureen, watching intently as Derek pushed the box further out onto the grass, then flopped on the edge, panting. 'It's covered in mud!' she squealed, waving her hands about in front of her face.

'It has been buried in the ground for over three hundred years,' said Derek, too exhausted for sarcasm.

'Oh God – I'm going to get covered in it, aren't I!' she moaned, itching to see what was inside, but mortified at the thought of ruining her nails.

'Yes, I would think so,' said Derek. 'But think of it this way, Maureen. You'll be able to afford the best manicurist in Yorkshire afterwards.'

'To hell with it!' she said, grasping the corners. 'It's not every day you find a fortune is it?' She thrust a fresh hand through the muddy rent in the lid and rummaged inside for a few seconds, pulling out an engraved gold wrist chain, a large sapphire ring and a palm full of small coins in gold and silver.

'Oh Derek – look at these! They're absolutely beautiful! I can't believe I'm holding treasure in my hands!' she beamed, mesmerised by the light playing on the jewels and precious metal.

Derek was lost for words, then suddenly became very nervous.

'Maureen, I think we should empty it and clear up here as quickly as we can. Ever since we've been here, I can't escape the feeling that we're being watched. We don't have too much time left before it gets dark; we'll have to hide what we can't carry and come back for it.'

'Whatever you say, Derek,' said Maureen, slipping the ring on her finger and admiring the jewel.

'I'll give you my rucksack. Can you empty the box first,

and then I'll start filling the hole in. We'll put the empty chest back into the hole at the bottom, then the litter and tissues on top a few inches under the surface. Don't put too much in the rucksack in case it splits. I can only carry about half of what's in there; and be careful not to drop anything on the ground around here, whatever you do.'

'What's 'appening?' asked Brian quietly, fidgeting with the keys in his pocket.

'She just pulled out a handful of coins from that box they brought out of the ground. Something sparkling too.'

'Let's 'ave a butchers…'

'Just a sec!'

'Don't you 'ave to be somewhere?'

'If you think I'm off anywhere now, you're very much mistaken.'

'So what about your date with Lucy?'

Dave grumbled and appeared to speak, although the words sounded as though they had been mashed and blended by some invisible baffling between his throat and the tip of his tongue.

'I saw 'em first. 70/30.'

'You what!' said Dave, breaking off his gaze.

'Thirty per cent.'

'Oh no Brian, we're going to divide it three ways. Equal shares. A third for you, a third for me and the rest for Albert.'

'Give an old drunk like him a fortune in gold and jewels, are you out of your mind! You seem to have forgotten I had to beg you to help me out tonight.'

'Keep your voice down! Whatever we get in cash for

whatever comes out of that box, gold, silver – if that's what it is, we give some to Albert. Fair's fair. The old sod needs a bit of luck, he'll be as chuffed as a fox that's found a kebab, we'll mekk 'im promise not to tell anyone of course. Just a few quid. We'll just say you've had some luck on the pools and want to share some of your good fortune. We don't have to tell him where the money really came from. Agreed?'

'We'll have to leave soon, before they do,' said Brian, reclaiming the binoculars.

'I'll go and make our excuses with Albert.'

Lindsay Boldwood relieved himself generously over the half millstone embedded beneath the decorative aggregate laid upon Mr Fothergill's rockery, preparing for another attack against his stout bay window. The scent of human flesh was devouring him like a fever, but the old wooden window frame had held firm, teasing and maddening him, whilst he took the full force of more high velocity bullets, any of which would have bought him a priest and an undertaker as a member of the human race. But he shrugged off the trauma of the bullet wounds, healing in werewolf form with supernatural speed.

'It's coming again…'

'I know, we don't need bullets, we need a frigging flamethrower. I don't know how much longer I can hold it off, Charlie. I'm gonna shake the hand of your joiner, if we ever mekk it out of ere alive.'

'My sister's a hairdresser, she…'

'Your sister is a friggin 'airdresser! That's just what I need to hear right now,' he said, groaning.

'She always leaves a box of her things in my understairs

cupboard… I'm just thinking aloud that's all,' said Mr Fothergill, rushing into the hall. 'There must be some hairspray in there…'

Ian snorted with derision and looked down his sights. 'I'm gonna die 'ere wee a bloody idiot.'

'Here's our flamethrower!' called Mr Fothergill, coming back into the lounge with a box full of jumbo size cans of hairspray, shampoo and perm solution. It might shrug off the bullets – but it won't like this. Have you got a lighter?'

'Are you out of yer mind?'

'Hairspray is extremely flammable – these are all pressurised. All you have to do is hold a naked flame in front of the nozzle of one of these, aim and press – and WHUMPH! A flamethrower! When that thing rushes us again I'm going to burn its bloody nose off.'

'Well, seeing as we don't have a silver bullet, you can kill it with a can of friggin Elnett.'

'It's coming…'

Lindsay Boldwood sprang forwards and crashed against the window, jarring the thick blown glass panes, clamping his jaws over the end of the rifle as Ian pulled the trigger. The bullet punched a hole the size of a child's fist in the top of its skull, spraying freckles of blood and gore over the glass.

'Pull it out!' cried Mr Fothergill.

'I can't! Just spray the damn stuff,' yelled Ian, locked in a tug of war with the werewolf and the rifle sling.

Mr Fothergill flicked Ian's lighter and held it in front of the broken frame.

'Nothing's coming out!' he snapped, panicking.

'Shekk the bloody can! Quick!'

'Oh God yes! – Sorry!'

115

Seconds later a huge tongue of flaming napalm engulfed the lower part of the bay window, setting fire to his elephant's foot plant and a stack of carved wooden coasters from Brittany.

'You've set fire to your bloody window you bloody numpty!'

The werewolf roared in agony and snatched up a small fairy with a fishing rod beside the pond, hurling it over the front wall, then dived into the pond head first, its head wreathed in smoke and sparks, just as the ambulance rounded the corner and bounced onto the flagstones at the designated parking area, beside the picnic benches.

'I've emptied it, Derek, I got about a third of it in your rucksack, the rest is in the tent bag.'

'Good. See if you can find a hiding place for it nearby, with plenty of cover. Somewhere we can recover it from quickly.'

Mr Boldwood's fourth attempt to break into Woodbine Cottage had ended again, in failure, and now the arrival of two more humans in an enormous white metal box with flashing lights and an ear-splitting melody of shrill sirens was not reassuring. No matter how delicious his prey smelled, it was not going to present itself in a way which facilitated him eating it without being burned alive, shot again, or run over and crushed, so he voiced one last howl of fury before sprinting away along the pavements beside the road, looking for an escape route to an environment which offered him the opportunity to conceal himself from prying eyes, a place where he could stalk and ambush his next meal and hold the advantage of surprise. A new scent from behind the front of the high street aroused his glands, drawing him down a narrow weed-filled cutting between the vicarage and the end wall of a terrace of tied cottages, and onto a flat field of small allotments, where a Gloucester saddleback pig was nose-deep into a pile of vegetable peelings, tied to an old iron stake with a length of frayed nylon parcel string and an old dog lead, and blissfully unaware of its predicament.

'I think it's gone. I think the ambulance must have scared it.'

'Charlie – will you put down the lighter and the can of 'airspray. You're mekking me nervous holding on to that flame right now.'

'OH! God I'm sorry. I didn't even realise I…'

'Why don't you stick the kettle on, Charlie. I think we could both do with a brew. You did good with the flamethrower, I have to say. Credit where it's due, son.'

'Thank you Ian. I feel rather a fool. I haven't been very helpful have I.'

'Charlie, without you and this old rifle of yours we'd both be dead. So don't be so 'ard on yer sen. I'm sorry I shouted at ya by the way. I haven't been as respectful as I should have, and me in yer 'ouse an all. But I was in a panic. I weren't thinking straight. Sorry.'

'That's very good of you to say so, Ian. Would you like a whisky before the kettle boils?'

'Now you're talking. We haven't done too badly have we, you and me. I bet there's not many folk who can say they've seen off a werewolf. The police have just turned up out front ah see – late as usual. This is gonna take some explaining.'

'The Ambulance crew saw it, they nearly ran over it – they'll back us up.'

'I wouldn't be too sure.'

'Well, they nearly squashed it mounting the kerb. I don't think I'll be keeping my coasters or the plant. I've been eighteen years growing that. I'll be dead before I can get another looking like that,' he said whimsically.

'At least we're alive. Let's gather up these cartridge cases and hide the rifle, before those coppers come poking around in your lounge.'

'What the hell was that thing we nearly ran over. Did you see it, Shaun?' said the petrified driver of the ambulance, peering out of the windscreen.

'I know what I think it was – what do you think it was…'

'I was asking you.'

'You saw as much of it as I did, so we've both seen it, haven't we?'

'Where's it gone?'

'I think it went up the high street and down a cutting between some houses. God Almighty, I'm don't think I'm going to sleep tonight,' said Barry, the other paramedic. 'Are the doors still locked?'

'I could murder a bacon sandwich,' thought Derek, hefting his rucksack of coins and jewels over his aching shoulders. 'Are we ready, Maureen?' He sighed.

'I've hidden it under the rotting log with the split down the middle', she said, puffing. 'It's easy to find. There's a crowd of mushrooms on one side and a bank of nettles on the other, over by the tree line. It'll be safe under there.'

'I hope so.'

'Derek, cheer up for goodness sake – we're rich! We can

retire and live in luxury for the rest of our lives. You don't have to look as though you've eaten an onion.'

'It's a bit more complicated than that, Maureen, You can't swap this kind of fortune for cash at the bank. Or spend it in Debenhams. We'll have to declare it, there'll be an investigation, some convoluted, drawn out valuation, publicity – I'm not so sure I want to go through all of that.'

'Debenhams, PAH! It's John Lewis and Harvey Nicks for me from now on. Who's to know if we kept some back for ourselves? We don't need to declare everything,' she said, still admiring the ring on her finger.

'We'll get a reward, I'm absolutely sure about that – eventually. But how am I going to explain how we knew where to look?'

'Well, what about that map you found? The one in the linen chest.'

'It only gives the general location. How am I going to explain how we found it at the first attempt? People just aren't that lucky.'

'You could say you found it with a metal detector.'

'Ahh, I hadn't thought of that…'

'I am good for some things you know, Derek.'

'I didn't think you could find metal objects that deep under the surface inside a box with a metal detector. Are they really that good?'

'Believe me, Derek, you can find things as small as drawing pin with one of those. My ex-husband, God rest his soul, had a mania for detecting. He went on so many of them battlefield tours to France, he ran out of space in his passport for all the stamps. All that digging did for him in the end though, poor Rodney.' She sighed.

'I'm sorry, Maureen, I didn't know you were married – did he have a weak heart?' asked Derek, moving off.

'Oh no, the silly sod hit the detonator of a mortar shell with his spade. Saved us all the cost of a funeral, there weren't enough left of him to put in a shortbread tin. The Mayor and Mayoress of Ypres sent me a lovely letter of condolence – and a picture of the crater.'

'They're moving,' said Brian.

'Shall we split up?'

'Split up?'

'Well, one of us can follow them, and whoever stays behind can get that tent bag they just hid.'

'Follow them and do what? Knock 'em over the head with a branch? They could be meeting up with other people on the way back – then we'll be right in the shit. No, we'll stick together Dave, tekk what's left and disappear quietly. No risks or complications.'

'I suppose you're right…'

'Course I am. Look – let's just keep things simple for ourselves. Go and get the bag and I'll keep a lookout.'

'I'm not going ovver there. I've got me best shoes on. You've got the hiking boots on.'

'All right then – but don't disappear. If you see anyone coming back brekk a twig or whistle or something.'

'I'm not going anywhere, Brian. You'll be fine, there's nobody around, just go get it.'

Tony Binnie checked the torch in the top box of his black Honda Super Dream, closed the lid and threw his leg over the seat, pressing the electric start button on the handlebar. The bike burbled into life and he revved the throttle, looking behind for any signs of smoke from the exhausts.

'Well yee shut the freggen dooor Anthony! An keep yar ruddy fumes oot ma ketchen!'

'I'll nay be long ma peytull.'

'Gate shum melk orn yer way.'

'Aye, ah will.'

'An daynt fall off that theng agayne.'

Brian pulled a handkerchief from his pocket, folded it in half and wrapped it around the fingers of his right hand, carefully lifting the damp end of the rotten log beside the bank of nettles, taking in the footprints immediately around the area of the old tree trunk.

'Bingo!' he whispered to himself, seeing the green canvas bag on the carpet of rotten bark underneath crawling with woodlice. He grabbed the ties near the top seam and pulled the sack towards him, gauging its weight.

'Right, watch where you're stepping...' he mumbled under his breath, backing out of the undergrowth, shaking off a few damp scraps of decaying wood from the holdall, before bringing it over his shoulder...'easy does it.'

'Are we taking the gig to town tonight my love? I shall need an hour to make my toilet and chose a dress?'

'I was in two minds today whether we should. On reflection – I think it a good suggestion, Fenella. I should like to take some port – it has been a most trying day at the magistrates, though one does one's best to be just and fair and direct one's peers in these endeavours. But one must also bear in mind the need to fulfil our daily quota and do our bit to help keep Australia British. Even if we should only populate the wretched place with scoundrels and administrators – I cannot decide which is worse.'

'May I ask what transpired during your last day of jury service, my husband? If tis' not too unpleasant to recount?'

'There were a few lighter moments that stuck in my mind my love, perhaps twill do me good to unburden myself from the affairs of the day. We had some amusement in our work at last toward the last part of the afternoon, before tea and biscuits at four. A fellow was brought before us for playing a *hit record* during the early hours of the morning at great amplification, incurring the wrath of his neighbours. The judge and jury were full of spite after suffering the playback – it was impossible to argue for leniency – I myself could not recall a more dreadful melody. The performer and author of the piece was a gentleman of Mediterranean descent – the colour of an overdone Yorkshire pudding wearing a hairpiece as stiff and sculptured as a banister rail. He is to hang on the morrow. If only we could have brought the *artiste* himself to justice, then we would have had cause to celebrate a double sentence, but we must be content with setting an example.'

'Were any of the prisoners sentenced to transportation, my darling? I hear the voyage is long and rough in the southern oceans from the writings of Captain James Cook – do you recall our happy visit to his old lodging house in Whitby town?

'I do recall the house, it was enviously situated, was it not? Concerning the prisoners, we had four in all, my sweet – rustlers of sheep. To my consternation, rather than accept the sentence handed down, one of the fellows begged for a capital sentence. His cries were most upsetting to his companions.

Would anyone else, I reasoned, not want to live and make a new life in the colonies, instead of having one's life snuffed out at the end of a rope? But the fellow was deaf to our entreaties, I had no idea the lager was so bad. He was still calling for mercy as they took him to the cells – begging for a last taste of English grog. One would have thought he would be more concerned about the nature of the wildlife of Australialand. We heard from a former colonist that their house spiders are exceptionally large and hostile – as wide as a lemon drizzle cake! There is also I am told, a carnivorous reptile called a Crinkledile, which lurks in puddles and small streams, and has more teeth than a bandsaw. I should not venture out of bed without my musket and a suit of Grandfather's armour if we had to suffer such things in England!'

'Is it wuth checken oot d'ya no thenk? The man's a fool, but ah cannae help thenken he wuz on tae sumthen.'

'Well I can't get away tonight, Tony. We've got the Sixth form end of term party at the Corner Caff, and we're booked up solid. On top of that, we've got all our regulars – we're just too busy. I could spare a couple of hours tomorrow night, before eight.'

'Well, I may go masell the neet.'

'Okay. Well I'll catch up with you sometime tomorrow. Ring me at home if you get lucky.'

Mr Boldwood had eaten well, though he still had a murderous appetite for more bloodshed and violence. He was only beginning to understand the extent of the bloodlust inside him, and a strange keening. With naught to trouble him except the fading ache of the bullet wounds, he followed his instincts and took off along the bridleway into the trees which led on to the old railway line and then to the coastal path.

'Weyll, let's hay a wee look doone the field o'shite,' muttered Tony Binnie to himself under his helmet, leaving his friend's taxi office on Westbourne Grove. Half an hour later he switched off the ignition, turned off the petrol tap and heaved his motorcycle onto its centre stand. He left the Honda in darkness at the kerb on the higher part of Pitt Lane before lumbering off into the trees beyond the car park. The woods were deathly quiet as he crunched along the path, relieving himself briefly against a tree as a cloud of bats rushed past him overhead, close enough for him to feel the draught from their wings. Within a few minutes, he came to the second stile, where the Pennine Way crossed the narrow footpath which climbed up to Filey Rd. Looking about, he found his bearings and rolled another cigarette, taking his time, then suddenly picked up the faint noise of voices further down the trail, where the path descended sharply to the right under the trees. Quickly, he threw his roll-up away and hid in a rut within a thicket which overlooked the bend on the trail.

Mr Boldwood's ambush was swift and bloody. His unwitting victim caught the briefest glimpse of a looming black shape, rising fast behind his right shoulder before the monster clamped its jaws around the bristle-covered folds of his generous neck. A reflex punch thrown by the Glaswegian in his cadaveric spasm connected painfully with the werewolf's jaw, slamming a heavily set sovereign ring into its rear molars in the short time before his head was separated from his shoulders and flew from the thicket, bouncing along bare earth towards the curve on the trail.

A short muffled scream from downwind confirmed that Scots Tony, or that part of him that was usefully recognisable, had bumped into two of his old comrades in arms. His eyelids blinked twice before falling shut as his disembodied head rolled to a standstill, his tongue falling wet from his mouth, jerking momentarily – as if expecting to moisten a stamp.

Mr Boldwood, suddenly alert again, angled his ears to the source of the scream and emerged slowly from the thicket, sniffing the air. Derek and Maureen met him in the moonlight in front of the head of their colleague, which had come to rest on the earth like a large and bloody full stop. Their eyes grew wide momentarily, then the two Satanists ran for their lives. Mr Boldwood, repelled by the scent of Aramis and Tramp, growled half-heartedly and returned to the corpse of the Scotsman.

'Come on Bri! Shift y'sen.'

'Just a minute – did you hear a scream?'

'Eh?'

'I heard a scream. Dint you hear anything?'

'The Ramones left me deaf, dint they…'

'I definitely heard a scream – a scream, cut short.'

'Foxes probably – come on.'

Several minutes passed, as they continued twisting and weaving through the trees and the undergrowth which seemed to reach out to brush them as they passed, while they strained to see the ground in front of their feet. Then Brian stopped again.

'Brian – come on!' snapped Dave in exasperation.

'Keep your voice down,' he hissed, squatting. Bringing

his index finger up to his lips, 'Look – in the middle of the path – what d'you think that is!'

Dave stood up straight and took in the sight of the decapitated head upon a crimson stain blocking their progress. He jerked his head around, then crouched down very slowly, looking at his brother with his mouth wide open, looking distinctly queasy.

'I think it's real. Dave?'

'I don't know – is it? What..?'

'We should turn back…'

'Turn back? We're nearly there aren't we?' he said weakly.

'Think – where's the body?'

'How the frigg should I know, is it really real?'

'If the body's not next to it, then somebody put it there, dint they. Someone *put it there*. This is way out of my comfort zone. Someone's left it as a message. Like head-hunters mark their territory – with other people's skulls. What in hell is going on down here!'

'The car's only a few minutes off, we don't have to walk past it. We can skirt around it through the woods…'

'Whoever put it there is probably in the woods.'

'Shit!.. Shit! Shit!'

'We're gonna have to double back on ourselves, then tekk a chance and walk up the cobbled path past the white beach shop hut and the toilet block at the bottom of the hill. It might be the most exposed way back to the car, but I think we should tekk a chance on being seen and get away from 'ere as fast as we can.'

'Okay, well no one's going to see us until we're near the top now, it's too dark. We could stuff your rucksack in the skip at the top of the cobbled path by the caravans, then cover it with rubbish while you go and get the car. I can stay in the shadows at the back of the beach shop and watch it. At least we won't be carrying anything if a patrol car comes past snooping.'

'Or we could just leave it in the shadows, with the rucksack, in the long grass by the fence. There might be all sorts of rubbish in there. Paint, broken glass, you don't want to put your hands in anything like that do you? If you make loads of noise putting it in, someone might come out of their caravan and see us.'

'Yeah. I hadn't thought of that. Best put it in the verge then, eh.'

'I'll bring me car up to t'bus stop, kill the lights then give you the nod when I've checked the road's clear. We'll drive back through Cayton village, rather than Gunstone. We better not tekk any chances.'

'You looking so dodgy, like you do.'

'Ha Har. Right – let's get moving…'

'Are we off back to yours first?'

'I thought we can hide the coins in one of the red tool boxes in the garage. They're all tough and they're lockable, until we decide what to do next. There's one with a Carnaby Raceway sticker on the lid. I'll stick it in there.'

'My share too?'

'Don't you trust me?'

'I spose… they've all got stickers on 'em though haven't they…'

'Well, we can put some in one and some in another. Makes no difference.'

'Just make sure Danny doesn't open one when he's fixing Deano's car.'

'We can argue about all this later.'

'No Brian, we sort it out now.'

'Keep your bloody voice down!'

'What would Mam and Dad have wanted… What would they say if they knew you were keeping it all for y'sen?'

'I didn't say that, did I. I said 70/30.'

'I can't understand why you think you're entitled to two thirds of it. Why are you being so damn greedy?'

'Dave, I saw it first, I'm not being greedy – fair's fair.'

'Fair's fair! You might have noticed they were digging for something; it was me who sussed it might have been something valuable.'

'Oh – and I wouldn't have come to the same conclusion then, come on…'

'You're just splitting hairs. Who saw what first. The point is, neither of us could have gone down there and got our hands on it alone.'

'Oh, why not?'

'Because you need someone to watch your back. And you're not convincing walking around here as a lone camper. People don't go off camping on their tod. They go with their mates – family, or at least one other person. No one goes camping on their chuff. It looks suspicious, it's… weird.'

'All right, all right.'

'So, we split it three ways – right. You asked me to help you out tonight.'

'All right. Agreed. Satisfied?'

Derek and Maureen were almost speechless. Their frantic sprint across the last few hundred yards of uneven ground had all but finished them off; fighting for breath, they lay exhausted, slumped against the timber uprights of the style on the edge of the car park, over which they had stumbled and collapsed, unable to go any further.

'Swear to me Derek, after tonight – no more occultism.' She gasped, falteringly. 'I've had all I can take…'

'Whatever that was – it was nothing to do with us.' He spluttered, clutching his chest. 'I need my inhaler.' He groaned, pushing himself to a more upright position, wheezing like a leaky accordion.

'Mine's in the car,' said Maureen, panting 'in the door tidy, driver's side.' She moaned, dropping her car keys in Derek's lap. 'If you can make it – I can't. I swear to God, I never want to see another one of your bloody grimoires as long as I live. It's going to be pizza, trifle and Coronation Street every Tuesday and Friday from now on.'

'Maureen…'

'Don't put a name to it Derek. Just don't.'

'I was going to say, I think you've sat in a puddle.'

'Oh sweet Jesus, I thought I'd wet myself. Now I've got a wet arse as well.'

'I'm going to the car,' gasped Derek attempting to stand. 'We should be moving…'

Mr Boldwood dragged the limp carcass of his prey deeper into the thicket and began to strip his prey; before gorging himself on the soft parts of the Scotsman, accidentally swallowing the corpse's pager, a miniature biro from a betting shop and a packet of Fisherman's Friends. They were not at all easy on his palate.

Four miles away, inside the foggy interior of the Kings Arms in the town centre; Dean and Amie were discussing how to exact revenge upon a shoplifter had stolen an embroidered gothic mini dress and bodice from Brian's shop.

'If that little bitch comes in here wearing it tonight she'll be going home dressed in the bin liner.'

'Amie, if you've got anything planned it'll have to wait. Besides, nothing's gonna happen in here; this is one of my best pubs and we're not getting barred for roughing up that little cow, so button up.'

'So you planned to do what?'

'Well I thought I'd shoot 'er in the head as soon as she comes through the doors. What d'ya mean – " So you planned to do what?" Two of my girls are coming in to catch her in the bogs and roll her up in parcel tape and cling film. Then we're dropping her off at the goods yard in the station in a reinforced cardboard box. We're posting 'er to Aberdeen. Nice and cold in Aberdeen.'

'Sorry… I defer to your seniority Dean. What was Brian planning to do? I didn't tell him I was going to do anything – but it's like a point of principle.'

'I never ask… It won't be very pleasant, he carries grudges like a camel.'

'Do you think he'd like the dress back?'

'Well, I said I thought we might be able to get it back, but he just gave me a funny look. You were a dog handler for two years weren't you?'

'Yeah, Dobermans, mostly. A few Alsatians. Boet was my first dog, the last after the parade ground incident. I can't believe they kicked me out – they set me up for a suspension. I know that now. Bastards! Breaking the rivets on my lead and taping a dog whistle in the mouthpiece of the Tuba – he just went crazy – you know the rest of the story.'

'Did he already have children? That Commandant van Dulmen?'

'He was a jerk. Look Dean, I promise I won't put my nail file all the way up her nostrils if I get to her first. Just a few centimetres. Did you know that she fancies Michael? I caught her giving him a sticky look.'

'No way! She better pray Fenella doesn't find out. She'll die the death of a hundred hat pins. I think they're coming out tonight...'

'In here?'

'Maybe. They might be hunting tourists first. They sometimes follow the Ghost hunt and scare the shit out of the punters. You've got to give 'em credit – they do look they've been exhumed.'

Derek inhaled a second dose of Maureen's Salbutamol inhaler, savouring the magical effect of the mist as it dilated his airway. He closed his eyes and took a long deep breath, feeling the tightness in his chest and the ache around his ribs subside as cool life-giving air flowed back into his lungs. For a few minutes they sat in silence in her Cavalier, not saying anything at all, doors locked behind the steel and glass.

'I know this might not be the right time to mention this, but...'

'But you're going to say it anyway – the answer's no. Not tonight, not tomorrow, not ever. You're welcome to it – the rest of it. But me – I'd like to be alive to spend mine.'

'I was going to...'

'Derek, it's very thoughtful of you, but...'

'Maureen, it's all right. I wasn't going to ask you if you'd come back with me to recover the rest.'

'Well that's a relief.'

'I'll make sure you receive a fair proportion of the settlement after it's been sold.'

'Oh I'll make sure I do.'

'Well, it's just between you and me now anyway – and anyone else we might have to include. There won't be anything coming to that bunch of cowards who ran away last night,' he said, with controlled disdain, remembering their brethren from the coven.

'What do you mean, anyone else we may have to include?'

'I'll need to bring in someone with the expertise to value it. Someone who's not going to go to the authorities and the newspapers. Do you remember Alan Chipping? That chap I represented a couple of years ago, from the Crescent Museum. He was put on trial at York Crown Court for selling some of the museum's artefacts from their archives to a private collector. He always wears a tweed three-piece suit, a good shirt and bow ties – well spoken, but a little too bumptious and confident.'

'You were thinking of asking *him* to look as the coins and jewels?'

'Well, he owes me a favour. You remember the outcome – we spent a lot of extra time on his defence. One doesn't want to be on the losing side in Crown Court. It seemed the best outcome we could expect in the beginning – after a cursory examination of the file the best we could expect was a suspended sentence. He would have lost his job and his livelihood. But when I pressed him for mitigating factors, he told me he'd just discovered one of the trustees had been doing the same thing, so I suggested Alan get him to testify that he had permission to loan the three items in question for study – in return for his silence. As luck would have it, the buyers were other academics in his field. Alan got to them before the investigators and they closed ranks. They gave evidence to support his assertion that the items were only on loan, on an unofficial basis, which isn't unheard of in their profession. It didn't reflect well on the police and the CPS in court.'

'Derek, I need a cup of tea. And Bert needs a wee. We'll go back to mine and I'll put the kettle on; so unless you've got to get home we can talk about it there.'

'I can spare another hour or so, I think.'

'Don't say anything about that thing we saw tonight. I don't want to have to think about it again. Ever. Where are we going to put this rucksack?'

'I'll put it in my filing cabinet in the study at home. No one else goes in there. It'll be as safe as it can be until we need to move it elsewhere.'

'Well all right. I've got no objections.'

Chapter Four

Wednesday

Lindsay Boldwood was not a tall man, from the outside at least, but to his family and friends his lack of inches scarcely registered. He was strong, kind and resilient, a man to depend on, but not a man to cross, a man whose character had been shaped by institutions. Eleven years in Barnado's homes after a chaotic childhood, victimised and neglected on a commune in Wales, twenty-two years in the Royal Navy, and at forty the Landlord of the Shirestones Hotel in Cloughton, on the doorstep of the North Yorkshire Moors. In many ways, the pub trade was like the Navy – the hours were long, the duties never varied and he was generally confined to one place. The world outside, such as it was, now came to him, a completely opposite state of affairs when he thought of the Navy. But Boldwood drew strength from repetition, from order, from lists and rotas, from the certainty that tomorrow would be very much like today, which was why he had never married. The opposite sex were baffling and unpredictable to him and caused him to be wary of relationships, though he often felt lonely, especially after losing the comradeship he had come to depend on for so many good years in the Navy. He had toyed with the idea of having a dog, but settled on a cat, an old tabby that he had christened Bagshott. The cat looked after itself, it was aloof but affectionate, and they rubbed along together quite amicably. And they never had mice.

Being used to such convivial surroundings, it was something of a shock to him when he awoke on a stinking cot of hay and wood chippings, cold, naked and aching in every joint and sinew he possessed. Though his feet and ankles were very warm, as they were; between the paws and under the chin of a Canadian timber wolf, which immediately raised its head and began to crawl up his legs on its belly, shooting out its steaming tongue towards his private parts. Another tongue from some other creature behind him, which he guessed was another wolf, began to valet the back of his head with the exfoliating power a particularly abrasive bath sponge. Even for a dog lover, the reality of his situation was causing him the most extreme mental discomfort, as he desperately tried to piece together the timeline of events that had brought him to such an unwelcome and embarrassing tryst. A quick examination of his surroundings confirmed that apart from his new companions, he was alone, on a flat ledge under an outcrop of rock, looking down over a contoured enclosure ringed by a sweep of high steel railings. The sun was just over the horizon and from his years of experience at sea, he guessed it was between six and seven a.m. Before he could properly understand how he had come to be naked in what was undoubtedly a pen in the local zoo, he knew that he had to escape as quickly as possible. Moving as stealthily as he could after saying goodbye to his new family, Lindsay emerged from the outcrop and saw a metal gate some ten or fifteen yards away, beyond a jumble of tree trunks and boulders. As he made his way closer to it, taking a handful of tainted straw from the ground to cover his modesty, he saw that the padlock was undone, though the long bolt was still firmly in its collar on the opposite side of the galvanised door frame. An electric cart, piled high with plastic feeding tubs and nylon sacks, had been left fortuitously a few feet beyond the door. As quietly as he could, Lindsay drew back the bolt, holding the rod off the metal collars with the palm of his hand, then pushed it aside and stepped out from the wolves' pen. He listened for a few minutes, standing still, then caution overcame him and he moved towards the cart, wincing as his bare feet were stung on the gravel. He almost cried with relief when he spotted a clean green fleece pullover and a pair of black canvas trousers hung over the seat. By chance, there were also two new pairs of wellington boots on the flatbed at the back. Neither pair were his size, but he borrowed the larger of the two pairs, tucking in the freshly ironed trousers. Then he began to retreat towards the car park, keeping his eyes peeled for the staff or any visitors, putting as much distance between himself and the horrible awakening he had suffered as swiftly as his legs would take him.

Dawn came with rooks to the last remains of Tony Binnie, And a caravan of beetles. The lifeless head that had caused so many years of irritation and mischief was now just another snack for the scavengers of the wood. The largest and boldest corvid had settled on the top of his scalp, and started to peck at his eyebrows, but its breakfast feast had begun to wobble, then suddenly toppled over as the bird took flight squawking with disappointment, the head rolling off the path and bouncing down the ivy covered bank, where it came to rest in a bed of nettles and woodland compost.

Lord William Henry Warner Woollens, the first son of Lord David Peregrine Warner Woollens and the present occupier of Charlwood House, stood in front of the tall windows of his breakfast room looking out onto the lawns and grounds of his estate, adjusting the focussing wheel on his racing glasses; seeking to bring the stranger padding furtively towards their car park into sharper focus.

'Haskins, fetch me the cordless telephony would you, there's a good fellow.'

'Certainly, my Lord.'

'I'll have some more bibblycoffee too if you please.'

'Yes, sir. Do you have any preference for your evening meal tonight? Cook informs me he has to go to the market in Pickering this morning.'

'I think I shall have the rabbit in Old Peculiar, with roasted vegetables and those wonderful sweet potato croquettes. Lady Woollens will have the same, pea pay purr position.'

'As you wish sir.'

'I don't recognise this fellow making his way to the house, Haskins,' said his Lordship lazily, just before his butler could escape the room. 'I can't recall us having any vertically-challenged beardylady chaps working on the staff, he could be the perfect fit for our beloved Edith. A companion for our loyal Rhinetosserous.'

'Sir, I am a long way from the window,' said his butler.

'May I have some more coffee drips too?'

'Yes, sir. I was just going to get a fresh pot – and your medications,' he added, leaving the room before his eccentric employer could interrupt him again.

'No, I've definitely not seen this fellow before. Wait a moment – he's not coming to the house – he's heading off down the drive.' Then a violent flurry of feathers in his peripheral vision made him turn his old Leica binoculars towards a side terrace. 'Do you know, there's a wolf beside the pond, Haskins.' He added, as an aside, 'It seems to be in possession of one of the peacocks... Haskins?'

In the Binnie household meanwhile, the whereabouts of the head of the family was causing some concern.

'Gate yer braykfust oot the cupboard son, ahm jusht tae the phone a wee mennett tae find oot where yer pa is. Tell yer bruther tae hurry up enn the bathroom.'

'Aye Ma.'

'Can ah speak tae John there?' asked Mrs Binnie as the phone was answered at Beehive's taxi office on Vines Square at the end of Lower Gunstone.

'It's me Mrs Binnie, do you need a cab?'

'John, dedd yee shee ma huhzband lasht neet?'

'Hang on, I'll put you on the extension...'

'Mrs Binnie?'

'Aye ahm stell heer. Have yee sheen Tony?'

'He dropped by here on his Honda late yesterday. He asked me if I'd go back to the plateau with him to search for that thing Beautimann was after, but we were just too busy, Then he said he was going to go down on his own I think.'

'He dedd, dedd eee? He told me an' the weans he wuz off tae the pub tae play pool after he'd shtopped off at yoos an thayne he wuz gonnae call enn at the minimarket on the way hame.'

'Did he not come home?'

'The rotten stenken barstudd...'

'He might have had an accident, Mrs Binnie. Have you checked with the hospital?'

'An accident! I'll make shure he has a freggen accident when he gets back hame – the double crossen lyenn ★★★★. He told me he wuz taking the two of uz, Tommy Mac an' Gelda back there taneet. Wee a daytectar an sumthen tae degg weth.'

'I'm sorry Mrs Binnie, I don't know what to say. I hope he's not in any trouble.'

'Enn trouble? He's no been oot o' trouble sense he wuz enn short troosers, John. You don't know Anthony like I know Anthony. Anyways, I appreciate yer 'ornestay, by the way.'

'All right Mrs Binnie, I'm sorry there isn't anything else I can tell you, but that's as much as I know.'

'Aye well, thanks anyway John. I'll no keep yee, ahv got the bearns tae get tae school. Ahl gate hes wuk tae call the devious barstudd on hes pager.'

Around the same time, the phone rang in the Beautimann household on Long Acre and was answered by the lady of the house.

'Hello – hoh. Who's speaking?'

'Hello Sophie – It's Maureen, is Derek there? I wanted to speak to him for a few minutes – if it's convenient. So sorry to disturb you both… work… is he enjoying his holiday?'

'I think so. He's not had a very good night last night though, and he's still got some of that dreadful rash on his forehead. It doesn't look as angry as it did yesterday, thankfully; he swears it's an allergic reaction to something in my shampoo. He could do with a nap this afternoon by the look of him, or he'll be falling asleep in front of the news. Just let me check he's decent. Can you hold for a moment?'

'Yes I can. I'm sorry to bother you this early by the way…'

said Maureen. A minute later she heard the sound of their phone being picked up and a tired sigh.'

'Morning Derek…'

'Oh hello, Maureen. Was there something you needed from me?' he replied at top volume, for the benefit of his wife who was trying to draw the zip of her tote bag before leaving for the sports centre.

'I was wondering what we were going to say to Isla about Tony.'

Derek waited for a few seconds before replying, hoping his wife would go before he had to get into too much detail.

'I think we'd better keep that little secret to ourselves, don't you? I don't mean to sound callous, Maureen, but it's not our problem,' he said disdainfully, rolling his eyes, feigning irritation as his wife grinned back and waved her fingers then opened the door to the hall.

'It's somebody's problem though, isn't it? He's dead. It's all right for you to be flippant, but I've got to face her at Weightwatchers every week.'

'You could always stop going for a while.'

'Stop going – it's one of my nights!'

'Then you'll just have to learn to keep it to yourself. I can't quite comprehend why you'd think telling her what's become of him would be a good idea. It's an insane suggestion quite frankly. It's not as though she'd be grateful for the description of his end.'

'You never liked him, did you?'

'I'd be a hypocrite if I pretended I was in mourning wouldn't I? He was always trying to upset someone, us I might add, and draw attention to himself with his smutty little asides and juvenile sarcasm. He behaved like a clown most of the time, except when he was behind the counter in that grubby video store of his. But it seems he wasn't the clown we all thought after all doesn't it? He certainly knew we were onto something, as it turned out. Having said that, I wouldn't have wished that on anybody, but what I think or ever thought about our Mr Binnie is immaterial. I think this is more about you.'

'I beg your pardon?'

'Difficult as it may be, this is something you'll have to learn to keep to yourself, unless you want to be drawn into a murder inquiry and all that entails. It may also mean we lose the gold. Is that what you want?'

'I wonder if he's still down there,' said Maureen morbidly.

'I'm trying not to dwell on it. You'd be wise to do the same. No doubt someone will come across what's left of him today or tomorrow.'

'Was he a Catholic?'

'I've no idea…'

'Are you going to call that Chipping fellow today at the museum? About the…'

'Not over the phone, Maureen…'

'Oh Lord! Sorry – I'm forgetting myself!'

'I'll call him after nine. I'm going to see if I can meet him somewhere out of the way. I was going to ring you this morning anyway, because I might need to borrow your dog at lunchtime.'

'*You* want to borrow Bert!'

'Hi? Is Brian in?'

'Who's asking?'

'Robert. Robert Rudding – I've got some of his stuff. Is that Danny?'

'Yeah. Brian's left.'

'Look – he was supposed to collect it last night. He must have forgotten. I just can't keep it at my house any longer – can I drop it off?'

'Yeah. Bring it over. Bader Drive. Number 55.'

'I know it. I'll be over in a few minutes.'

At Charlwood House meanwhile, there were more unexpected guests.

'I'm sorry to disturb you m'Lord, but two gentlemen of the police are here wishing to speak to you regarding an escaped bear,' announced Haskins the butler, showing his head through a gap in the door to the large study room on the east wing.'

'We don't have any bears, Haskins,' was the brusque reply from within.

'Yes sir, but the gentlemen are adamant.'

'Why don't they speak to Harrison. He's in charge of the animals for heaven's sake – rowlyblind.'

'It's Wednesday, sir.'

'Ah, so it is. What happens on Wednesdays?'

'It's his day off, sir.'

'Can't they speak to the other keepers?'

'I've rung the office sir, but no one's there at the moment. They're probably in the elephant enclosure.'

'Well you'd better show them in then, Haskins, if they're here, but it's not very convenient.'

'No sir, of course.'

Lord Warner Woollen's butler closed the door briefly and beckoned the two policemen who were surveying a battle-scarred suit of armour hung nonchalantly at ease, resting its brutal mail gauntlets on a great broadsword, in front of a rack of halberds and lances.

'Gentlemen,' he began, addressing the officers, 'there are a few niceties to take into consideration when you are in conversation with Lord Warner Woollens. My Lord suffers from a form of aphasia – a communication disorder caused by a historical concussion. From time to time he may say something quite unexpected: a made up word or phrase, usually something with a strong childlike resonance. In all other respects he is as sharp and lucid as any man his age with the advantages of a good education. We do come as a pair though – he likes me to accompany him when his wife isn't available to translate. Not that his speech is indecipherable, far from it, but he needs the reassurance and company of those who know him well, in any situation where he may be required to speak. I think it's only polite that you're forewarned. If you're ready now, I shall introduce you.' Haskins tapped his knuckles gently on the door and pushed it ajar. My Lord, the policemen are ready, sir…'

'All right. If they're ready for me, I'm ready for them, but don't disappear, they'll think I'm doolally tap – pea pay purrr position…'

"This way gentlemen, Lord Warner Woollens will see you now,' announced his butler, leading the two men over the threshold into a huge library cum sitting room.'

The policemen entered the study, examining the dimensions of the room and its eclectic collection of artifacts with sweeping glances and obvious envy.

'Hello my Lord, my name is Detective Sergeant Broadhead, and this is Detective Constable Fu.'

'Fu? Cantonese eh? Well, good morning to you both, I

hope I can be useyfully gentlemen, I didn't realise our police force was so cosmo – copolitan. I went to Tibet in my twenties – on an expedition, from Porterhouse – to search for the Aboriginal Snowman. Two weeks of fruitless hiking, though the scenery was rather good – breath-taking, if I remember correctly. Developed a lifelong passion for goatie cheese. We sell lots of it from our farm shop here… Lord knows what it's done to the arteries, but I'm told a good Clerr Claret cleans them out.'

'DC Fu's family were from Tibet, my Lord,' said Broadhead, 'weren't they, son?' Detective Constable Fu said nothing, but took out his notepad and fidgeted with the clicker on his pen.

'Is he indeed! You must come to tea and we can talk about our expedition. My man Haskins will arrange it – you must see our Hefflephants and our Black Rhinetosserous Edith. Dribblyberries! What do you say?'

'Very little…' muttered Broadhead out of the corner of his mouth.

'The bear, my lord,' said Haskins, bringing his master back to the subject in hand.

'Bear? We don't have any burr – bears – Lady Woollens wanted one of each but we're waiting for some paperwork. We had an enclosure built, but it's empty. We're a bear behind. In a manner of speaking.'

'What about wolves, sir?' asked DS Broadhead.

'Wolves?'

'Yes sir. Do you have wolves here?'

'A fewsies.'

DS Broadhead stared at the neat but hirsute man in front of him, in a way which would have indicated to all but the most stupid human being that he was expecting a little more in the way of detail.

'And how *secure* are these animals, sir?' The third word was forced out between his teeth like the pip from a grape.

'Very secure, Detective Sergeant...' replied Haskins.

'I'm sure Lord Warner Woollens can speak for himself,' snapped the policeman, a little too sharply.

'All our animals are housed in enclosures that exceed the statutory minimum requirements for the safe keeping of wild animals – according to current legislation, slation,' said Lord Woollens confidently, reading from a white cardboard crib sheet which his butler was holding up behind the backs of the two officers.

'What about the one with the tranquiliser dart in its side that's laid out outside with the peacock in its mouth?' This time, the sergeant had omitted to use the word 'sir'.

Neatsfield Estate, three miles south west of Whitborough, had been marked out in the mid 1930s and completed in time for the Second World War. Built to satisfy the need for more modern middle class and lower middle class housing, the wide avenues and streets serving its detached and semi detached homes, anticipated the growing popularity of the private motor car. Each house had its own drive, a large back garden and a smaller garden plot to the front to act as a buffer zone for each property from the surrounding roads and pavements. Equidistant from Higher and Lower Gunstone, the two main arterial roads into Whitborough, with link roads to both, it was encircled by a mixture of common land and farmland. Shortly after the war, the council added three hundred corporation houses on farmland adjoining the first development, almost doubling the size of the estate.

It was from the former to the latter that Robert Rudding drove with Brian Drake's illicit merchandise, but as he travelled down Bader Drive towards Brian's house his heart skipped a beat. A police car had stopped on the opposite kerb, and the driver appeared to be in conversation with a pair of very stocky young men with short haircuts. Unwilling to panic, Robert drove on as calmly as he could, watching his speed and looking straight ahead, then kept going until he reached the junction of Bader Drive and Wissler Avenue. Turning right, he cleared the junction and spotted a phone box at the end of the street.

'Whitborough Museum Chambers reception, Charmaine speaking – how can I help?'

'Hello. I'd like to speak to Mr Chipping if he's in the building. On a private matter,' said Derek, pacing the carpet in his study with the phone cord stretched to its limit. 'It's Derek Beautimann, his solicitor.'

'He's in the archive this morning, Mr Beautimann. Hold the line and I'll transfer you, sir.'

'Thank you.'

'Hello – Derek?'

'Hello Alan, can you meet me at lunchtime today?'

'Today? I suppose so – where?'

'You're going through Kenwith Ravine with your dog first, presumably. At lunchtime?'

'Well, that's what I'd planned. But…'

'I'll meet you at the end of Dunn Rd, just before the coach park. About quarter past?'

'Well yes, this is very informal?'

'I need to speak to you where we won't be overheard.'

'All right, how long would you like?'

'Twenty minutes, no longer than that, I imagine.'

'All right, if that's what you'd like – I'll see you there.'

Robert dialled the number for Clash City Records, looking nervously over his shoulder, then checked his car as the phone rang.

'Clash City Records,' said Brian, answering the phone as he checked his wallet.

'It's Robert, Brian, I'm round the corner from your house in the phone box. I've just tried to drop your stuff off. But there's some police outside and a couple of blokes that look like bouncers.'

'WHAT! Outside my house! What are they doing? Are they going inside?'

'No. They're in a car. They're talking to some big blokes on the pavement in front of your place.'

'But they've not gone in the house – the police.'

'I don't know, I don't think so…'

'You mean you don't know…'

'Look, I only just drove past. The coppers were in the car – the other blokes were beside your fence on the pavement. They were talking to each other across the road.'

'You've got my stuff in your car?'

'Well I haven't brought it into the phone box with me – of course it's in the bloody car. I can't keep it at home anymore. I thought you were collecting the bloody stuff last night?'

'Don't take it back to the house…'

'Well, what am I supposed to do with it? I'm not leaving it in my car – what if I get stopped?'

'Use your imagination – take it somewhere nobody will think of looking. Just don't take it back to my house. Is Danny's Capri on the drive?'

'Is it blue?'

'Yeah, he must be at home still – where's your car now?'

'I've parked it on Wissler Avenue. I just told you – I'm in the phone box.'

'Leave my stuff in your car and go around the back of the terrace. You can get in our back door through the garden – by the side gate on the snicket. Tell Danny to get the tool boxes out the garage and get 'em stowed somewhere safe. Then hide my gear. You can tell me where you've put it later. Just don't hide it somewhere obvious – got it?'

'Are you gonna pay me for this?'

'I'll consider the favour you owe me paid off.'

'This is an extra, Brian.'

'We'll argue about this later, Robbo. Just get to the house and warn Danny sharpish.'

'Lindsay! Where've ya been! We thought you was dead!' cried Ian, smiling with relief as his employer Mr Boldwood appeared suddenly, striding into the yard.

'What the bloody hell 'appened here?' he asked, looking mortified as he ran his eyes over the smashed planks of the toilet block door propped up against its frame, and the crime scene tape stretched across side of the annexe. 'What do you mean – you thought I was dead? I've been mugged. What's all this?'

'Somebody got carved up in the toilet block last neet.

There were blood all ovvert walls, an ont floor… the police are treating it as a murder. But there's no body. They couldn't find owt except a loada blood and strips of skin. What are you doing in them clothes?'

'I got my head kicked in by hunt saboteurs,' he said, lying as bravely as he could, still unsure as to what had happened to him. 'I came out of the bogs last night to chase some bloody foxhounds out of the yard, ran 'em up the street then came across a gang of long hairs an' bloody anarchists outside the shop. They asked me if they were my dogs, then just jumped me before I could open me mouth. Stole me clothes, me wallet and dumped me unconscious at Charlwood Zoo.'

'Well you better tell the coppers when they get back this morning. Or ring 'em now.'

'So are they coming back to look at all this?' he asked, frowning, waving a hand at the wrecked door.

'They said they were sending a forensic team 'ere today, sometime this morning. We'll 'ave to use the front door on the high street, we're all right to go inside that way. Can't use this bit til the this yellow tape comes off. But the inside o' the pub's covered in our fingerprints already anyway.'

'Is there any damage inside?'

'Nowt that I could see, though I've not been up top.'

'Well I've got to get in to get a shower and get into some clean clothes.'

'I didn't wanna say, if there were anyone else 'ere – but you really stink of dogs. Did you know you've got hay stuck in your hair – you look like you've kipped in a barn.'

'I haven't got any scratches on my face, have I? It feels really hot and itchy. I feel like my bloody skin's been scraped off with a blunt knife.'

'You look fit as a buck rat. If anything, you've got a bit of a glow about you actually, Lindsay. Apart from yer after shave.'

'While I'm in the shower, can you phone Trapnells and get them to come and fit us a new back door this afternoon. I want something sturdy this time, not another one of those braced tongue and groove things, something solid, hardwood. A new frame, new locks, front and back. If they can't come today or tomorrow, then call Des Mountain, in Sandsend. Des will fix it for us if they can't. Will you stop staring at me like that.'

'Sorry Lindsay. You've, you've got…'

'What?'

'You've got curly hairs stuck in your teeth, mate.'

'Oh God, I feel sick…'

'There was a wolf here last night,' said Ian, suddenly sounding very uneasy, 'after you disappeared. I caught it in the cellar, it was after the mince.'

'A wolf! Are you pulling my leg?'

'That thing in the cellar weren't like them from the zoo up road. It were more like a cross between a wolf an' a bear. I saw it, so did your nephew. Charlie next door saw it, the ambulance crew saw it. I put over thirty bullets into it and it lived. How could that happen, nothing could have taken that and lived? Nothing. It…' Ian began to cough.

'BULLETS! AMBULANCES! What's been happening, Ian? What's the matter?'

'I thought we was gonna die. I thought you was dead. Me and Charlie locked ourselves in 'is house, he had an old 303 he kept from Korea, we were shooting it – but it just kept coming. It just kept on coming… it was only the ambulance turning up and his bloody 'airspray that saved us. We were running out of bullets. We only had about ten rounds left. Charlie got taken to the hospital, he were in shock. We both were.'

'HAIRSPRAY?'

'Charlie was using this big can of 'airspray, like a sort of flamethrower. It was trying to push through 'is window to grab the rifle. So he used it to singe its friggin nose. I don't really wanna go into it anymore, Lindsay... Do you need to phone the brewery?'

'Why – was there any stock damaged?'

'I don't know, but the scullery door's been trashed, and there's Bolognese sauce and splinters all ovver the floor in the cellar. The bloody thing ate most of me mince.'

'BEE... BEE BEEP!'

'What's that?'

'I don't know – something in one o' these pockets maybe,' he said, frowning.

'Sounds like a pager or summat, Lindsay. Lindsay, are you all right ? You look a bit pale.'

'BIP, BIP – BEE BEEEEEP!'

'I need to get to the bathroom, Ian, I feel a bit queasy all of a sudden. Can I have the key?'

'Sure. Look – I'll check the pump room and clean up down below before I call Trapnells. There'd better be one of us around out the back when the coppers turn up again. Go and have a shower. I need to go home meself at some point though.'

'Okay. By the way, I'd appreciate it if you didn't mention I got mugged. It's not something I want to become common knowledge around here, it's a bit embarrassing. I'll find some way of getting these clothes back. Thanks for being here by the way, I'll make it up to you at some point.'

'There were no one else. What could I do. If it's all right, can I get off when you've cleaned y'sen up? I'm wired. I've been up all night.'

'Why don't you use one of the guest rooms.'

'Thanks Lindsay, no offence, I appreciate the offer, but I'd rather go home.'

'All right, I'll be as quick as I can.'

Mr Boldwood stopped momentarily on the landing at the top of the second staircase, as he always did under the picture of van Gogh's Starry Night, to get his breath, only now he wasn't out of breath. Puzzled, he pulled back the sleeve of the fleece to check the pulse in his wrist which was normally racing when he reached his rooms, but it was as flat as the wooden boards under his feet. If he hadn't been so eager to get to the toilet, he might have taken more time to think about why this was so unusual, but instead he went straight to the bathroom. There seemed to be something very hard and alien moving along the tunnel of his rectum that could not be classified on the Bristol stool chart, but could certainly be identified by British Telecom.

Whilst Dean and Michael where otherwise engaged below, Dave and Brian were discussing the previous night's events and Robert's revelation in one of the long derelict rooms above the shop.

'You're pacing…'

'What?'

'You're doing that thing you do…'

'I can't sit still and think like you. I need to move about when I'm thinking about stuff. I'm trying to think how we can get the gear back when the woods are closed off.

Someone's gonna find that head today, I'd put a bet on it. On top of everything, I've got to meet that pillock Phil Kennedy at the top of Coldharbour at one o'clock. I was expecting to have something to give 'im. He won't be too chuffed when he finds out I've got nowt but thin air.'

'Well I'll just spectate then, shall I, while you wear out the carpet. What's that for?' grumbled Dave as Brian shot him a flinty look. 'Just because I'm sitting down doesn't mean to say I'm not giving this the same serious consideration you are. Don't get yourself so wound up! Sit down, relax – and a solution will present itself. It's safe enough for now. It's in a bin liner stuffed behind the barge boards. Even if it's noticed, people will think it's just rubbish. You're not seriously thinking of going back there are you, anytime soon?'

'I need to think, Dave.'

'Is there owt in there tying it to you?'

'No, but there's fifteen different orders in it.'

'What are you going to tell these blokes who've paid you already?'

'I don't know. I'll think of something.'

'Well, you could just tell them it was damaged or out of date or something, pay them back. Just don't stall 'em. Forget about what you've lost. We're well up on this trip with this holdall. I don't know what you're selling that shite for anyway. Now we've got bouncers outside our house, this is getting out of control. It's more trouble than it's worth, or do you like being Doctor Jekyll?'

'I'm just a bit tense, after last night.'

'Oh I can see that – as tense as a pig in a catapult. The way I see it Brian – with all that's gone on, assuming they find the body that's missing its head – we're going to need a general panic before we can get back anywhere near the surf hut. Give Kennedy and the other blokes their money back – you could tell 'em the cops got to it before you did. We've got bigger things to think about and we don't need any other distractions. There's not been a murder, let alone a decapitation, around here in years. Those twerps from the Gazette will be crawling all over the bloody woods when somebody reports that thing, like fleas on a cat.'

'A general panic?'

'What?'

'A general panic. Like a bomb scare.'

'Just a minute – you're not suggesting we…'

'Why not?'

'What – cause a bomb scare? Just for a bin liner full of steroids! Are you nuts?'

'Why can't we? I paid for that stuff. It's mine and I want it back.'

'Because! Because we own a record shop. Because you're a petty crook. Because I'm in the pool team. We don't make bombs and blow people up! You can't even bake a friggin scone for Christ sake! Why are you smiling?'

'If the police got a call about a real bomb in Whitborough, they'd have to cordon off half the town. Think of the disruption, it'd be chaos, so many bureaucrats and agencies tying themselves up in knots, tripping over each other … hours and hours of delays. Traffic jams for miles.'

'I can't see the point of all this – talking about this as though it's something we'd ever get involved in. You'd need more than a bomb scare anyway. You'd need some other disaster or emergency going off at the same time to clear the police and forensics from the woods, unless you've been hiding an arsenal in the shed.'

'I haven't, but Vernon Hooper has.'

'Vernon from Manor Farm? He's long gone, Brian. He hasn't been seen there for years. Where the hell would he have got a bomb from anyway? He's a bloody farmer.'

'I'm not leaving that stuff to rot under Cayton Bay surf hut. Besides, I've got a reputation to protect. People rely on me. I can't just let them down, it's not good business. Someone at the surf club is bound to find it sooner rather than later, they might even sell it on, or take some of it themselves.'

'Well it won't kill 'em, will it. They'll just get really bad acne and go bald prematurely.'

'Just listen to me a minute – d'you remember years ago, Dad told us about that Heinkel Bomber that got shot up and crashed on Vernon's land in 1941, near Nalgo? Dad told me he'd been poaching nearby, checking his snares when the plane came down; he'd seen Vernon arrive with his two brothers carrying shotguns, big tough-looking bastards the Hoopers were, back then. Anyway, Dad said as soon as the Germans saw them coming they ran off into the trees. Dad was hiding in a culvert beside the field with little Terry Rutter and Pete Woodrow. They watched the brothers steal a machine gun and some bombs from the plane before the police and the Home Guard arrived.'

'But why would they want to steal stuff like that?'

'Vernon was selling all sorts on the black market in those days. Grandad said he wanted the gun and the bombs to intimidate people who'd crossed him. Dean's Grandfather Ludwig was one of the crew on that plane.'

'Dean's Grandad!'

'Yeah, he was a bomb technician in the Luftwaffe. Spent the rest of the war in that camp near Malton, off the Pickering road with the rest of the crew.'

'He got caught then?'

'Oh yeah – they came out of hiding and surrendered once the Hoopers had gone. England must have been a bloody paradise if you were a German during the war, if you weren't a Nazi…'

'So where are the bombs?'

'Still at the farm – and I think I know where.'

'What about the Hoopers, Brian?'

'Vernon's been living with his daughter in her cottage out on the Abbotsham Road since his brothers got sent down in the sixties. The farm was too much for him on his own. He rented the barns out to the classic car club for years, and the paddocks and stables to Georgina William's riding club. I think he tried to sell the place, but there was a lot of subsidence at the gable ends, big cracks in the stone courses – a blocked septic tank and a ghost, apparently. Vernon probably made up the ghost story to stop people breaking in, but some of the neighbours say they saw some queer lights inside there at night … it's derelict. I think he forgot about the war.'

'We should go and see Dean's Grandad. I want to know if those things are safe to move.'

'Why don't you do that, you two get on, don't you.'

'Hang on – why me? It's your idea.'

'Dave … please. I don't think his family wants to speak to me since the house party. He thinks we're a bad influence.'

'Yeah, I could understand him thinking that. I'll try – but don't get your hopes up.'

156

'I'll go to the city library in Leeds tomorrow and have a look in the local history records after I've been to the record fair. See what I can find out about unexploded bombs in the war records.'

'You are nuts, Brian – you know that don't you?'

'Listen – old Vernon used to take care of his guns. I'm sure he knew what he was doing when he stored that machine gun and those bombs.'

'All right, let's just say we find these things. What then?'

'Well, we've got to get them as close as we can to a main road in the town for maximum disruption. Give them a shallow burial and leave enough of the casing breaking the surface for the police to spot them.'

'And?'

'An anonymous call to the police, from a concerned citizen walking his dog. The dog smells something in the ground and starts digging – uncovering more of the bomb.'

'It sounds simple enough, but…'

'What?'

'I just think…'

'What?'

'I don't know. I'm not… it's plausible, but…'

'People find stuff like this all the time on building sites, in their gardens, the sand dunes. Hand grenades, old bullets, it's not unusual. There's that glade of tall trees beside the old railway arch, just off High Gunstone.'

'Yeah, but you'd have to get there at night. There's too much traffic going past during the day. Another problem with that place is lots of people take their dogs there last thing. What about burying it near the bridge supports under Valley Bridge? Not town end, the other side. There's plenty of cover, the top part's completely obscured by bushes and it's far enough from the road, but close enough to get to easily. We can park near the top of Swinbrook Road, there's some steps leading down to the bushes next to the old drinking fountain. If we time it right and make sure there's nothing coming up the road we'd only be exposed for thirty seconds at most. How heavy *are* these things?'

'I don't know. That's what I'm going to try and find out at the library.'

'Well, they used to use winches and pulleys to put these things in the planes, Brian. We're going to need something to help us carry one. Have you thought about that?'

'We've got Grandad's engine trolley in the garage. I've got to get below soon,' said Brian, switching his train of thought, 'Dean's kidnapping his ex. I've promised him a mock trial as long as he doesn't involve me in the execution afterward. It's a friendly kidnapping, by the way. She's a drama student and they want to act out a scene she's going to do for Rag week at college for charity. She gave me a script but I lost the bloody thing, so I'll have to improvise.

'Well, I suppose the bloody farm hasn't blown up yet, has it. Who are we letting in on this?

'Just you, me, Dean and Grandad – for now.'

'Are you going to tell Michael or Amy – or Danny?'

'No, not if I can help it. We could use Dan if need be, but I'd rather not. I'm not saying they'd let slip to anyone else – they wouldn't. But something tells me they wouldn't want to know anyway. Intuition I suppose.'

'What about later. What if this escalates?'

'Look. This is what we'll do…'

'I never thought you'd suggest we meet in a place like this, Derek. The dog rather suits you though. They calm you down, pets, don't you find?'

'I'd appreciate it if you didn't smirk, Alan. It's not mine. I borrowed it.'

'Is he all right, your little chappie? He's looking a bit sorry for himself. Terriers are usually so full of vim – is he off his food, or has he had the snip?'

'Never mind the dog. And don't put your fingers near it – it might be small, but it bites like a pike.'

'Did you hear that siren a minute ago?'

'No, I didn't, I was listening to Tubular Bells. Can we get to the matter in hand Alan, I didn't come here for my health.'

'Well, if you're not here to socialise, I hope you've brought some carrier bags, he looks fit to burst, the poor lamb. What's his name?'

'Carrier bags?'

'Carrier bags – for collecting their doings. It's considered beyond the pale inside the dog community to walk away and leave it anywhere on terra firma. You wouldn't believe the looks I've had when I've forgotten mine. Ostracised – for months I was. By the turd martyrs.' He sniffed. 'I always double bag, me. Well, you can't be too careful. One little hole…'

'I need some information from you or one of your colleagues. A discreet professional opinion,' continued Derek, ignoring his friend's interruptions. 'That's why I asked that we meet here.'

'I thought you'd have a good reason for coming here. It's not exactly you, walkies around the coach park, if you'll pardon the observation. But if you didn't want to be seen, then you've picked the right place. There are plenty of trees around the margins to hide behind, as you can see. And the coaches... We can go on the verges, if you'd rather?'

'Alan, some coins have come into my possession. I'd like your opinion on their value. I believe they're Spanish, Elizabethan.'

'Now there's a contradiction...'

'I meant the era.'

'Ahhh.'

'They're gold.'

'Are they now!'

'This thing swallowed one of them.'

'Well, Derek, this explains everything. Nobody I know would turn down the chance to walk a mongrel that shits precious metals. Would you like to take Tilly for a while instead?'

'No, I wouldn't. Look – how this mangy thing comes to have swallowed a coin is irrelevant. I have more than one of these, Alan.'

'More than one in the dog?'

'A few. He just ate one of them.'

'Well, I can certainly try. One of my colleagues in York could give you a firm valuation, he's used to be an archaeological metallurgist. But now he just specialises in coins. Do you have one with you? Apart from in the dog I mean?'

Derek reached into the back pocket of his slacks and held up a coin between his thumb and forefinger, in front of the face of his friend, whose eyes grew wide as his hand reached out to hold the gold.

'May I?' said Alan, clearly mesmerised.'

'I'll want something in kind – of equal value. Cash will be fine...' said Derek, holding back.

'Derek, we *are* old friends ... *this* is valuable ... Spanish, undoubtedly.'

'Yes, we are. But the first time we met, I was defending you for fraud.'

'A man must sometimes bend the law, to make a living, where the ground is cold and the grass is sparse – I wasn't made to live in poverty. How much would you like? Your hands look very raw, have you had a reaction against something?'

'You could say that. Two hundred pounds.'

'Two hundred pounds!'

'Two hundred. I could go elsewhere, Alan, but as you say, we are old friends and I'd appreciate your discretion. I'll pay you five percent of its real value for a fair valuation, agreed?'

'And the others...'

'If the conditions are right, at a later date. I'm not going to commit myself to anything.'

'It's very unfair to tease a man when you've stoked his appetite, Derek.'

'I dare say you'll recover, like your wallet. Are we agreed?'

'I suppose you'll be wanting some money now, and a carrier bag?'

'I'd rather not have the carrier bag.'

'You'd rather not think about using it, you mean, though in your case there really is money in dog shit, Derek.'

Thirty minutes later, the three thespians took their positions in the front space of Clash City Records and began a read-through of the trial scene.

Brian began the proceedings. 'All rise, this Kangaroo court is now in session.'

'Be seated,' interrupted Dean.

'What?'

'You're supposed to say be seated ... I think.'

'Are you? Am I? Sorry Deano – I lost my notes.'

'Just make it up.'

'You're right, we'll make it up. I am the judge – after all.'

'Your Honour.'

'WUURRGGHHHMMM!'

'Please be silent, Miss Clayton – you are speaking out of turn,' said Brian, adjusting his imaginary robe and half moon spectacles. 'Mr Beadle – please continue.'

'Thank you, my Lord. As I was saying ... before I was so rudely interrupted.'

'"Hear hear!'

'AHEM! It will become apparent...'

'Crystal clear,' said Brian with a flourish of sarcasm.

'If your Honour would kindly shut his cakehole,' added Dean. 'It will become apparent,' he continued, 'that the accused did wilfully, maliciously and resentfully withhold certain duties and services that are fundamental to the existence of a normal, healthy...'

'NORMAL!'

'...relationship between two headbangers.'

'Please explain to the court the exact details of the offence,' said Brian, getting into character.

'The offence, your eminence – and I need not stress the seriousness of the crime was and remains the refusal to take into her mouth certain vegetables. Err, a carrot and sprouts, belonging to the victim.'

'EH?'

'Err, me your grace. She wouldn't lick me popsickle.'

'OUTRAGEOUS!' mocked Brian, cracking the countertop with his gavel. 'And can you relate to the court the circumstances relating to the evening on which the offence was committed, please be brief.'

'Willingly m'lud.'

'Pray continue, Mr Beadle.'

'So, the victim – him being meself, had showered and dressed in a clean ripped Hanoi Rocks tee shirt and black jeans. I was clean shaven, sober – mostly – and ready for some action.'

'And you used shampoo and soap presumably?'

'I certainly did, Imperial Leather, your Grace.'

'UPON MY WORD, I used it myself! And the accused refused to grant you a…'

'Blow up, m'lud.'

'A blow up, Mr Beadle!'

'MAAARRRGGGGH!'

'Miss Clayton, if you please!' said Brian forcefully. 'Mr Beadle, I see no good reason for continuing with this case. The facts are incontestable, the charges most serious and grave. The accused is clearly guilty. She has been shamed in silence by…'

'The gaffa tape, m'lud.'

'Indeed. By the gaffa tape you have so expertly applied earlier. As the judge presiding I shall now pass sentence…'

'MMMMMMMMM!'

'Miss Tereasa, Melody? Clayton – I see at least your parents had a sense of humour. Having heard the most disagreeable evidence against you, I feel compelled to apply the heaviest tariff available to me, young lady, against your person. You should clearly be ashamed of yourself.' Brian then selects a black lace glove form the clothing accessories rack and places it carefully over his head. 'As a jumped-up chauvinist pig.'

'And kidnapper…'

'And kidnapper. Thank you Mr Beadle. You will now be taken from this place, thence to another place. And there, inside that space, Mr Beadle will introduce some ice cubes into your bra. Then you shall have your ears filled with mustard sauce from Feaney's caff.'

'WURGGGHHHH!'

'Calm down, girl! Anyone would think we were asking you to give favours to a complete stranger. MR BEADLE! Bring on the cubes…'

'Yes, your honour!'

'Derek, it's Alan.'

'Alan – so soon. I presume you've been able to get in touch with your friend, the numanatist – the coin expert…'

'Yes, he can meet you on Thursday at lunchtime – in York. I thought you'd like to get things moving.'

'York!'

'Derek, he's only agreed to this as a favour to me, so you'd better be polite. I might add you'll be expected to pay for lunch and all his drinks. May I recommend the Blanc Chemise restaurant on Goodramgate, or the Slaughtered Lamb on Gillygate. Smile and be gracious and I'm sure you'll find him most helpful. He'll want one of the best coins for his private collection, so don't forget, whatever you do. His name's Lawrence.'

164

'Take a stranger out to dinner – at my expense? Is this some kind of joke…'

'You're skiing off piste on this one, aren't you, Derek. You wouldn't drop this in my lap if you weren't, you old rogue. Am I getting warm?'

'This is all going to be declared to the proper authorities…'

'But not just yet eh? I don't blame you. I'd do the same, keep a little back…'

'It's not like that.'

'If you want to drag us into it when it's still not been declared, then I don't see why we shouldn't have a piece of the action. Don't forget we're taking a gamble, doing this behind the backs of the proper authorities. You know the risks as well as I do. This donkey wants more than a stale carrot. And don't treat me like an ass. By the way he's what they call a numismatist. He's a member of the British Numismatic Trade Association. 'They're quite a rare breed.'

'You don't say…'

'Alan, he's very good at what he does, you're very lucky he's willing to give you his opinion on an ad hoc basis, believe me.'

'Oh I feel it.'

'Just be there on time.'

'What's his surname?'

'Baston Demarque. The family were Huguenots. Protestants. Doesn't speak a word from the old country though. Let me know how you get on.'

'I hope he's discreet.'

'He's as buttoned up and as secretive as you dear, you'll get on like a couple of twins.'

After a long soak and a wash and brush-up in the privacy of his rooms at the Shirestones, Lindsay Boldwood decided he needed to get out of his hotel for a few hours, while the police forensic team finished their examination of the toilet block. Despite feeling abnormally energetic and vigorous, he still felt very tense, and had not had his usual morning clearout, though he had been amusingly gassy in the bath. He took the bus to Whitby, enjoying the change of scenery, and visited the Co-operative, after a stroll around the harbour, then went to Gallants Chemist to get something for his upset stomach. It was only as he was passing Dipsy & Cote Bakers that he remembered he'd not eaten all day, then realised he wasn't the least bit hungry.

Lindsay approached the counter in Gallants and smiled at Joyce Shuttleworth, who often came to the Shirestones with her husband Joe and their children for their Sunday lunches and birthday parties.

'Hello, Lindsay, what can I get you?'

'Hello, Joyce.'

'Are you all right, love?' she said, picking up on his awkwardness. 'Forgive me for saying, but you look a little out of sorts… not in a bad way.'

'I'm not sure – I think I've got a bit of acid. I just don't feel hungry…' he replied, making a circular motion over his stomach. 'I can't put my finger on it.'

'Oh…' said Joyce. 'Any other symptoms?'

'I'm a bit slow this morning,' he whispered, leaning over the counter. 'I think I need something to move me on … if you know…'

'We've got just the thing,' she said benevolently. 'Milk of Magnesia. It'll settle your stomach as well.'

'How much is it?'

'One ninety-nine a bottle. Or two for three pounds.'

'I'll just have the one Joyce, thank you. I thought that stuff was just for babies, I can't remember why though?' he chortled, then grimaced as he felt another spasm.'

'No, it's for all ages, adults as well as children. You might have had it as a child, most people have at some point... is business good?'

'Business? Oh yes. We're doing well. We're full at the weekend, got a coach-full from Fort William, though we've had a bit of vandalism recently, in the toilet blocks. The joiner's coming this afternoon to fit me a new back door, and some other bits and pieces. It's all in hand. Can't say I'm best pleased.'

'Oh love, I am sorry. I hope the police catch them. What a shame, Lindsay, especially with Easter so close. I hope you get it spick and span in time, I'm sure you will.'

'Thanks, Joyce.'

'Are you taking anything else? Ibruprofen...'

'Ibru... what?'

'I'll take that as a no, then. Any kidney problems – regular stomach pains?' she asked, dropping his purchase into a tall smooth white paper bag.'

'No. Not until this morning.'

'Make sure you drink plenty of fluids when you're taking it. Have some when you get home, then again before bedtime. You might feel a bit drowsy, but it works a treat.'

'All right, Joyce, thank you.'

'I'll see you soon.'

'I'll look forward to it. Hello to Joe and the boys.'

Unknown to Lindsay, the compounds in his medicine

would also prevent a repeat of the previous night's carnage, inhibiting the influence of the Lycanthrope virus to an extent where only a partial transformation was possible, during his deepest sleep cycle, keeping the residents of Cloughton and Whitborough safe, but ruining his sheets. By the next morning it would look like he'd been wrestling a huge Alsatian under his duvet.

Dave knocked on the door of Dean's Grandfather's house on Boxtree Hill, then stepped down away from the door to a respectful distance while he waited for the elderly war veteran to come into his hall.

A blurred head appeared behind the obscure glass in the upper door. There was a short pause as the lock was disengaged and then the door swung open, revealing a slim well-dressed man with a neatly trimmed white beard and fine silver-rimmed glasses – guarded, with a diffident air, but at the same time confident and enigmatic.

'Come in, Mr Drake, my grandson said he had a play to practice for tonight, so couldn't be here with us, but I'm sure we can manage without him. Come into the lounge, it is on the left there,' he said, pointing to the doorway of a large well-lit room with two large sofas and several comfortable armchairs. 'Would you like a drink?'

'Oh, thank you, I'll have a black coffee Mr Kalbach – thank you. Where would you like me to sit?'

'Sit where you may, Mr Drake, my chair is beside the round table.'

Once they were settled in their respective chairs, Ludwig Kalbach began to speak, moving straight onto the subject of his time in the Luftwaffe through an introduction to life as an ex-prisoner-of-war in a foreign land. Dave listened intently, taking small sips of coffee.

'I tried very hard not to look back, when it was all over. For me, it was an easy decision to stay in England. Ingrid and Peter – my son, Dean's father – joined us here too, as soon as they could. We did not want to go back to ruins, to hardship, Armin and I. Armin was one of our crew, we were kept together near Malton, off the Pickering road. This country has given us everything, though I cannot deny I had a good life before the war. We lived in Wegberg. We were the busiest surveyors in Westphalia, my brothers, my father and I, overseeing Germany's modernisation, marking out the routes for the new autobahns. We had cars from the government, a great privilege then. But our neighbours were jealous. The Sommers were the most jealous. Their daughter Heidi was a bad sort, a witch in the League of German Maidens. She told the authorities that we made disreputable remarks about the party and said unpatriotic things. All rubbish! But we were investigated, so I joined the Luftwaffe to shut them up. It was not a hard decision for me, I had always wanted to fly, and the uniform was very smart. Ingrid, my wife, liked me to wear it always, even at home.'

'What did you do in the air force, Mr Kalbach?'

'I was an air navigator. I directed the plane, and I looked after our bombs. There were lots of munitions.'

'All sorts of bombs?'

'Many, many bombs, ja. It was important to me to be the best technician, this is how you stay alive. I thought if we crash, we will not go boom! Our crew were chosen to appear on the cover of Signal in the fall of 1940, perhaps because our pilot and co-pilot were so handsome, nevertheless a great honour for all of us. But we would never return to Denmark for the pictures.'

'Signal?'

'It was like the Lufwaffe's version of Hello! People who know me now know that I was not a Nazi, but we had been treated badly after the Great War. When a nation of proud peoples was so humiliated, it made it hard for the voices of reasonable men to be heard. Extremism flourished and grew like a cancer. I never liked him, Hitler. He was to us like a headmaster, or a pedantic council official that you make fun of, who suddenly wakes up as master of the world. I do not like people who shout and rant, but chance and luck were on his side, at least in the beginning. It was impossible to speak out, because he was never challenged or faced down. And so triumphant! Unbearable! This Scargill fellow reminds me of him. All finger pointing and yelling, pushing his fringe back from his sweaty face. The same sense of entitlement. But I digress, let us talk of other things, not jackbooted political psychopaths and Union Barons. Dean my grandson says that you wanted to ask me something about our aeroplanes for your nephew's school project, ja?'

'Yes, that's right. Was it a Heinkel that you flew, Mr Kalbach?'

'Yes, but I was not the pilot. I sat behind and plotted our course. The crews used to call the pilot's seat the zahnarzstuhl, the dentist's chair, because it was the most dangerous place to sit when you had a Hurricane or a Spitfire flying straight at you.'

'Our nephew Peter has got to make a five minute presentation to his class on one type of German bomber from the Battle of Britain. He was very excited when he heard about you, Mr Kalbach. But we weren't sure that you would want to talk about it.'

'I would not have, ten, twenty years ago. But I feel now that we must pass on our stories to the next generation, so people do not forget, however uncomfortable it makes us feel. I will tell you anything you ask. But I will not talk about the lives we may have taken. Or the destruction, it is still too vivid, even after all this time.'

'Thank you, Mr Kalbach. Peter wanted to know where you flew from, and what your bombs looked like.'

'What they looked like?'

'Just what colour they were. That sort of thing.'

'Our Kampfgeshwader – or Wing, I think is the English equivalent – flew from Aalborg in Denmark over East Anglia, Lincolnshire and Yorkshire. East Anglia was very beautiful to us. You have very fine churches in Norfolk. We loved their flint and brick houses and cottages, the farms, the fens – so pretty. The landscape was to us so lovely. Sometimes we flew north to Teeside also. Yorkshire of course is the place I have lived, we were ordered to attack airfields and infrastructure for transport. Railway yards, bus stations, factories…'

'What kind of bombs did you drop?'

'You would have made a good interrogator, Mr Drake.'

'Our nephew is really interested in the war.'

'Well then, we had incendiary bombs, air mines, and high explosives. The Heinkel could carry several types of munitions. We had bombs from 48kg to 2000kg. The Heinkel could carry up to 2000kg in total, but on our last flight, when we were shot down, we were carrying 55kg SC50 II bombs in our racks. The bombs were usually dunkelgrau, pardon me, dark grey or dark green, sometimes sandy grey. These

were dark green, with yellow stripes on the tail section – am I
boring you, Mr Drake?' he asked, noticing Dave's uneasiness.

'No! No it's really interesting. Please – go on.'

'If you are sure?'

'Yes. Absolutely. Peter will be riveted.'

'Well then. Now, the b…'

'The bombs with the yellow stripes on the tail.'

'You are a good listener.'

'Thank you, Mr Kalbach.'

'So, they are about three and a half feet long.'

'Can you remember anything else about them?'

'They were released by the front gunner, who would use
a remote toggle switch as he looked through the bombsight.'

'Were they safe to handle? Or move, how would…'

'They were loaded from a cradle, Mr Drake – we would
not carry them. They were not dangerous until they were
fused. We would not move them when they were fused in the
racks.'

'Would these bombs be safe to move today? If you found
one stored. Or buried even?'

'If you found one, then you should get away from it by
running, as if a car is chasing you, Mr Drake.'

'Even if it were properly stored, indoors?'

'Do you mean in a museum?'

'Yes, it could be a museum – would it be safe to leave the
fuse in?'

'That would be most unwise, who would do it? Only a
madman! Our bombs were not made to be stored with their
fuses inserted for long. These were produced in their tens of
thousands, to a price. Not built to remain safe for years. Tell
your nephew – if he ever finds one, not that he will – to leave

it alone and tell the police. I hope their teacher will explain this also.'

'Oh, I'm sure that they will, Mr Kalbach. Thank you for being so detailed.'

'You have an interest too? You are leaning forwards when you listen, with the most careful expression Mr Drake?'

'Oh yes… I've always been fascinated by the war. Fascinated.'

'Of course, it is an interesting subject, if you enjoy history. I am pleased you realise its importance in world affairs. My grandson has told you the story of our capture?'

'Just the basics.'

'Then you know our plane survived.'

'Really?'

'Some of our bombs were stolen.'

'Stolen – really?'

'And never recovered. Two of our machine guns also.'

'*Two?*'

'Yes but only one was reported. Strange, is it not? Some men with guns came, before the Home Guard and the police. We were also armed. But a pistol is not a great deterrent to a man with a shotgun. We did not want to fight, and we were badly shaken after the landing. So we left the plane, taking our code books and orders to the woods to burn them. Luckily they did not follow.'

'It is, very strange.'

'Well, look how long we have been talking, it is time for my bath,' said Dean's grandfather, rubbing his knees after his cuckoo clock sprang back to life. 'I have to do this always, before I stand, Mr Drake. I am like your Barry Sheene, I think. But my age catches up with me, bodies grow old, and stiff. You will have similar burdens yourself one day.'

'I am very grateful you took the time to talk to me, Mr Kalbach.'

'Gut. If you nephew has any more questions… Tell him I wish him well with his presentation.'

'Well, thank you again. That was very useful,' said Dave, moving towards the kitchen. 'I'll see myself out, Mr Kalbach.'

'Be careful, Mr Drake.'

'Your steps aren't slippery, Mr Kalbach. It's stopped raining.'

'I did not mean the steps. Goodbye.'

Back in the Binnie household meanwhile, things were about to get a great deal worse after another telephone call. 'Isla? It's Else, love. Elsie Cakebread, are you on your own pet?'

'Else? Oh hi hen, long time no see – Ave jushed gort tha bearns sent. Ett's nice tae hear yer voice. Ahm sorry I've no had time tae…'

'Isla – I don't quite know how to break this to you, love. But I've had a message from Tony. I don't mean to pry Isla – but when did you last see him, pet?'

'A message? Yuv no sheen hem enn pearson, then?'

'Did you two have an argument, Isla?'

'Weyll, he's no gonnae gate any favours frum me when he gets enn.'

'Did you say you were at home, love?'

'Aye…'

'I don't quite know how to break this to you, pet, but I was having a soak at home last night, and a bit o' me time, when I had one of me visions. I saw your Tony. He's crossed over, Isla… He says he's been killed – by a wolf. You need to call the police…'

'Crossed over! Are ya pullen ma leg, Else? Yer no right enn the heyd, hen?'

'Look, I can't do this over the phone, hun. I'd better come over. Don't go anywhere – I'll be twenty minutes.'

At Whitborough Hospital, on Andrews Avenue, two of the senior men from the local police station had arrived to interview the two traffic policemen after their period of isolation.

'Can I help you?' Asked the stocky receptionist, looking up as the shadows of Sergeant Broadhead and Inspector Marshall fell across the visitors book.

'Hello... Patricia,' replied the inspector, reading her name badge with the eagle eyes of a trained observer. 'We're here on the invitation of Doctor Rowbotham, one of your consultants. We've come to interview two of our officers who were admitted on Wednesday morning. I'm Inspector Marshall, and this is Sergeant Broadhead,' he explained, pausing to let her examine his warrant card. 'Could you let him know that we've arrived?'

'I'm afraid he's not here today, gentlemen, but we do have one of the registrars on in his place, who'll be able to answer all your questions. Follow the yellow tape on the floor which will take you to the ICU units on the ground floor.'

'Is there somewhere we can get a cup of tea or coffee nearby?'

'There's a drinks machine on the ward, Inspector.'

'Is it free?'

'No, there's a small charge. Was there anything else?' she asked, covertly assessing the next person in the queue behind them.

'She's fierce,' observed Detective Sergeant George Broadhead. 'We could use her on our front desk, Ray.' He added, as he ambled away from the reception cubicle with his Inspector, Ray Marshall.

'She's probably more at home here, she's got more people to intimidate. I don't think she'd like our customers, they'd give her the hump.'

'Have you met this Rowbotham, the consultant?'

'We had a conversation. On the phone.'

'I hope they're awake.'

'If they're not, then you can wake them up, George. Knock a mug over, or kick the bed frame accidentally on purpose. Either way, we're not leaving without a statement. Once we've got that we can make our excuses, when we've got what the paperwork the chief wants. I'm not hanging around in this place longer than we have to.'

'I wonder how long they'll be stuck in here. Hasn't Deighton already had two days on the sick this month?'

'His wife's just had their first baby, so it must have been a lack of sleep I reckon, rather than a genuine sickness. He's got a clever tongue, that one. Keep an eye on him George, much too slick with his answers. Doesn't appear to be rich in common sense though – which is a worry.'

'You can do a lot with common sense. I'd rather work with a copper that's got a bit of common sense, than some bloody twit from university. He's got a degree in economics apparently.'

'Well, that's going to be as useful as a spaghetti fireguard. We can only pray that some of Dodd's finer qualities rub off on our new virgin.'

'Paul's wife Martine says A&E was overflowing with

people from the Duchess and the Technical college since yesterday lunchtime. Same symptoms, some mystery virus. It's not pleasant by all accounts, fever, some people hallucinating – stuff coming out both ends. It's a bit odd, they're two miles apart at least. Environmental health have been in to take samples. They've closed down the kitchens temporarily.'

'Environmental health?'

'No, the owners. It's better they do it before anyone else does.'

'His wife's on the staff here?'

'Yeah she's an auxiliary.'

'It's a big place, this hospital.'

'Yeah, easy to get lost unless you follow the tape. Follow the yellow brick road…'

'Oh, very funny. Is this it?' asked Marshall as they turned a corner and reached the end of the tape.

'ICU. Yep, this is it. They might want us to take our shoes off and put something on.'

'Put something on?'

'Yeah. Like the disposable one-piece coveralls forensics use. They're to stop germs that people carry in getting into the cubicles.'

'They're not going to make us wear a bloody mask as well, are they? I certainly hope not – I can't talk with a bloody gas mask over my face.'

'No, but we might have to talk to them through a plastic sheet. They could be in one of those plastic tents. The ones with air filters and zips at the corners.'

'Well I hope they're not that ill, George. It makes me think we're going to catch what they've got too. No wonder his lordship doesn't want to come here to question them.'

'Inspector Marshall? Sergeant Broadhead?' asked a young nurse at the reception desk window.

'Is it that obvious?' said Marshall jokingly, trying not to sound self conscious.

'I'm sorry, gentlemen,' said the nurse, smiling. 'I wasn't trying to be presumptuous. It's just that we've been told you were on your way here by reception. Would you like to follow me, please?'

'Yes, of course nurse, after you,' said the inspector. 'Will you be wanting us to take our shoes off?'

'There are some infection control guidelines we'd like you to follow. The doctor will explain,' she replied, walking quickly into another wing and then stopping in front of a set of swing doors. 'Wait here please.'

'I'm getting more uncomfortable the longer we spend here,' grumbled Marshall, fidgeting in his mac pockets. 'There's something very odd going on in this town. I can feel it in my water. Call it intuition, but there's a connection between what happened to Dodds and Deighton and that nasty business at the pub in Cloughton. Two separate incidents, different times and locations, but both outside of our experience. Outside of the norm,' he said meaningfully, spacing the words for consideration. 'All the witnesses we've had were scared – very scared. I've seen it in soldiers that go to warzones, people that witness death, they never really come back whole – as the same person. Normally you can expect a bit of deference when you interview someone for the first time. That chef couldn't have cared less who we were, where he was or what we were about to ask him, one word answers and a distinct hunted look – as if he'd been through something he'll take to his deathbed. That paramedic Shaun and his mate Barry Griffin weren't exactly forthcoming either. There's a big heap of trouble coming our way – mark my words.'

'And a shit storm of paperwork,' said George, huffing, trying to find enlightenment in the plethora of guidelines and protocols on the signs screwed to the walls. 'I'll bet you a night in Luchinelli's that someone at the Zoo's involved. Fu's caught the scent of something. Bright lad.'

'I wouldn't bet against it.'

A few seconds passed before a young male doctor emerged from a side door.

'Inspector Marshall, Sergeant Broadhead? My name is Alex Weeton, I'm the registrar, would you like to come into the office? I'm afraid it's a little rudimentary, but it's just for a moment, please take a seat.' He motioned to the two plastic chairs in front of a simple office desk. 'I understand you're here to interview your colleagues Mr Dodds and Mr Deighton, and take some paperwork.'

'We're here to collect their statements and ask them a few basic questions, yes. We only intend to stay as long as that requires,' said Marshall.

'That's what we understood from your superintendent inspector. I expect you're curious to know how well you colleagues are?' he asked breezily. 'Both of them are awake and lucid. We're treating them with broad spectrum antibiotics; we have a no-touching protocol in place for visitors and families at the moment, just as a precaution, – but it seems they are recovering well.'

'Can we see them now?' asked the sergeant.

'Of course gentlemen, if you would like to wait outside, Matron will take you through. There are some sterile shoe covers and gloves you will need to wear, but other than that you may go through as you are.'

'We'll probably need half an hour each, said Inspector Marshall. I trust we won't be interrupted. We're still on police business; our conversations need to be confidential.'

'I'll see to it that you're not disturbed. Just inform the nursing station when you leave, gentlemen. I hope we've done all we can to make them comfortable.'

Five minutes later the two policemen were ushered into the room occupied by Sergeant Dodds, who was propped up in bed reading an Alistair MacLean novel.

'Ahh, Dodds. How are you feeling?' asked his superior.

'Good sir,' he said putting down the book. 'I'd kill for a decent newspaper though. Can't say I'm too happy about being cooped up like a bloody lab rat, but I expect you'll tell me it's for our own good. Are you here for the statements? I finished mine yesterday.'

'Have they given you any indication about how long they're going to keep you here, Cliff?'

'No, nothing. They were quite candid about our toxicology reports. Face to face. I'm afraid I lost my temper and told them they'd better take some more blood or I was going to sue them for defamation – calling me a monkey shagger! Then they came back and said the lab in Leeds made a mistake – we had some kind of snake venom in our bloodstream. No trace of the bloody monkey virus they were so sure we'd got – oh no. I think they've got monkeys working in their lab. Monkeys with degrees. But I get the impression that now we're on the antibiotics and improving, they don't really know what else to do with us. I think we're here just for observation now. That's what I think.'

'Well, that's reassuring. What I mean is, we're relieved you're both getting better, aren't we George?'

'Absolutely, sir. The lads have had a whip round, and we bought you some magazines and some sausage rolls from Derrigans Cliff. And a couple of cheese and onion pasties and some proper tea bags. Paul's wife says the tea's a bit anaemic in here.'

'Well fellas, that's the best thing I've heard today. I'm really touched. Really I am. You've cheered me up, God knows I need it. I've been gagging for a proper brew. The food's not too bad – I've had worse – but the tea's like piss. Bloody awful.'

'So they reckon you were both bitten by snakes,' said George.

'That's what they reckon. They told me I'd had a bit of a reaction to the venom, but then we got stung by some weird flies or wasps beforehand. I think we kicked a wasp nest myself. Either me or wet nose next door. The funny thing is, I haven't got any lumps where they bit me, like you normally get with a wasp sting. My hands and head just looked like I'd been dipped in Ribena or summat, and all my skin's been peeling off where they were crawling on me. It's faded a bit since, mind. I looked like the end of someone's…'

'Yes, well I've seen an adder myself on the coastal path, our spaniel must have spooked it. Luckily she was on the lead and I pulled her back just in time. You don't see them until you're on top of them. It must have been an adder, I assume. Or more than one…' said Ray, hypothesizing.

'That's what I think,' said Cliff. 'And I reckon that's why we were hallucinating, though I don't want to go into that too much. But I reckon it was that that caused us to crash.

The odd thing is, they can't find any trace of a snake bite. They haven't looked *everywhere,* but there's no bite anywhere that I can see. They haven't told us anything about what happened.'

'Well, you collided with a minicab on Lower Gunstone, just before the rise into Wheatcroft Dip. The accident investigators estimate you were doing between 20 and 25 mph. But the taxi driver was over the speed limit, by some margin. They estimated his speed was close to 55mph. He crept over the white line before the top of the rise opposite Crossways Motel and hit your front quarter. Luckily he hadn't taken any passengers. He's here in the other wing. We interviewed him and he's admitted speeding and careless driving. He couldn't really argue otherwise, with all the evidence.'

'How is he?'

'Oh he'll live. He'll lose his licence – but the doctors say he'll walk out of here, eventually.'

'Which cab company was he driving for?'

'Quick Cab.'

'The worst in Whitborough.'

'By a long way. We'd had them all once or twice. They won't be around too much longer, we'll see to that. Including that moonlighting bus driver that works for 'em. He's the biggest maniac in town.'

'We'd like to stay a bit longer, Cliff, but we need to talk to Deighton too, and get your statement back to the chief. I'll come back one evening when I'm off shift, is there anything else?' said Inspector Marshall.

'I really appreciate all the food and the tea bags fellas, but no. If I recall anything that I've left out in the statements I'll fill in the other blanks and get in touch. Thanks for the chat too. It was good to talk to you and George. I haven't been in here that long, but I'm fed up to the back teeth already.'

'Well, don't go running off, Cliff. We'll see you soon,' said Inspector Marshall. 'We'll show ourselves out,' he said, winking at Sergeant Dodds. 'Right, George,' he muttered, 'let's go and see what our graduate's been doing with his time, while he's been propped up on his arse.'

Moments later, the two officers opened the next door further up the corridor and peered in.

'Now Deighton, feeling better I hope. Ready to climb back on your horse?' asked Inspector Marshall in a fatherly tone, with a perceptible acidic inflection.

'Yes sir, I feel well enough to walk about – but it looks like we'll be stuck here until we've finished the course of antibiotics and they've found out for certain what we've been suffering from.'

'You'll be out soon enough, lad. Did you manage to finish the statement we left with you?'

'I did sir, it's as definitive and detailed as I can recall, under the circumstances.'

'Definitive eh? And detailed. Well, it should be worth a read...'

'Sir, may I say something off the record?'

'Concerning who?'

'Sergeant Dodds, sir?'

The two senior men's eyes met momentarily, although Deighton missed the exchange, reaching for a cardboard folder in his bedside cabinet.

'This would be about what, exactly?' asked the Inspector, hoping the young policeman would unravel enough rope with which to hang himself.

'I'd rather speak with you alone, sir…'

Sergeant Broadhead looked at Marshall again, but this time they did not try to conceal the exchange.

'Sir, I know the sergeant is a friend of Sergeant Dodds, sir, I'm…'

'It sounds to me, Deighton, that what you are going to say to me about Sergeant Dodds is going to put him in a bad light. Or am I mistaken?'

Deighton blanched and tried to avoid the withering stare of the sergeant, which seemed to be scorching the paint on the back of the bed frame behind his head.

'Deighton, if you have a legitimate grievance against one of your colleagues, that could include myself, Sergeant Broadhead here or Sergeant Dodds, then there are proper ways of dealing with your concerns. What we don't do in the Police Service is try to smear other men's reputations with off-the-record briefings and intrigues – do I make myself clear? We know most of what happened. We know that you were driving the vehicle. You were seen by two telecoms engineers from BT bundling the sergeant into the back of your patrol car and driving away – and I quote "like Oliver Reed leaving a country house party". NO calls were made for assistance, NO calls were made for an ambulance. Does that refresh your memory?'

Deighton, momentarily lost for words, looked like a man who had just turned a corner into a tight alley and seen a lorry bearing down on him with no visible means of escape. All the bombast was rushing out of him like the air from a burst tyre.

'Hand me that file would you George,' asked Inspector Marshall. 'This won't take a moment.'

'Sir?'

'Shut up.'

'Sir, I've got a right to be heard.' His elders and betters gave him another look, which made it clear he was about to be brought to down to earth.

'I'll tell you what's going to happen now, Deighton. You can have your statement back, we'll leave two blanks for you so you can have another think about the events the night before last. Make it as definitive and detailed as you like. Sergeant Broadhead will come back and collect it tomorrow afternoon after you've had something to eat. Perhaps you'll be able to recall some other facts and details in the extra time. I'm sure I'll think of something you can do for me in future as a reciprocal favour, son. Well, we'd love to stay, but duty calls.

Just one other thing. Our little empire isn't much, lad. We're not a big station, but we are good at what we do in Whitborough. That's down to teamwork. If you're not a team player, we can't use you. We don't tread on the next chap.'

Chapter Five

Thursday

Derek sat cross legged on a buff colonial chair in the front of house lounge of the Blanc Chemise restaurant on Goodramgate, hiding his face and torso behind a spread-eagled copy of the Daily Telegraph. His eyes moving along a track from the columns on the upper pages to the full length glass doors at the entrance onto the street. A young waitress on reception looked up and gave him a kindly smile to put him at ease, though he found himself dodging her eyes and raising the newsprint another inch. Then a shadow fell over the top of his shoulder, taking him by surprise.

'Mr Beautimann?' enquired one of the waiters, 'My name is Anton.'

'Ermm, what is it?' he replied guardedly, hiding stubbornly behind the paper.

'Mr Demarque will be a few minutes late. He called to say he's in traffic, sir. May I get you anything while you're waiting? Would you like to look at the menu de jour, or the a la carte?' The waiter tried to peer discreetly over the headlines as Derek drew the paper closer to his chest.

'No, thank you,' he said quickly, trying to bring their conversation to an end as swiftly as possible. 'I'll wait. Thank you for the message,' he added, in a cutting tone of voice which left Anton in no doubt that any further exchange would be pointless.

A portly, nondescript man in his late forties, in a smart navy linen suit and collarless shirt, entered the restaurant as the waiter retreated, and immediately fell into an easy though polite conversation with the maitre d'hotel. After an interval, the waiter reappeared and ushered him towards the lounge, moving swiftly towards the pair of Farah slacks, Marks and Spencer's socks and Chelsea boots resting beneath the screen of newspaper.

'Your guest, Mr Beautiman… Mr Demarque,' announced Anton coolly, before slipping away to attend the other diners. Derek dropped the paper unceremoniously onto the coffee table and stood up to shake hands with his host.

'Pleased to meet you, Lawrence,' he said formally. 'It's kind of you to see me. I'm in need of a discreet professional opinion. I assume Alan explained…'

'Yes, I must say, this find of yours has got me quite excited.'

'Oh?'

'Alan's a great friend. We've had a very enriching professional relationship, across the years – though I've become more of a specialist here. Alan's expanded his horizons and developed a much broader knowledge of archaeology. We've often been able to help people between us, from time to time. It would seem you've had some good fortune recently, Mr Beautimann. How did you two become…'

'I represented him in court. I was his defence solicitor, I'm one of the partners in the law firm Beautimann, Buerk and Trippe.'

'May I say, thank you for all your hard work, sir, and very well done. Have you had thepleasure?' asked Lawrence, nodding towards the tables.

'I can honestly say I've never been to a French restaurant.'

'If you enjoy rich food, Mr Beautimann, then this is as close to heaven as anything you're likely to try, at least in the British Isles. Their chef is from Alsace, he's very um – well, we won't go into that – but immensely talented. The menu is tilted somewhat towards the dishes from that region, Lorraine and Champagne, whilst most of the seafood dishes you'd recognise as traditional to Normandy.'

'We're not so well served in Whitborough, though we have two reasonably good Italian restaurants – Lucchinelli's and Bertuccio's. And three good Indian restaurants.'

'Alan says Whitborough is full of them.'

'There are a few.'

'I must confess, I'm not a fan of spicy cuisine. It doesn't agree with my constitution,' he said, patting the front of his straining shirt. 'Did you bring a selection of the coins?'

'Yes, two of each type.'

'I think our table is ready,' said Lawrence, catching the approach of one of the waitresses. 'Shall we sit down and I'll look one over quickly before the menus arrive, to get the juices flowing,' he said, getting slowly to his feet. 'Do you have another appointment this afternoon?'

'I've got to collect my daughter Grace from her pony club at five thirty. Is the menu in English?'

'I'm afraid not, but there's a very brief description underneath the names of each dish. If there's anything which puzzles you, just ask. I come here rather a lot, so I'm familiar with most things. Their menu de jour is good, but we can order a mixture of anything from that or the a la carte. The pan fried scallops and the coq au Reisling would be hard to improve on, but don't let me push you into anything.'

The two men were shown into a booth behind a wooden partition, supporting a frosted glass screen. Awaiting them was a square table of reasonable size, beneath a crisp white tablecloth laid with silver cutlery, red napkins and a selection of wine glasses in various sizes. A pierced silver condiments rack containing a selection of oils, salts and saucepots occupied the centre. The waiter assisted them to their most comfortable positions, then offered them two menus, one for food and another for wine.

'Is it very expensive to eat here?' asked Derek, examining the table setting and furniture with a careful eye.

'Oh, not excessively so,' replied his host,'but I find that the more convivial the atmosphere, the more productive the man. I'm sure you'll find the food is superb; it's a very good place to conduct a little business, very discreet. May I see one of your coins?'

Derek could not suppress the feeling he was being groomed for the loss of a considerable amount of money, by a manipulative stranger who was holding all the cards and seemed from first impressions to be as least as avaricious and unprincipled as his associate. But he had come prepared to endure an expensive and unproductive afternoon if it ultimately contributed to his own self-enrichment. It was undoubtedly the same motivation that had brought the corpulent Lawrence Baston Demarque to their table. Derek withdrew a small compact and opened the lid, setting it down into the chubby palm of his host.'

'Oh my word!' whispered Lawrence, producing a small magnifying glass with a light set in the rim. 'Wonderful

189

detailing, I can tell you straight away that it's Spanish – struck during the reign of Philip the second, the king of Spain who tried to overthrow Queen Elizabeth the first. Alan was right on the money in that respect, so to speak. My next question is, are there many more? Was it part of a cache, were there any other artefacts found with it from the same period?'

'I can't answer that, I'm afraid.'

'It would help me a great deal to know, Mr Beautimann. Of course, I understand you may have your own reasons for not wanting to go into the circumstances of its…'

'I don't know the circumstances around its discovery, I'm sorry. I found them clearing out a friend's garage,' he said flatly, employing some of the tricks and techniques he had learnt observing successful criminals – their body language, speech and demeanour in court – in order to paint a false picture for his opponent.

'A garage! In a garage!' gasped his host, completely flummoxed. 'But…Alan…'

'They were in a dirty old cotton drawstring bag, under some old car parts. The kind of thing kids used to carry their PE kit in, in the 50s and 60s,' said Derek, savouring the effect of another low blow. 'So what would you value it at – at auction?' Then without warning he kicked the shin of his host with the unforgiving edge of his chelsea boot as the waiter sashayed back into their booth. He was almost starting to enjoy himself.

'OWW! Ouch!' groaned Lawrence, dropping the compact onto the white linen.

'Would you like some more time, gentlemen?' asked the waiter expectantly. 'Are you all right, sir?' he asked, seeing Lawrence flushed and obviously in pain, gritting his teeth.

'Come back in five minutes, would you Anton, thank you…' he said brusquely, covering the compact with his napkin.

'Perhaps I can get you a carafe – some water?' suggested the waiter, sounding concerned.

'No. Please… Thank you.'

'I will come back…' said Anton.

'I'm so sorry Lawrence, I didn't know what else to do – are you all right? He just appeared from nowhere – I was trying to warn you.'

'Just tap the cutlery next time would you please – or put your hand over your face and cough. Please don't kick me like that again…' he pleaded, taking a tissue from his pocket and dabbing his forehead.

'I'm so sorry, but I was just protecting our interests. I'm sure you're as keen as I am to keep this a secret. It might be easier if we went for a walk near the Minster, there's a large lawn where we could…'

'No, no. Perhaps we could just change places. Then I can see when anyone approaches,' said Lawrence, keen to keep his meal ticket inside the restaurant. 'You were right of course – to attract my attention…' he grumbled. 'The staff are very attentive.'

'Does one tip here?'

'Absolutely one does. It would be unthinkable – beyond the pale – not to. We certainly wouldn't get our feet under such a good table otherwise, I can assure you of that.'

'It's difficult to know when to. He's coming back – the waiter,' warned Derek, seeing a shadow pass on the other side of the glass as Lawrence snapped the compact shut.'

'Are you ready to order now, gentlemen?' asked Anton, arriving with his notepad.

'Yes,' said Lawrence decisively. 'I'll have the rye toasts with tapanade and a glass of Pinot Blanc.'

'And for you, sir?'

'I'll have some Perrier water…'

'Wine, sir?'

'No.'

'My colleague is driving home, Anton.'

'Very good sir. Would you like to choose a starter, sir?' asked Anton, looking at Mr Beautimann.

'Something inexpensive… the onion soup?

'Et le plat principal?' enquired Anton.

'Pardon me?'

'The main course,' explained Lawrence gently.

'What's rosbif alsacienne?' asked Derek.

'Horse.'

'What about Cassoulet de Leg – humes avec… or baeckeoffe?'

'Avec spaetzle au basilic…' added Lawrence helpfully. 'It's spring vegetable, beans and herbs with basil dumplings. Baeckeoffe is beef stew, cooked slowly, then sealed under a pastry lid.'

'I'll have the first one or we'll be here all afternoon. I'm sorry, but I'm just not au fait with French cuisine,' said Derek irritably. 'Are we having dessert as well?'

'Do you like apple tart?'

'I should think so…'

'Anton, I shall have the roast partridge and sauerkraut flambe with grapes, and a glass of Tokay Pinot Gris with my main. A side of perigord truffles and roast hazelnuts. And streusel for dessert. My colleague will have tarte aux pommes – thank you.'

'Very good sir. We have the first asparagus arriving later today.'

'Do you? I may come back again before the weekend.'

'It seems the first spears of asparagus are arriving this week, Mr Beautimann, I shall have to come back,' said Lawrence seductively.

Derek shifted position and checked his watch, resisting the invitation to comment, and hoping his silence would bring his host back onto the subject of the coins.

'Well, I think we have a few minutes now before the first course arrives,' he said, attempting to defuse the cold atmosphere around their table. 'Let me have another look at this find of yours,' he whispered, picking up the compact and magnifying glass once more. 'This coin of is of a type called a Doublon. It's gold, that's for certain, as pure as one would wish to find. When one of these turns up in England, one from this era – it always gets people in our small community excited. To find one has been found on the coast of North East England, especially when they turn up in quantity, stirs in me a very special kind of hope. Have you heard of the Treasure of the Mar del Norte, Mr Beautimann?'

'No, I haven't – the waiter's coming back.'

'Ahhh, our drinks – and the starters,' purred Lawrence gratefully, as the first course was set down before them. 'Anton, may we have an interval – before our le plat principal, say thirty-five minutes?'

'I will instruct the chef, sir.'

'I do like the fact that the food takes preference here,' said Lawrence. 'I don't enjoy a strict French service, it sometimes appears to baffle one's guests. The meat at 6, the starch at 2, vegetables at 10 o'clock.'

'I'm sorry – you've lost me.'

'I'm sorry, Derek. I was referring to the position of the food on the plates.'

'Lawrence, I didn't come here to learn about the finer points of food presentation, I'm here for one reason and one reason only.'

'Of course, I'm sorry, I'm such an incurable foodie. I sometimes think…'

'You were talking about The Treasure of the Mar del Norte,' said Derek assertively, instantly regretting the fluency and force of his pronunciation. He had given away his hand, but it was too late now for him to back-pedal. He was furious with himself for his impatience, which might now cost him dearly, but tried to preserve his mask of indifference.

'It rolls off the tongue, does it not?' said Lawrence. His voice had lost a little of its warmth now. His body language was more restrained, his bonhomie more guarded. 'Are you certain you've never heard the story of the Armada Treasure, Derek?' asked Lawrence searchingly.

'No, I haven't. Could we just get back to the question of its value,' he asked wearily.

'I'm sorry,' said Lawrence slowly, though his mind was racing. Perhaps I'm wrong – he wondered, perhaps he just picked up on the correct pronunciation instantly; a solicitor would do that all the time, he reasoned. Perhaps I'd better stop prevaricating before he walks, he thought to himself.

'The value…' said Derek, toughening his tone of voice, catching the scent of doubt and hesitation in his opponent, made keen by all his years in court. It was time for him to go for the throat.

'It's worth, I would say, is in the region of five thousand

194

pounds, to a private collector. But I can only give you a true value for a single coin,' he said, dipping one of his toasts. 'You have a problem, Mr Beautimann – more than one coin is a problem.'

'Go on,' said Derek.

'How many more do you have. Ten? Fifty? A hundred?'

'Why is that relevant?' asked Derek, treading carefully.

'The more there are, the more people will presume they were found as a cache. If a great find like the discovery of the Treasure of the Mar del Norte were not reported to the proper authorities, if the finder, or finders were to attempt to sell some of the cache without declaring it first, they would only be able to sell a very small amount before the market closes. A treasure such as this cannot be sold off without it becoming public knowledge within a very short space of time. If you attempted to offload it – perhaps that's not quite the right term, if you'll forgive me – you'd be at a massive disadvantage. My advice is to declare it. Do you really want to be looking over your shoulder day and night, for years into the future? You might even be putting your own life at risk, there are many people who would kill without hesitation to possess it. It would become an intolerable burden. You may only receive a fraction of its value as a reward for its recovery. But that's a price worth paying, believe me.'

'Thank you for being so candid. If I'd heard you say those words in court, I'd say they were the words of someone who was speaking from personal experience.'

'There's something else I think you should know. I can't attest to the legitimacy of it, but nevertheless I think you should be aware of it.'

'Oh?'

'Alan may have mentioned I usually take a small fee for my advice. In this case it will be the meal, and only the meal, Mr Beautimann. I won't be asking you for one of these coins. I'm a superstitious man. You might think superstitious people are deluded, I don't know, but that's the way I am and I'm not going to change.'

'What do you mean, exactly?' asked Derek, becoming intrigued.

'The treasure is cursed,' said Lawrence, closing the lid and pushing the compact back towards his guest. 'I don't want anything more to do with it.'

'Cursed?'

'There are many valuable things in the world of antiquities and collectables with unlucky histories, Derek. Do you believe objects can be unlucky for their owners? There are powerful arguments, for and against. I have a good life, I love my career, I've become very comfortable financially. Why would I take a risk just for one coin? Everyone who has come into contact with this fortune has died within the year. The crew of La Ramblas, the ship that transported it, Sir Henry Kettlewell, who recovered it. Lord Fothergill the commander of the garrison who despatched it to the King, his couriers. The King himself. Put it back in the earth, if that's where it came from, and forget you ever laid eyes on it. That's my advice.'

'I see.'

'A description of the original box in which the treasure was kept survives in the archives of the British Museum in London, together with a drawing...'

'A drawing...?'

'A plaque was fixed to its lid, of which there was also a

sketch. A plaque with a Latin inscription, if my memory is correct. The inscription read "hic natus non possidebunt Angliae et vivat." It means – no man born of England shall possess me and live. But that's not as interesting as the curse on the gold itself, before it was minted. It was stolen from the Maya – and it's their curse which seems to concentrate people's thoughts. So, you see – it's doubly unlucky.'

Brian and Dave made a sharp right turn, between two waist-high ivy-clad dry stone walls, a few hundred yards past the Landkey Arms on the northern outskirts of Whitborough, then drove slowly down the tight track of Limers Lane, leading to Manor Farm. The narrow ribbon of elderly tarmac, shielded by high earth banks and bounded by dense hedgerows had a permanent mohican of rough grass and weeds bonded to the cracks and fissures on its pitted apex.

'So, are you going to let me in on the secret of the old empty farm?' asked Dave as he tried to make sense of a tangle of webbing belts on his lap. 'Which clown tied this lot up?'

'You did – you nicked 'em when you got kicked out the Army Cadets and shoved 'em in the loft.'

'Oh yeah, I did, didn't I,' replied Dave, grinning. 'I must have stowed 'em away so Dad didn't find out I'd pinched 'em. I knew they'd come in useful one day. Don't remember stowing them in this state though,' he grumbled, rummaging through the knots. 'Is this the only access road?'

'Yep. One way in and out. Unless you've got a land rover or a tractor to go cross country.'

'Did you say the classic car club paid Vernon to store their cars here?'

'Yep.'

'It's a bit out the way, innit?'

'I guess some people like that. Safer up 'ere than somewhere in town.'

'Spose so.'

Manor Farm had been one of many local properties built by French prisoners of war, transported to Britain after the Battle of Waterloo and set to work under the supervision of the British Army. Built in the style of a Cornish longhouse, it sat commandingly at the top of a long flat moraine, a mile inland from the coast to which it ran parallel. An L-shaped copse of Scots pines and holly protected its walls from the chill of the strong easterly winds, though most of its windows looked westward over the fertile undulating plains to the front. Behind the main farmhouse an open rectangular courtyard enclosed by an unbroken wall of two storey outbuildings and barns added to its sense of isolation. It had the feel of a barracks or a prison, surrounding a parade ground, which of course it was when it was conceived. But as a farm it was serviceable, if rather rigid in its layout.

'I brought some bedding and the air bed from the loft, to pad out the floor of the van.'

'Our bedding? The pillows and the quilts?'

'Look, we don't want to take any chances, do we. Besides, if the worst happens, what are you going to need pillows and a quilt for? Oh, I borrowed the small settee cushions too.'

'That's my settee…'

'I'll tekk it all to the launderette when we're done – don't frett. I took the dog's bed too…'

'So what's Snowy sleeping on?'

'Your summer quilt. Sorry.'

'You're not gonna tell me you're putting these things

in our 'ouse, because you can piss right off. Where are they anyway?'

'There's a secret chamber between the house and the barn. The only way in is by a concealed doorway behind the track of the sliding doors. The only way you'd spot it is by standing at the back wall and looking over the track of the door panels. One side is two sections longer than it needs to be on the left. There's nowt to see from outside.'

'You admire the bastards, don't you?'

'It wasn't built by any of the Hoopers, Dave. It was part of the original farm. They just made the most of it when they discovered it.'

'Ahh, right.'

'The last but one panel on the left hand side has dummy hinges on the first joint, where it's attached to the next one in line. They look like regular hinges, but they're fixed with pins that tap out with a hole punch. Take the pins out and push on the wood, then push the door away from you and there's a false alcove inside. It looks like stone but it's painted plaster and covered in grime and cobwebs. That's how you get in. That's where they kept all their black market contraband.'

'Like a priest hole for stolen goods.'

'A priest hole... oh they'd have loved that,' said Brian, stepping out of the van.

'Ooo are you?' Asked a tall, portly plain-faced man in an old tweed suit and a tatty cardigan jumper, stepping down from a hayloft onto the cobbles, holding a twin barrelled shotgun.

'We might ask you the same question,' said Brian, bluffing, caught off guard.'

'I'm the one weet shotgun laddie, an' it's ma farm – so I'll ask t'bloody questions. What are yoo two doing 'ere? An keep yer 'ands where ah can see 'um.'

'He's got a hearing aid,' whispered Dave, trying not to move his lips.

'What's that?'

'My brother's scared of guns,' said Brian, trying not to antagonise the man he guessed was a farmer.

'Ah daynt think I 'eard yer right when I asked yer what you're up to up 'ere. Ya daynt look like bloody grocers ta me. I've not ordered n' fruit an' veg.'

'We're only borrowing the van…'

'Borrowing it? Nicked it more like… Get yer arses ovver theer byt trough,' said the farmer, jerking the shotgun towards a large rough hewn stone sarcophagus filled with slimy water.

'We borrowed it to collect some of our dad's tools. He used to keep his bus here…'

'Bus?'

'His Leyland PD2. The green single decker? We're Wilf Bullock's sons. I'm Eddie. This is Peter,' said Brian, still trying to convince the older man they weren't the opportunistic thieves their host suspected them to be. 'He left his spark plug wrench, a torsion bar and some long wheel nut spanners behind ages ago. But he's only just missed 'em. He asked us to see if we could bring them home, on the off chance they were still here. He can't get spares for 'em, they're too rare – that's what we came up for, that's all. Otherwise we wouldn't have had to drive up here.'

'You're Wilf Bullock's sons!'

'Yeah, but we're not really into buses, like Dad was. We were hoping there'd be someone here that could show us where he kept the old girl. That's what he called it… I think.'

'Aye, that's yer fatherr right 'nuff – well, tell im ee's welcome to drop by and see us any time. I'm Ian, by the way, Vernon's younger brother. Pleased ta meet ya, lads.'

'Do you think you could point that at the ground…' Said Dave, staring at the pregnant barrels of his gun.

'Bloody 'ell… Where's me manners eh?' said Ian, lowering the gun and propping it against the wall. I'm afraid if ya came ta see Vernon, he's not 'ere no more.'

'Dad said he lives with your sister in her bungalow on the Abbotsham road.'

'Aye. Bin there ten year or so now. We've bin trying to sell t'old place, but it's still ont market – if yer intrested? Needs a wee bit o' work mind, but nowt too 'ard fo' someone that knows reet end of a ladder.'

'Dad said Vernon told him the place was haunted.'

'Haunted? Well ah dint know 'bout that. I've not seen n'ghosts when ah've bin 'ere – anyroad. An' ahm 'ere 'alf week sometimes. I'm glad you two are 'ere as it 'appens. Before I show you where yer fatha used to keep 'iz bus you can 'elp me lift me new gate on its 'inges if ya daynt mind lads, it's just ovver theer see…' said Ian, nodding towards a chained-galvanized five bar gate leant against a wall on wooden chocks. 'It needs lifting on t'post ont far left o' that pen full o' hay bales, see.'

'I think we can manage, can't we?' replied Brian, trying hard to sound agreeable.

'That's grand lads, ay – ah'd be reet grateful. Once we get t' bugger on, could y'ang on forra bit while I go get me mate up 'ere wee is welder, Ah meete be an 'our or so, but ah'l see thee reet wee ya fatha'z tools. If ya daynt weld mushrooms on top o' t'pins, gates g'missing, see. No end o' thieving bastards round 'ere. Ah dint wanna get t'bugger on then lose it.'

'I think that'll be okay, eh Pete?' Said Brian, kicking his brother's shoe.

'Oh aye… no problem. We can wait a while.'

'Grand. I'll get me keys.'

Ten minutes later Ian Hooper was climbing into his old Land Rover bound for Hollow Hills Farm in Flat Fields, after leaving Brian the keys to the big barn.

'Has he gone?' asked Dave, opening the back doors to their van.

'He's going now, just waving at us – wave back.'

'Okay.'

'Could you back the van up to the doors while I get the padlocks off.'

'Brian?'

'What?'

'Did you bring a hole punch and a hammer and pliers?'

'There's a toolbox in the van.'

'Yeah – but we need a hole punch and a hammer at least to knock out the pins on the false panel.'

'Shit… I didn't look – sorry. I'll check the toolkit…'

'If there's no punch we can use a big nail at a push. Get the padlocks off and I'll check the toolkit. Where is it?'

'It's the big ply box over the wheel arch.'

'If you get the doors open – have a look around inside, see if there's anything lying about we can use.'

Brian looked at the rusty old keys on the hoop of string and held the padlock, moving the swing plate cover away from the lock aperture with his thumb before pushing one of them home. There was some stiffness, then a pleasing click before the mechanism disengaged and the padlock clattered onto the algae-stained flags.

'You all right?' asked Dave, looking backwards.

'Yeah, but it might need the two of us to push these doors open,' he replied, squatting down to pick up the padlock, noticing the condition of the wheels at the bottom of the first set of doors. 'These castors look as if they've seized up.'

'Only in bloody Yorkshire…'

'Eh?'

'Nothing. Hang about, I've found some pliers. And there's some WD40, thank God.'

A few minutes later after a lot of effort and curses, the two brothers got into position inside the barn with the doors closed, ready to tackle the enigma behind the hidden entrance.

'Do you know how it swings out now?' asked Brian. 'There's a catch of some kind at the bottom.'

'Ball and cup. Clever,' said Dave, shuffling his feet as he knelt down, trying to get comfortable under his brother. 'When I push the wheel plate down with this file – give the door a shove. There's a sprung bearing fixed in an insert plate, at the bottom edge of this panel that's held in a collar, attached to the wheel assembly. It should pop out and the door should spring free once I depress the wheel plates… ready?' said Dave, kneeling below his brother, whose palms were resting on the panel.

'Set,' said Brian. 'Ready when you are mate.'

Brian pushed hard on the wood and the door gave in with a weak groan. Beyond the threshold small furry bodies scurried across the stone flags in the gloom seeking cover as the two humans stepped over the door track into the old recess.

'Blimey, check out these spiders webs,' said Brian. 'It's creepier than the shop.'

'Did you see a broom nearby?' asked Dave, looking at the alcove in disgust. We'll have to clean all this crap off before we can see the wood underneath.'

'There was one near that old garden furniture back there, Dave,' said his brother. 'I can see some of the painted stone under here,' he added, peering through the sagging cobwebs. 'It's quite well done. If the paint wasn't so cracked and flaky around the door joints it'd be quite convincing.'

After a brush down, the door in the alcove revealed nothing else, other than the finer details of its fading mural. There were no visible handles or studs over its surface, it appeared to all intents and purposes a perfect blank.

'Oh great!' said Brian, looking to the rafters in exasperation. 'What now?' Then he spotted a small alcove two feet above the brick arch, with a D-shaped handle hanging within, attached to the filthy cord of an old rope. 'Dave – look, up there. That's gotta be it – the way in. Let's get that saw horse in here.'

Five minutes later, they were standing inside a single storey brick outhouse, illuminated by an elderly light bulb wired up to a black Bakelite switch, attached to what appeared to be an old chopping board fixed onto the wall, from which a flat black cable snaked up onto the rafters and through a rent in the peak of the gable end. The room was lined with a wide worktop of thick planks at waist height, laden with dusty boxes marked 'ORDNANCE' in stencilled letters. There were dozens of pressed steel ammunition boxes, boxes of thunderflash grenades, pistols and rifles, sealed crates of Mills bombs and a Panzerfaust, resting in a pram.

'Bloody hell…' whispered Dave.

'Look,' said Brian, 'under that bedspread…'

'Maureen. It's Derek. I'm in a call box in York station. I'm about to set off home soon so I'll be brief.'

'What did he say about the treasure…'

'It seems our good fortune has put us in something of a predicament.'

'Oh..? *Get squeaky bally!*'

'Pardon me?'

'I'm talking to Bert, Derek.'

'Well, put him down. This is important. Alan Chipping's colleague tells me we may have become the unwitting subjects of a curse by becoming its temporary custodians. It seems that our treasure comes with a special health warning. He's as certain as he can be, from the few things I showed him, that we've recovered items linked directly to the original burial, if you'll pardon the expression. But he doesn't want anything more to do with it. Historically it's been rather unlucky for anyone who's been linked to it. In fact, he advised me to put it back where we found it – are you still there?'

'A real curse…'

'Well – yes. He was rather unequivocal. I'm at a loss to know what to say.'

'Well, I'm not superstitious.'

'Come again?'

'I'm not superstitious.'

'Maureen, I don't think being flippant about a disclosure like this is the right way forward.'

'I'm not putting it back for nothing and no one. You do what you like with your share Derek, but I'm not losing the chance to be rich beyond my dreams because of some old wives tale from some silly academic I've never met.'

'He's not a "silly academic", he's a respected authority,

and I think his refusal to take anything relating to it speaks volumes about his belief that its possession is potentially quite harmful.'

'So it's fatal is it … to keep any of it. That's what he's saying? NO! DOWN! Sorry Derek – keep going.'

'He quoted some words from an inscription on its lid, the one that was covered in mud, recorded on a drawing at the British Museum, which read – "No man born of England shall possess me and live." Those were the words of the curse. He was quite positive about that. The treasure has something of a reputation for bad luck within their fraternity.'

'No man born of England – I'm not a man.'

'Granted, but I would imagine the wording alluded to both sexes when it was written. He also revealed there is a lesser known curse associated with the gold itself that came from the Mayans, that may be equally serious … I really don't know what to do.'

'GET SQUEEKY! We can sell it can't we… then it won't affect us.'

'It's not that simple. Will you please not shout like that, you nearly burst my eardrums.'

'I'll put him in the kitchen in a minute – sorry. He's being a right little bugger. How long have you had those coins that you showed me, before we dug up that chest.'

'A few months. Since last November, but…'

'Derek, it seems to me you're still very much alive.'

'Yes, but…'

'So it's a load of hokum, isn't it. He's probably hoping you'll put it back so he can dig it back up again and keep it for himself. GOOD BOY!'

'MAUREEN! If I believed that I wouldn't be taking time

to explain this. Are you discounting what happened to Tony Binnie?'

'No, of course not. But he never laid eyes on any of it. There – he's in the kitchen, all right?'

'We don't know that. What we do know was – he was in the same area as we were, at the same time. That's not a coincidence. Did he recover something we didn't find before he died? He was at the gathering. We need to think about this and discuss what we're going to do – but not over the telephone. We're going to need some powerful talismans to protect ourselves – as quickly as you can get them please. In Hebrew, with a form of the Tetragrammaton. Go to Violet, Violet Penrose until Eileen gets back from Tenby. Don't let her give you one of those Egyptian ones she's been scribing – she got the pictograms mixed up.'

'I'll go and see her tonight…'

'We need to meet before we go back to work. What about Sunday?'

After nearly crippling themselves moving two high explosive bombs by car, Brian and Dave had decided they would need a more suitable means of transportation for the next phase of their plan, and were calling the one and only person who might be able to help them at such short notice.

'Albert? It's Brian. How are you, mate?'

'Brian… I'm tekking a few days off if it's about yer lawn. Is that why you're ringing?'

'No no. I'm just ringing to ask you if you'd mind lending me and Dave your van and trailer tomorrow morning again quickly – as a favour. We'll have it back on your drive before 9. We're stuck – that's all. You'd really be helping us out Albert –

I don't know who else to ask... We'll give you something for your trouble. How's thirty quid sound?'

'Thirty quid? What are you moving?'

'Moving? Oh! Err, we're moving a cooker. A cooker. We don't need any of your mowers or tools, Albert. Just the van an' the trailer. Will you help us out?'

'Thirty quid?'

'You can have it cash or cheque?'

'No cheques, cash. Cash is fine, Brian. Very generous, yeah. You'll look after it?'

'Oh absolutely. Absolutely.'

When d'you want to pick it up, lad?'

'About five.'

'What – tonight?'

'No, in the morning.'

'Five in the morning – by eck... you'll excuse me if I don't see thee off. I'll leave the keys under the frog by the pond.'

'The frog? It's not real then?'

'You daft bugger Brian – it's green. Wee white spots. I got it fromt garden centre on Higher Gunstone. Are you going far? Only if you are, can yer put some diesel in it.'

'We're just going into town, Albert.'

'Good job you've nay grass to cut. Reckon there'll be a mist ashore tomorrow. Ya won't be able ta see yer 'and in front of yer face.'

'You don't say...'

Chapter Six

Friday

Fortuitously, the next morning another dense sea fret was rolling inland, reducing visibility to less than thirty feet and compelling the few vehicles on the roads to slow down significantly and use their headlights. It was the perfect weather for the type of work where you didn't necessarily want to be seen, and the kind of weather that keeps curious eyes indoors, or looking straight ahead.

The Charlwood Estate's gardening van and trailer arrived on the upper portion of Swinbrook Road just as the sun rose, easily finding a large unclaimed stretch of kerb close to the top of the road where it intersected Shillbrook Avenue, opposite the old public drinking fountain, by the steps to the gardens, beneath the Ramsgill end of Valley Bridge. Brian and Dave pulled on their woolly hats and wound scarves around their faces before stepping out of the van and checking the area, shaking out their legs in their dark green overalls.

'Looks good. Let's get rid of these bloody things. I'll drop the tailgate, and you steer Dad's trolley off the ramp. We'd better just do one at a time,' said Dave.

'Okay. We could just use one of 'em for now. Pull the engine trolley back here, then we can move it the rest of the way between us.'

'All right. What are you doing with the other one though? We aren't taking it home, are we? Are you gonna call the coppers when we get back?'

'We'll hide it in the woods at Oliver's Mount. I think we'd better use the call box on Emery Row.'

'Don't forget to rub your prints off it, mind.'

An hour and fifteen minutes later after much of sweat and toil, one of the German bombs was resting peacefully in its shallow grave in the mossy soil and leaf litter near the bridge supports.

'Good morning, Whitborough Police, Sergeant Moyne speaking. How can we help?'

'My dog's uncovered something that looks like an unexploded bomb. He was digging behind the holly trees and bushes, under the big bridge at the quiet end. It's a greyish green colour, and there's some peeling yellow paint on the back on some fins, the bits sticking out the ground...'

'Under Valley Bridge, sir?'

'The big one you drive across. Not the footbridge.'

'That'll be Valley Bridge, sir. Can I take your name?'

'It's Mr Diddicott.'

'Diddicott... Double d and t?'

'Yes – yes.'

'And your address sir, please?'

'Look – I don't much care for this giving my address business. It's very Orwellian. Anyway, it should hardly matter to you. I don't live here, as you've probably deduced by now – I'm on holiday.'

'It's standard procedure sir, in case we need to follow up our enquiries. We do need it for our...'

'Well, you'll just have to do without it, won't you. I've taken the time to call you and let you know I found this thing. Now why don't you do something about it, rather than interrogating me like some jumped up little Stasi bureaucrat – goodbye!'

Valley Bridge, conceived by the Victorians and opened by the Edwardians, spanned the Kenwith valley gorge between Whitborough town centre and the older Georgian suburb of Ramsgill. Its foundation stone was laid at the top of a small cliff beside The Stella Maris Convent on Late Lane, and the last kerbstones came to rest on the opposite side of the gorge next to The Atkinson Grimshaw School of Art and Technical Drawing, where it met the longest stretch of Northdown Road. Built to take the main influx of traffic from the south and connect Lower Gunstone to the town centre, it copied the style and form of the great Italian Alpine railway bridges, of which we may see so many fine examples in the film documentaries of great railway journeys. To come upon it by the road from the South bay was to experience one of the most breathtaking sights in North Yorkshire. Over two hundred and fifty feet high at its mid point, its balustrade pillars carried the same tall gas lamps that so enhanced the span of Westminster Bridge. A robust cast-iron lattice screen of scooped lozenge-shaped piercings under flat-top bull-nose capstones bridged the gaps between each pillar, allowing pedestrians and children on the wide pavements either side of the central carriageway a safe glimpse of the view along the valley to its smaller sister bridge in front of the sea, without having to peer over its topsides.

'Respond, all cars in the vicinity of Valley bridge and Ramsgill. Code 10. Repeat, code 10, Over.'

'Charlie 1 to control, our ETA is minus 2 minutes, over.'

'Charlie 1, report your status over.'

'Confirm we have just attended a minor RTO. No other engagements, over.'

'Proceed to bridge end of Swinbrook Road and Shillbrook Avenue. We've had a call from a member of the public, his dog has uncovered a device buried behind holly bushes under bridge supports. Witness reports it is grey or green in colour, yellow identification markings on the rear uppermost section. Probably of military origin.'

'Recieved and understood. Has the army been informed, over?'

'UXO protocols procedure has been initiated, awaiting response, over.'

'If this isn't a false alarm it's gonna ruin everybody's day. Some of these old EODs are tricky bas…'

'EODs?'

'Explosive ordnance devices. Another term for UXO's. This'll be number two for me, Danny.'

'What, in Whitborough?'

'Yeah, we got called out to Oliver's Mount a few years ago now, when some contractors were putting the footings in for the new radio mast. Now if they'd used a local firm, one of the older ones, they'd have known they needed to do a ground survey, with magnetometers. But the bloody council used some goons from Leeds because they had more plant and manpower – and shit for brains. Anyone round here could'a told 'em there were a radar station up there in the war, if they'd done their homework properly and asked about. The Jerries bombed it five times, but it were never out of action for long. It were the Staxton Wold of World War two, the radar could catch the Nazi bastards coming in a sweep from Sandsend to Hornsea. Anyways, when they were marking out the trenches for the foundations, they hit an old SC250 bomb with the digger. Luckily it were a dud, or they'd all 'ave been playing bloody violins on a white fluffy cloud. It could 'ave have flattened the war memorial and Mountside cafe, an' all the trees round about no problem. That's the kind of thing you're up against. The krauts used to paint the fuse designation letter in a circle on the nose. Sometimes if the mark survived the fall our boys would know what they were dealing with – most of the time. But some of these things were set to explode up to 72 hours after they were dropped – or they could have anti-tampering fuses with two circuits and mercury switches. These things get more unstable the longer they're left, because the detonators and the main charge deteriorate, especially the ones with chemical fuses.'

'How'd you know so much about these things?'

'Me brother-in-law's in the Royal Engineers, 33 Regiment. They deal with all the air-dropped stuff from the war. Most of them are disabled remotely with robots now. That big bastard at Oliver's Mount had a spike on the front. Graham – the brother-in-law – told me the spikes were fitted to detonate the bombs on impact, but that thing just buried itself.'

'When did Brian say he was coming in to pick you up?'

'Not sure. After twelve I think. All depends on how much he got done yesterday. He's going off again, straight after he gets the other keys and his dinner, after he drops me at theirs.

They were tekking Albert's trailer back, then doing summat else. They borrowed some of his tools I think.'

'I just can't see Brian with a spade.'

'You'd be surprised.'

'Maybe I wouldn't. Is Danny fixing your exhaust at Brian's?'

'Yeah, the silencer collar bracket cracked. Here comes our first customer,' observed Dean uninterestedly, glancing outside through the bay window. 'There's a lad too,' he added, speaking to Michael in the basement through the shop's intercom.

'Have you been lighting tobacco leaf down here, Beadle?'

'I only had a few drags, Mike. Barely half a roly.'

'Well, come down here and suck it back in then. The air hasn't changed down here since King George was on the throne.'

'Got to go Mike – customer.'

You cheeky ars…'

Clash City Records first customer of the day was a young tourist in her mid twenties, with a dark bob, Audrey Hepburn style sunglasses and headscarf ensemble, dressed in a black blouse and capri pants with leopard print flats and matching tote bag.

'Oh, hello – I thought you were a northern outpost of Madame Tussauds when I saw your monk in the doorway there. He's quite sinister, isn't he? An odd thing to have to welcome you, if you don't mind me saying. Do you have any posters?'

'He's called Gregory.'

'Gregory? Was some historical figure in Whitborough?'

'Gregory Rasputin, the mad monk. He brought down the Russian royal family.'

'Yes, I have been to school, though it was a few years ago. May I have an answer to my question?'

'We've got about two hundred posters, miss, rock bands and punks bands mostly, that kind of stuff.'

'Can you show me? I wanted a poster of Bryan Ferry.'

'We got two Roxy posters, they should be in the first ten sleeves... Sorry – can't leave the till. The rack is halfway down on the left behind the belts. There's another downstairs in the basement too but it's full of punk and sh..., other stuff.'

'Mummy! Can I go down, Mummy, please Mummy?'

'Well I suppose so, I'll have to stay here and endure searching this contraption that passes for a poster display – and Timothy?'

'Yes, Mummy?'

'Don't run. You've got enough scuffs on your knees. No more...'

Several minutes passed. Then the stomp of little shoes was heard scampering up the staircase.

'Mummy! Mummy! Come look – there's a scary man in the basement,' shouted the boy, breathless, stumbling over a carpet gripper at the top of the stairs.

'BE CAREFUL!'

'Mummy! Come see!'

'I'm looking at posters darling...'

'But Mummy!' he hissed again, drawing close to her and pulling hard at her trousers.

'Don't grab, Timothy! What have I told you!'

'Sorry Mummy, but he's really scary.'

'Oh for heaven's sake!'

'Watch my purse please!' she called back at Dean as she

215

was whisked towards the stairwell by her young son. 'It's on your poster rack!'

'Any minute now,' whispered Dean as he heard the boy and his mother hit the bottom step. After a pause, there was a short scream and the sound of scrambling feet. The lady appeared at the top of the staircase and started to sprint towards the door, barely glancing at Dean, followed by her young boy, who grinned at him briefly as he was pulled out in the slipstream of his mother.

'Hey Mike, you just made us a few quid again,' said Dean over the intercom. 'I'm looking in the purse as we speak… Forty quid up! Minus my commission. Come up and I'll get us some teas before I head off.'

'You can stay behind the counter. I'll go after I've roped off the basement, Brian asked me to get him some lunch from the Irish poisoner, so you can drop it off at their house after you leave.'

'He likes to gamble, doesn't he. What wrong with Hollands?'

Ten minutes later, round the corner in Corfe's Cafe, Michael was carefully observing the birth of Brian's lunch. 'Madam, I should like a smile with our food; there is no love in that sandwich. A dry stone waller would have taken more care…'

'A what!'

'Observing your food preparation, Eilis, is not an activity for the faint hearted. The tomato was terrified, the lettuce was lacerated and the cheese looks as stale as a trawlerman's socks.'

'Feck off, Michael.'

'Also, your mustard is French. Brian can't abide French mustard.'

'It's not fer yoos?'

'No, Eilis.'

'Chroist, I woulda tayken a bit more toime widdit, if oid known yoos weren't stuffin' yerr face.'

'We'd like three teas too, without a slick of oil on the surface. If it's not too much trouble.'

'Fussy barstudd, aren't yerr.'

'You are, as always, sophistication personified, Eilis.'

'Stophistication is it? Not in my feckin cafe.'

'Do you have any soup?'

'Maybe…'

'Fresh soup?'

'Straight from the can. We got Heinz, or Baxters.'

'What kind?'

'Surprise soup.'

'Surprise soup?'

'No label, we buy it in bulk. Every can's a surprise.'

'Well. We must try some one day, is it six pounds?'

'Gimme foive. Terry will make yer drinks,' she said, nodding to her assistant, 'you got margarine on yer spectacles Tel,' she shouted, inches from his hearing aid, 'clean yer bloody glasses, so you can see what yer doing, ya bloody fool.'

'Beg pardon?'

'CLEAN YER FECKIN GLASSES!'

In his office at the police station, Inspector Marshall was deep in thought, chewing his biro and re-examining pertinent witness statements connected with the Shirestones incident with Sgt Broadhead.

'Not again?' he groaned as his phone sprang to life.

'It's the Royal Engineers sir, a Captain D'Ascoyne, they're at the bridge,' announced his secretary after a pause.

'D'Ascoyne? All right, Delia…'

'Inspector Marshall?' asked the Captain, hearing the inspector cough and clear his throat. 'I'm afraid you'll have to close the bridge and all the approach roads for us. The residents overlooking us at the top quarter of Swinbrook Road will need to be evacuated while we make it safe.'

'It's real then?'

'Yes, German undoubtedly, standard light HE.'

'Light?'

'One of the smaller types, 55kg. But it's very close to the bridge structure. We'll see if we can disable it remotely, but if not, one of our chaps will have to go in with a St. Christopher and crossed fingers.'

'What?'

'Their St. Christopher's medal. Patron Saint of Bomb Disposal.'

'How long will you need to close off the area for?'

'We could be finished in two hours. On the other hand, it could be four or five. It all depends on the position of the thing in the ground relative to the fuse cover. And the type of fuse. How was it found?'

'Some holiday maker's dog uncovered it.'

'So there would have been some agitation around the casing – well, he's a very lucky dog.'

'Well his dog's alive – but we're having a very unlucky weekend. I'll send down some more manpower and crowd control barriers before I call the Highways department.'

At Charlwood Zoo, Brian and Dave had managed to pass themselves off as reporters from the Gazette to scope the pens before they attempted to recover their troublesome property, using their mock up press passes made by Michael while flaunting Dave's Pentax SLR with its enormous Tamron lens. They were given to Erica Ireland, a school leaver from Pindred Comprehensive School on a two week work experience placement, who escorted them to Edith's enclosure, where Lord Warner Woollens was busy helping one of the other zookeepers to cast savoy cabbages, chard and spinach into the Rhinos' feeding ground.

'Excuse me sir... my Lord?' asked Erica apprehensively. 'There are two men... There are two journalists, a journalist and a photographer here from the Gazette to see you – Ibrahim asked me to introduce them to you, my Lord,' said Erica, alluding to the Office Manager. 'I'm sorry. This is Daniel,' she said, 'without the camera, and this is Simon – with the camera. I'd better be getting back.' She tried not to make too much eye contact, tugging her sleeves over her hands.

'Stay with us Erica – there's no need to be shy, young lady, I'm sure Ibrahim can manage by himself for a while,' said Lord Woollens, rolling a cabbage towards a bare patch of ground before cleaning his hands under a standpipe. 'Our Office manager comes from Kenya,' he continued, addressing Dave and Brian. 'He used to keep Edith and her kin safe from poachers, back in her native Africa. Isn't she magnificent? They say a mature black rhinetossceros with a good heart can reach thirty-four miles an hour on the hoof.'

'Really,' said Brian, swallowing involuntarily, 'thirty four miles an hour...'

'Can't see a bloody thing though. Near sighted. But they do have superb hearing, to compensate. Have you ever seen such beautifullyfull ears?'

'No, I can't say I have, my Lord.'

'They swivel independently of each other, like directional microphonies…'

'Fascinating…'

'They can pick up the sound of a predator hundreds of yards away in the bush.'

'Predators?'

'Oh yes. You wouldn't think so, would you? But big cats will stalk the mothers downwind to try and get to their calves. You wouldn't want to approach her from the front though. Suicide… They're very conscientious defenders of their own ranges, but she'll let Debra and I approach her, as long as we move slowly and stop every few feet so she can pick up our scent. We raised one before as an orphan, so I suppose you could say we've been surrogate parents. But there are times when even we don't go near her. We're trying to draw her out at the moment with some tempting greens, so the other staff can go in and clear her dung. It's almost as good as potash is for improving the yields. We don't interfere with the other piles around the perimeter until they build up as a rule. Rhinos use it to mark out their territory, so we allow her to leave a little at the boundaries – reduces her anxieties.'

'May we go inside the enclosure with you, my Lord?'

'I only go inside on my own or with Debra, gentlemen. But no one is allowed near her at the moment.'

'Why is that?'

'It's ladies day,' he said flatly, although it seemed to Brian and Dave as though he had suffered a peculiar facial tick.

'Ladies day?' said Brian, biting his lip.

'Time of the month – got the decorators in. Not safe to approach – she'd charge a paper bag at the moment. And her farts are up too, which always makes her a little testy. Well, it was nice to beetle you, gentlemen. We always welcome the press-press. Erica will be your guide for the rest of your visit. If you have any questions, she'll be very happy to help. Erica, do you think you can manage?'

'I think so, sir. If not, I'll ask one of the staff.'

'Good girl.'

'Are we all right to take some photographs of the rhino, my lord?'

'Make sure you turn off the flash on that camera first, or she'll charge you down. I can assure you it may well be the last thing you do as a three dimensional object. Ask the staff if you have any other query queries. Toodle dip.'

'He's crackers,' said Dave.

'Shush. Just pretend to take a few pictures. Then we'll get back to the car. We know where the toolbox is now, so don't fanny about – just be quick and let's get going,' whispered Brian.

'All right all right. Are we skipping the rest of the tour then?'

'Too right. We'll make our excuses. Just say we've got a meeting with the picture editor.'

'I can show you the elephant enclosure after you've finished taking your pictures, we have wolves and wildcats too,' said Erica shyly, trying to stir their interest.

'I don't think we'll have time to do much more luv, thank you all the same. We've got to get back for a meeting with the picture and features editor. No rest for the wicked, I'm afraid. Is this where you'd like to work when you leave school?'

'Yes, I'd love to get a job or an apprenticeship here. I want to be a vet.'

'Well Erica, thank you very much for introducing us to Lord Warner Woollens – a very entertaining gentleman.'

'He makes me laugh,' she said, suddenly regretting the comment. 'I didn't mean he was funny. I mean, he says funny things – I'm not making fun of him. You won't…'

'Erica, we're only here to write an article on the rhino. We're not bad people, you won't see anything you say in the Gazette without your permission,' said Dave, trying to soothe her paranoia.

'I'd be really grateful if you didn't…' she said starting to weep. 'I'm sorry – I say really stupid things sometimes when I'm nervous. Please, please don't print what I said.'

'Here love, have some of these,' said Dave, passing over a packet of tissues. 'I promise, we won't print anything you've said. Thank you for the introduction, and all the best for the future, we wish you all the best for your future, don't we Br… er, Daniel.'

'Absolutely,' said Brian gently. 'I'm going to kill that little bastard,' he added under his breath.

'Thank you, Simon. I really really appreciate it. Would you like me to walk you both back to the car park?'

'No luv, we'll be fine.'

'Goodbye then…' she said timidly, walking away and dabbing her eyes.

'Bloody hell, we only came here to take some pictures,' said Brian, embarrassed at the display of emotion. 'Since when do you buy packets of tissues?'

'Since I started needing to buy tissues to clean me camera lens.'

'You can get proper wipes at camera shops.'

'Well, I've got these too.'

'Well, we got away with it, just. I can't say I'm looking forward to the next bit. I think I'd rather face the hormonal schoolgirl again. The thought of going inside that thing's territory is making the hair on the back of my neck stand on end. He did say there was just one of them, didn't he?'

'I only saw the one – I think.'

'If it wakes up while we're in there, we've got no chance. Did you hear what he said about it? It'll reach thirty-four miles an hour on the flat. That's four miles an hour faster than one of those choked mopeds. Faster than the Pizza delivery. Four wheel drive with a horn like a…'

'Rhino?'

'Exactly…'

'Look, it's gonna be dark by the time we come back, Bri. It can't see that well.'

'It doesn't need to. It's got ears like a bat and a nose like a shark.'

'Will you stop it?'

'Stop what?'

'*Externalising* your anxiety. It very wearing…'

'Sorry, let's get out of here, shall we, and collect Deano.'

'Brian – I really think giving laddo that Panzerfaust is a bad idea.'

'You worry too much,' he said unconvincingly. 'Anyway, it can't be avoided now. Look – I thought we could park up behind the main street in Cloughton, then set off from there when it gets dark, after we do all the other stuff. I just think it'd be smarter to stay local and cut down on the travelling early evening, keep our heads down.'

223

'Sounds good to me. You'd have thought Robbo could have found a safe spot in town, instead of this place. What was he bloody thinking? Putting it in a friggin rhino enclosure in a zoo.'

'I know exactly what he was thinking. I told him to be imaginative and put it somewhere no one would dream of looking. He's getting his own back for the soaking he got at Cayton Bay, the devious little shit.'

'It wasn't your fault they capsized though, was it? It was Neil. He should have been rowing and reading the water, he's the bloody fisherman.'

'Exactly. If the lazy bastard hadn't got our nephew to do all the hard work, they would have kept their feet dry and got me my stuff, before he hit the reef or the sandbar, anyway same difference…'

'No, they aren't. Waves break up messily on a reef – you get white water. Sandbars are different, they're smooth and the water just runs over clean. Impossible to see in the dark until you're right on 'em, no surf see?'

'Thank you Dave…'

Dean used the wrecking bar to prise the planks from the long box at the back of Brian's garage. After removing the second plank and setting it down beside the shelving racks, he reached in and felt for the stock and barrel of the machine gun under the rough wool of the army blanket. Then he drew the bundle towards the gap in the lid, setting it down to get a better grip, then he picked up the gun again and drew it out, putting it in front of the crate, which he then transferred onto the floor. He looked over the tool racks for a knife to cut the string ties binding the blanket. Underneath the green wool and the oiled paper, the MG81, the Lutfwaffe variant of the MG34, was as clean and corrosion free as the day it was uncoupled from its mounting in his Grandfather's aircraft. It appeared unmarked and intact, so he returned to the crate and knelt down, reaching inside to find the ammunition, a 50 round drum magazine of 7.92mm ammunition, which was similarly wrapped inside an old gas-mask box.

Picking up the MG again, he gently lowered it down into the suede covered chocks of a padded vice, aligning its centre of gravity to the mid-point of the indented strip stamped on the top edge of the jaws. He tightened the vice firmly enough so he could fasten a modified Bren gun bipod stand to a lug at the end of the barrel – and practice attaching the magazine. Then he took out Brian's notes, picked up the package he had left for him and sat down on top of a space hopper.

'Cool,' murmured Dean, picking out a black silk balaclava with a thin red stripe down the middle from the folds of brown paper. There was also a black army surplus combat jacket, some leather gloves and black combat trousers, and a whistle… 'He's off his trolley, my boss,' grumbled Dean. 'Still – a hundred and fifty quid, an' a couple o' tickets for Motorhead, an a pay rise… Worth a sniff. I suppose there's summat in here to tell me what the friggin whistle's for.'

Carr Wold Parkway was built over the site of a former LNER marshalling yard at the junction of Lower Gunstone and the A64 York Rd, where they met the B777 to Filey. It had been sold to the local corporation by British Rail in the mid 1960s as surplus to requirements, as more and more freight began the transfer over to road haulage. It was then remodelled and used as a bus station and depot until the local bus company relocated their operation to Whitborough town centre. After being returned to council ownership, resurfaced and landscaped, it was redeveloped once more as a potential business park, and was now home to several businesses, all connected to the motor industry.

The main offices and waiting rooms in the Art Deco styled former station were now the home of Bol d'Or Motorcycles, who sold new and second hand Moto Guzzi, Ducati, Laverda, MV Augusta, Kawasaki and Suzuki motorbikes. The bus garage and workshops had been converted to house Thunderbird Autos – an Anglo American classic car business, alongside Paint Perfection, a paint and body repair shop. Clarke's Motor Services, formerly of Pratchett Place in Whitborough, moved into their former parts and utilities outbuildings. There was also a new ranch-style Mexican restaurant and cantina called the Four Horsemen, which played film scores from westerns like the Magnificent Seven and Sergio Leone's Spaghetti Western movies, an Esso petrol station with a shop, and a Little Chef. A fifteen foot high grass bank, planted with pampas and ornamental grasses, surrounded the site on three sides, sheltering the concourse from the heaviest winds and lending it a South American feel, which was reinforced by islands planted with tall grasses around rockeries studded with alpines and hardy cacti.

Dean walked calmly up the outer incline of the right bank, close to the front pavements of the Parkway just after five o'clock, and placed the MG81 in the thickest clump of evergold sedge and fountain grass beside a mature pampas overlooking the front pavement, where the police positioned their vehicles beside the A64 slip road. He checked the two cars for any signs of occupation, then waited for the concourse to clear before disengaging the safety catch on the breech of the machine gun, then lined up the front sight on the nearest Vauxhall.

Constable Elland was crouched down by the rear offside of the second Cavalier, inspecting the side wall of the tyre for damage, when the firing started. It was by far the most unpleasant fourteen seconds of his time in uniform. Dean planned to leave one car as scrap and damage the other just enough to give him an edge in the ensuing chase he was engineering. There was also a BMW R100RT in police livery parked nearby as an unexpected bonus, which would soon become a burning wreck.

Dean pulled down his black silk balaclava, added a cheap pair of tinted sunglasses, then tucked the butt of the gun snugly into his shoulder, adjusting himself and the gun until he felt reasonably secure. Then he opened fire, raising the muzzle quickly to compensate for the fall of shot as he began to cripple the nearest Cavalier, putting three short bursts into the engine bay through the front wing and bonnet, and another into the white rear panel around the petrol cap cover. The back quarter section of the saloon exploded in flames, blowing the boot lid high into the air and setting fire to the tyres beneath, creating a choking black fog of flaming rubber. Then he switched his aim to the upper bodywork and roof, blowing out the emergency lighting, the windows and mirrors, making sure the adjoining car was similarly degraded. His last burst shattered the petrol tank and side panels of the BMW, spilling fuel over the engine casing and cylinder heads, which were still hot, and igniting the petrol, turning the pristine motorcycle into a fiery skeleton.

The cardboard kitchen roll liner he had added to the barrel as a flash suppressor was also now on fire, although to anyone who had not been close to his murderous work, it appeared to be just another piece of burning debris falling to earth. He quickly stamped it out, then pushed the gun back into the leather gun case, slinging it over his shoulder. His hands were shaking from the surge of adrenalin and exhilaration, coloured by the knowledge he had just ruined enough police property to cover three years' wages. Then he tumbled down the other side of the bank and sprinted along the edge of the culvert to the back of the site, ran the full length of the rear bank, then crept into the foliage on the far side, crawling towards the top to watch his handiwork. He waited for his heart to slow down while he stuffed his gloves into the pockets of his leather jacket and took out a miniature bottle of vodka, swallowing the contents in one long nervous draught.

PC Elland, curled up into a ball, eyes watering and coughing badly from the smoke, forced himself to go down onto his elbows, and look under the bottom sill of his ruined car to try and locate the feet of the gunmen, but the smoke made his task impossible. He suddenly felt horribly exposed, and decided to find a safer place to make his next move before he was found and executed by other terrorists. He saw that his colleague the motorcycle patrolman had come out of the Four Horsemen to guide him to safety, waving his arms, so he got to his feet, crouched down and sprinted towards the saloon doors of the restaurant on shaking legs and ducked inside, brushing off the glass granules covering his uniform under the impassive gaze of a long dead Texas Longhorn, and a wrinkled Mexican milk snake. Blood was starting to splash down from the left side of his head, pooling on his lapel.

'Awww, show Daddy poorly leggy...' Cooed Steve Wood

to his dog Peggy as she wriggled playfully on her back, snorting and sneezing with glee as the centre of attention, just as a blazing boot lid crashed onto the neat whitewashed kerbs outside Bol d'Or's plate glass windows. The terrified boxer ran for cover under the biggest motorcycle she could find, a 654 pound Kawasaki Z1300 and lay whimpering, while Steve dashed towards the bracket holding the fire extinguisher inside the front doors. Hearing the commotion outside, their two mechanics Don and Ken rushed out of the workshop to watch the unfolding drama across the square, through the branches of the enormous Monkey Puzzle tree on the roundabout in the centre of the park.

Dean crept into the now empty workshop and took the keys to a nearly new Kawasaki GPZ1100 from one of the hooks on the service board, stealing a black and red AGV helmet from a plastic chair by the metal litter bins inside the doors. Then he retreated outside to find the bike. He pushed the key into its slot below the instrument display, switched on the electrics and checked the fuel gauge, finding it 3/4 full. He pressed the electric start button.

'Don, did you hear someone start one of the bikes out the back?'

'Maybe it's Alan, come back to moan about his new brake pads.'

'I'm sure I heard a bike start. The service door's still open.'

'Shit. It'll be all right. I'll go an' check, you stay here with Steve.'

Dean adjusted the gun cover so it rested comfortably on the seat behind him, then gunned the Kawasaki's engine, peeling off left down the concrete slip road with its thick steel handrails. He roared past the front windows of the showroom towards the centre of the parkway, hurtling past the Cantina which was playing the theme tune to A Fistful of Dollars, over the flames.

'That bastard's got a gun on his back!' growled Steve Wood to Ken as Dean zoomed past.

'He's just stolen that bloody GPZ from our line outside,' called Don, who was cradling the other red fire extinguisher.

'He's what! Don't just gawp – go an' fetch them coppers.'

'But that car's burning like a torch!' said Ken sheepishly. 'It might set off the other one. How come the bike's burning too?'

'Someone was shooting at 'em from the top of the bank. You stay here then if you're too chicken. I'll go by meself…'

'Someone's shot them up?'

'That's what it sounded like.'

'One o' the coppers is running back to the car, look – the one that just dashed in the Cantina. Bloody mentalist, it's gonna catch.'

'He's going after our crim on the GPZ… In that bloody Cavalier…'

Constable Elland was driving outside himself, to stay within sight of the motorcycle-mounted terrorist who had tried to murder him so violently just a few minutes before, though another part of him, the sane, reasonable human being his friends and colleagues knew, was appalled he was risking his life again so soon after his first lucky escape, giving chase to the suspect on the red motorcycle. As the chase progressed, his anger was overcoming his training and better judgement. His primal instincts were rising to the fore and taking control. The fight or flight instinct buried deep inside every human being was rising towards its apogee within him and spurring him on. In the circumstances, his desire to take out his assailant by any means necessary seemed to him entirely reasonable.

It was a new experience hurtling past rural bus shelters at speeds well in excess of the national limits, close enough to see the mice leaping into the safety of the verges. But he reasoned that he could justify his actions as proportionate but not excessive if something went wrong. When it came to apprehending terrorists, normal operating procedures went out of the window.

The bodywork of his Cavalier had sustained a few cuts and bruises as he settled himself into some sort of rhythm in the first few minutes of the chase. The wings and bonnet panels were buckled, and bulged with hawthorn branches and the plump red hand of a Little Chef mannequin he had murdered wagged at him from the lip of the bonnet, where it had embedded itself during their fatal collision. The machine gun burst had had, up until now, no adverse effect on the handling of his vehicle. Most of the bullets had gone high. Those that missed the main body of the car had embedded themselves in the roof cradle, after chewing furrows in the roof wadding and roof rack track, though one round had pierced the upper bonnet vents and split the screen wash reservoir cap underneath. One of his ears was hanging off and the other one was full of lather.

Elland closed his eyes and swerved hard onto Butlins straight, sawing the steering wheel to stop the tyres sliding before he fed the screaming engine another gear and stamped down hard on the accelerator pedal. Up ahead at the edge of his vision he saw the rear brake-light of the motorcycle light up as the rider set the bike up to cross the John Paul Jones roundabout and rejoin the main road to Bridlington.

Dean decided the time had come to put some distance between himself and his pursuer. Crouching down behind the low plexiglass screen of the Kawasaki, he opened the throttle and watched the long white lines on the road blur and come together, concentrating on the contours of the landscape dead ahead, as it rolled into his vision, showing him where the road curved or tightened so he could adjust his position and speed. He was almost tempted to forget about the plan and let the copper chase him all over the county until the tank ran dry. But soon he was closing the distance to the trap he had set for the police within the old Victorian railway tunnel some eight or nine miles distant. He hoped he could soon draw another patrol car into the chase, from the layby used by lorry drivers for overnight stop overs beside Grizano's Italian takeaway, where the police often hid between the transporters, hoping to catch out unwary drivers or bikers rushing between the two towns.

As he flew past the line of parked trucks and cars with caravans, he glimpsed two traffic officers biting into their calzones, in front of a car transporter. The two men dropped their food and began to sprint back towards their car. Dean accelerated again and roared away.

A few minutes later, he throttled off and sat up into the wind as the tunnel and railway line came into sight. The wind caught his chest and rushed down his torso, almost lifting him off the seat. Braking hard, he went down through the gears, using the engine braking to scrub off more speed, eventually coming to a halt in the shadows at the mouth of the tunnel. Hopping off the bike, he flicked down the sidestand with the toe of his Doc Marten and took out his torch, walking further into the semi darkness, searching for the grimy black door in the wall. The stonework was dark and sooty, though several rivulets of water ran down from the brick arch overhead. Suddenly the torch beam caught the grimy outline of a brass handle which felt like ice in his hand. Once inside the chamber it was surprisingly dry and warm, around twenty feet long, seven or eight feet deep and about seven feet high, lined with stout painted tongue and groove panels and wooden boards over the ceiling, primed against rot by gallons of red lead primer. Its walls recalled an old railway station waiting room. A Tilley paraffin lamp had been lit and placed on a milking stool at the far end. The shelter had originally been built as a dormitory and cooking space for the railway engineers and construction managers at the turn of the century, so they could remain on site in warm surroundings during spells of bad weather, to study and rest.

Dean unzipped the holdall in the centre of the floor and took out the old anti tank weapon. Peeling off the greaseproof paper, he wiped down the painted steel and tried to remember all the information his grandfather's friend had divulged about its function and operation. It was reassuringly heavy, with adjustable sights and four range settings marked in luminous paint to enable soldiers to aim accurately in poor light or darkness.

In the closing months of World War 2, across the Eastern front, and during the battle for Berlin, Soviet tank crews had come to dread the Panzerfaust as much as a well directed Tiger or Panther tank, which were then too low on fuel and too low in numbers to make any significant contribution to the defence of the German Reich. Volkstrum and Hitler Youth units often rode towards the front lines on bicycles, with two of the weapons held by clips either side of their crossbars, hoping to kill Russian tanks, and self-propelled guns from the windows and doorways of abandoned houses, or from other hiding places within the denuded urban landscape of wartime Germany. They had become so successful that the Russian high command had been compelled to change their tactics, sending infantry teams ahead of the armoured units to flush out and neutralise any threat to their tank crews in an attempt to reduce their rate of attrition.

Cursing his luck, Constable Elland saw a police pursuit car from the Humberside force pull out of the long layby and truck stop a few hundred yards ahead of him and switch on its blue lights. As his radio aerial had been decapitated by a bullet, he had no means of communicating with any other pursuit teams. Basted in perspiration from his exertions, he drove on regardless, determined to stay in the chase, wiping the sweat from his forehead with his shirt sleeve before it ran into his eyes.

Dean emerged from the dormitory and leant the Panzerfaust against the wall. Doubling back to his stolen motorcycle, he pushed the GPZ1100 back out of the tunnel, then down the cinder track to the left of the bank and foundations. Hiding it behind a huge wall of ivy covering the borders of the path, he sprinted back into the tunnel, priming the Panzerfaust and resting it gently on his shoulder, lifting its nose towards a portion of the roof at the midpoint in the tunnel. Very carefully, he took aim and fired as the first car sped headlong into the black hole of the tunnel.

The projectile struck the roof just as the first patrol car reached the mid-point inside the length of the tunnel, triggering an avalanche of bricks, hardcore, fractured rock and a cascade of black gritty rainwater. Elland, now keeping pace close behind, swerved into the opposite lane to avoid a giant dagger of sandstone, which struck the tarmac in front of him like a giant's club. More bricks fell, bringing down with them a carpet of smaller rocks that pulverized his bonnet. The car slid to a halt, steam pouring from its grille, then the terrified traffic officer forced the door and fled towards the exit, holding his arms over his head.

'Won't it be full of water?'

'Nah. The Sea Cadet kids dry mop it every week and put an sock bag over the muzzle.'

'A sock bag? Who told you?'

'Me little brother's mate. He's in the Sea Cadets. The mop they use is over there on a nail under the Nissen hut's portico, bring it over and lean it on the barrel. We'll need it to push the wadding and the powder bag in.'

'Wadding?'

'Yeah. It's like padding, goes in after the powder but before the cannonball. Sit on top of the gun and get a can and sandwich out. Just act normal while I shove the powder in. That little tumbler I gave you is full of powder for the pan and chamber at the other end. Tip it down the hole, but leave some at the top around the edges, Amie.'

'Where's the rest of it?'

'In this bread bag. I need summat to prick it with…'

'Just use your finger.'

'Good idea.'

'There's a lot of it, Danny. Do you have to use all of it?'

'Well, this is what Brian gev us, so I guess it must be. Is anyone looking?'

'No, there's no one around, do you want the mop now?'

'Is it dry?'

'Feels dry – here, be quick.' Amie passed him the mop as he pushed his finger through the bread bag.

'Keep a look out, I'm sticking it in now.'

'There's no one about. What are you using for wadding?'

'Loft insulation.'

'Loft insulation, you crack me up.'

'It'll be right futt job.'

'Is it in?'

'Yep,' said Dan as he went into his bag for the wadding, jamming it into the barrel with the mop. 'Just the cannonball now.'

'Danny! There's a gang of kids and an old bloke coming up on the other side of the wall. Looks like a school party, they might be coming in here. We should hide.'

'Hang on,' he hissed, gritting his teeth, balancing the 63 pound cannonball on the edge of the muzzle before letting it roll down the barrel. 'It's in!'

'They're stopping at the gate, I think they're coming in.'

'We're done – let's go,' said Dan, grabbing his tote bag before starting a run towards the back of the barrack block. Amie followed him, glancing back to see if they had been spotted.

'Right, are we all here?' asked Mr Shannon, looking over the heads of the Year 4 History group from Horsforth Comprehensive. 'Good,' he said, after doing a quick head count with his pen. 'All present. Foster, pay attention. Now as you know, we don't have time to see the castle today, but we do have time to see a relic of the civil war before we finish for today. The Whitborough Sea Cadets have given us permission to view a historically important cannon used by Cromwell's forces during the conflict. It is very rare to see such old guns still intact, as most were melted down and used for other purposes when they were obsolete. So let's go into the parade ground and take a look.' He said, ushering his pupils through the gate into the compound where his class congregated around the old gun.

'Sir, there's some powdery stuff in the pan, look,' said one of the boys, bending over the breech.

'I very much doubt it's gunpowder, Matthew. It's probably flakes of paint or dirt.'

'Looks like gravy granules sir,' said one of the others, provoking a snigger amongst his peers.

'Baldwin, if you don't pay attention you can stay here and we can go over this again while the rest of you are enjoying the delights of Whitborough. Do I have your attention?'

'Yes, sir.'

'Right, now listen. I'll be asking you questions about this and the other things we've seen today; this may also come up in your exams. So listen carefully. Can anyone tell me the name of this gun and the reason why it's here? It's on your fact sheets, if you remembered to bring them. Elliott?'

'Is it a Royal Cannon, sir?'

'Almost right, but you've got the name back to front, this

gun was called the Cannon Royal. It was the most powerful artillery piece used by the Parliamentarians against the Royalist garrison here. It was brought to the town specifically to bring down the outer walls, so Cromwell's army could capture the Castle.'

'Sir... they had another cannon too, called Sweet lips after a prossie from Hu...'

'Bennett, I think...'

'It's true though – it ses so in this leaflet fromt library.'

'Thank you Bennett, your timing is impeccable as always, let's...'

'Doesn't look as though it worked, sir.'

'Allt walls are still up,' added another pupil.

'Some of the walls you see are not the original structures. The keep that we see here now, was almost brought down by guns like these. A large part of what you see today was rebuilt after the siege. Repairs and extensions or strengthening works have taken place here and on other sites throughout their history. What we see here today is the work of centuries, not a building as it might have appeared when it was first built.'

'So did they get in sir, the Roundheads?'

'No. The siege was broken when the garrison surrendered. They had run out of food and water, and realised that help was not coming. They surrendered in the summer of 1645, as you all know, or should know if you've done your reading. Come closer to me, so that all of you can see.'

'Can we go into town straight after, sir?'

'Yes Cutforth, you may. You've got four hours, that's all. So make sure you're all back here at the minibus at the right time, or you'll be walking back to Wykeham. So, here we have an example of a gun made from a single casting. Rather than the guns that were common during the medieval period that were made from two halves and then fastened together by thick iron bands, these guns were still smooth-bore but much faster in operation than earlier weapons. Once the powder chambers were primed, dry wadding inserted and their elevation set, the gun was loaded and ready for firing. Can anyone tell me what this is?' asked Mr Shannon, holding up a long piece of dried reed.

'It's a match sir, a taper. They used them to fire the guns.'

'Well done, Goddard. This is a piece of reed taper. Once it had been dried out it was the perfect way to set a flame to the gunpowder; we'll light this piece in a moment to demonstrate how these guns were fired. Because reed grows to such great length, it meant that the man lighting the gun did not have to stand so close to the ordnance when the burning end was put into the pan. When guns like these were made in greater numbers and the integrity of castings were improved, artillerymen began to use linstocks, which were pieces of wood with a whole drilled through them, for holding a match or cloth. Tabitha, this is for your benefit as well as the boys',' said Mr Shannon, addressing one of the other students who was staring listlessly at the ground. 'If you're not going to give this your fullest attention, then you'll be coming back to Wykeham with me. Elliot, pass me the matches from the map pocket of my tank bag on the bench there…'

A blinding white flash exploded from the muzzle of the cannon, and a pall of silence, which was not really a silence at all but the still centre of an expanding aural singularity that bleached out all other sound in its own hellish vacuum, sent shock waves across the parade ground, cracking the window panes in the Nissen huts and barrack building nearby, and rattling the casements at the rear of the row of the Victorian terrace houses on Paradise Lane, shattering the peace. The force of the recoil caused the gun to jump its blocks and roll down the incline onto Procession Way through the open gates, the old wheels and axles shrieking in protest. The gun's momentum scoured away decades of rust and corrosion as it picked up speed.

It took just three short seconds for the cannonball to reach HMS Heddon, a type 42 destroyer, from the Sea Cadets' parade ground on Whapple Bank, striking her first and second communication and radar towers amidships behind the bridge. Despite losing thirty percent of its velocity travelling through the tallest parts of her superstructure, the 63 pound ball of pig iron still possessed the power to deliver a large helping of death and destruction to anything within its trajectory, which was at that exact moment in time a Lynx Helicopter with a full fuel load, carrying the Mayor and Mayoress of Whitborough, the ship's Commander and the Town Clerk – with full stomach loads.

Several million pounds of expensively crafted components, two experienced naval officers, the helicopter crew and three experienced scroungers were suddenly broken up and violently scattered about, attacking the aft sections of the ship like a giant demented bead blaster. Every painted surface next to the blast swiftly disintegrated under the red hot raking claws of supersonic shrapnel and a few sharp fragments of some fine civic regalia, the Mayor's chains of office. The cannonball completed its arc by decapitating a show-off who was unwrapping a choc ice on his jetski.

Mr Shannon came unsteadily to his feet, looking out into the bay over the terrace of houses in front of them as a fireball erupted from the back of the Royal Navy Destroyer moored in the bay. Some of his pupils were quietly crying, some were sitting looking stunned on the asphalt, some were shouting at him. But he couldn't hear a thing. He couldn't hear his own voice. Then he became conscious that he'd wet himself.

Danny and Amie had instinctively ducked down when they heard the explosion cut through the air like a sonic boom.

'Now we're in it...'

'Oh my God! Look! It's hit the ship in the harbour,' said Amie, panicking. 'We're going to get locked up for the rest of our days!'

'No we're not Amie. We didn't fire it did we... oh no! That helicopter just blew up!'

'We've got to get out of here.'

'Don't run. Just walk slow. No one saw us on the gun.'

'Did you mean it to do that?'

'No, of course I bloody didn't. Course I didn't. Blow it up – yeah. Brian told me we'd break it or crack it, using all that powder.'

'Why put the wadding in then, and the cannonball – you idiot!'

'Because I needed to block the cannonball inside to wreck it. I brought some steel wedges and rods to put down after the ball to jam it like Brian told me to, but those bloody sixth formers got here before I could ram them in, didn't they.'

Meanwhile, inside the Bunch of Keys, oblivious to the destruction so near to them, the men and women of Brazen and Heddon were digging in for an afternoon of brazen debauchery. Tables were swung and slammed together, the dartboard and pool tables were mobbed and the Fairy Liquid uncapped behind the bar. The pub's regulars, who would have been drifting in quietly, taking a stool and making conversation, watched helplessly as the invading force took over their peaceful public house with barely a nod to its occupants or a note to the staff.

Normally the haunt of veteran school teachers, lecturers and grey-haired rock fans, the pub now resembled one of the naval drinking dens on Union St in Plymouth, full of hormone-rich hooligans with hard-ons, looking for a girl with a shiny handbag to plug themselves into.

On a soft leather bench in the mid section of the Keys, Petty Officer Robin Leeks began to swap stories with his girlfriend Georgie, a barmaid from the Equestrian public house on Arguments Lane, observing the cosmopolitan collection of beer mats that covered the walls. Directly in front of them, spread out on stools around the small tables or reclining on the benches, sat a party of marines from Heddon, drinking steadily in a blue haze of cigarette smoke as they worked their way down the pub's blackboard of guest beers, between trips to the men's where they sprayed the cracked porcelain like busy fire engines.

'Gerrush another bottle of that Kasteel shtuff again shomeone, ahm hoff forra piss fust tho… alwight?' said one of the young men, slurring badly as he attempted to stand and grab hold of the bar to steady himself before his walk, but he let his hand drop heavily onto the arm of one of the Key's barmaids, who screamed in pain as he pinned her wrist against the ridge of a glass ashtray.

'Whatcho screaming at! Silly cow! Never touched yer!' protested the marine, who then made the situation worse by lunging at the barmaid with his mouth open, waggling his tongue. 'Gish a snog darling,' though Amy Gallagher was not in the mood for any sort of clumsy approach from a member of the opposite sex, especially a leering drunk. Before he could muster another word, she cracked him around the head with her good hand, into which she had pushed another ashtray, sending him sprawling back over the tables amongst his companions.

At once the atmosphere in the middle section of the pub changed from one of woozy congeniality to belligerence and outrage. Although his comrades in arms had felt some sympathy for the girl, her overreaction had completely altered their disposition towards her, and she was doing nothing to calm the situation, continuing to glare at her assailant whilst arguing ferociously with his peers.

Richard Austin, the landlord, a man at least as big as Geoff Capes, heard the commotion and stomped down into the middle bar, wading clumsily into the fray with a disastrous opening comment about some elements of the armed forces giving the town a bad name. Already annoyed that the invaders were squeezing out his regulars, he was not in the mood to hear the navy's side of events. The inebriated marine provided the match that lit the fuse, by hurling abuse at the barmaid as he tried to make his feet. Austin, towering above the party like a grizzly bear, then uttered the words that every landlord keeps at the back of his mind for emergencies, on this occasion in the collective sense, then began to clear the benches using his bulk to bounce the marines towards the exit. So the navy went to war, hurling their stools over the bar to make space for a brawl. Petty Officer Leeks, until now a spectator, decided to intervene and appeal for calm, though Georgie his next and best was already under their table, searching for her hairdresser's comb and rape alarm. But Robin had discovered too late that he was unable to stand after four pints of Pebbletrees 'Owd Bob. His brain had withdrawn normal service and refused to animate his body in the proper manner, as it was playing twister with the millions of intricate connections inside his central nervous system.

On the sands of Victoria Bay, opposite the veiled broom cupboard of Cubitt Mekare the world famous Indian palmist, a fizzing orange claw of blazing scrap crashed through the balding roofing felt and the thin marine plywood boards of the deck chair dispensary roof, igniting a row of dusty Calor gas cylinders at the back of a stack of chairs. The subsequent blast sent a blizzard of bayonet-sized splinters and burning nylon weave over the bare arms and legs of the tourists watching the slow death of the town's adopted destroyer. Fred Chadwick, from Merton Drive in Farsley, dived into a sandpit a moment before the tail rotor from the Lynx passed over his windbreak, disembowelling a penny falls machine in the Viva Las Vegas amusement arcade. Panic gripped the crowds as burning shrapnel began to fall from the sky onto the beach, foreshore road and the pavements, still teeming with visitors tackling their cornets and back-combed candy floss.

'THE BLOODY SHITTING SHIT'S SHON FRYER!' yelled Sub Lieutenant Reid from the top tier of the pub, dropping his pager into a pint of Theakstons.

'EH?'

'WASSAT?'

'The bloody shit, THE SHIT'S SHON FIRE!' exclaimed the officer, scarcely able to believe his own voice, or understand it.

'The ship's shonfire shir? Did you shay it washshonfire?' asked one of the ratings, screwing up his face.

'YESH! SHOURSHIPS SHON FIRE!'

'WHAAAT!'

'Shitting ruddy shitcakes!' spluttered one of the wrens.

'MOOOOOVE! MOOVE!' yelled the junior officer, overturning his table. 'OUTSIDE! NOW!' he yelled, rising too sharply and knocking himself out on an iron shelf brace. There was a short pause before the beer-laden bodies of two ships' companies ran, stumbled and scrambled towards the exits, as the brawl between Austin and the marines continued almost unnoticed, the landlord clubbing the navy into submission with his huge fists.

Two milk floats, coming down the road at top speed, rounded the bend, swerving to avoid the sailors running out of the Bunch of Keys into the road, then high sided on a puddle of diesel left by a local bus, crashing into each other and overturning, throwing crates of milk and yoghurt over the already slippery tarmac. More of the ships' crews staggered outside, falling off the thin kerb into the road at the very moment a huge shoal of cycle racers rushed silently around the curve on the edges of their skinny tyres.

The event which would later go down in local history as the Milk Race Massacre was recorded quite by chance by an elderly resident of Whistler's care home, overlooking Parsley Sage Street, who was inviting the staff to admire his new video camera. Tony Bullock, the manager and his trusted deputy the home secretary, Jane Dickinson, had alerted Mr

245

Candy to the noise in the street below, and beckoned him to the large second floor bay window overlooking the pub just as the milk floats were heard accelerating towards the drunken melee.

The lycra-clad cavalry of the pelaton had opened hostilities with a blitzkrieg-like spearhead of irresistible speed and penetration, routing the shambling leaderless hordes of the navy, who were in the majority of cases only a few drinks short of a state of catatonia. The cyclists should have carried the day, but made the mistake of pausing to assess their casualties, losing the initiative and the battle at a stage when another push and some calculated aggression would have given them victory. But they were not military men, and were ignorant of the rules and strategies of war. The navy, brutalised but unbowed, began to regroup and take strides towards their attackers, who were worried enough to retreat and draw bicycle pumps, an ill-advised act of foolishness which only poured more fuel onto the fires of the navy's ire.

Consumed by a bitter determination to restore their injured pride, the sailors attacked as best they could, across a landscape of broken glass, broken men and mangled bicycles scattered over a slick of yoghurt, diesel and battery acid. The landscape of the battlefield was a guide dog's worse nightmare, a cornucopia of trip hazards and sharps. But after an hour and a half of gulping down the strongest ales that England and Belgium could provide, the attackers had all the anaesthetic a man going to war could ever want.

'Shall I keep it running, Mr Bullock?' asked Mr Candy, looking across to the manager of the home, who was watching the brawl with the expression of someone at once fascinated and repelled.

'Did you see what that man just did with that bicycle spoke?' cried Jane, peeping through her fingers.

'Has anyone called the police?' asked Mrs Candy, moving her head back and forth to try and get a better view of the carnage behind the throng at the window. 'Philly, call the police would you dear, there's a fight outside on Sage Street,' she shouted, trying to catch the attention of her friend, who was engrossed in a particularly tricky crochet at their table in the middle of the lounge.

'I'll be right there, dear,' she replied. 'Two ticks.'

'You stay there, Phillys,' said her friend April on the opposite side of the sofa, putting down a copy of Yorkshire Life. 'I'll go instead – I could do with the exercise.'

As more reinforcements trickled out of the upper and lower exits of the Bunch of Keys to bolster the big push, their opponents realised they had only a few more seconds in which to choose the direction of their escape, before they were trapped in front of the high wall which bordered the road and the cottage garden of the nursing home. Some turned and began to sprint or hobble up the hill, but the majority fled or limped down to the roundabout in Kenwith Ravine, leaving ten or twelve of their less agile colleagues facing the onslaught. Two of the cyclists who had lost their shoes had hurriedly dismantled a derailleur, and were using the sprockets as deadly throwing stars before they were rushed and overwhelmed. Then the last sparks of resistance were snuffed out under a flurry of kicks and punches.

'Whitborough Police, Constable Elland speaking. How can we help?'

'It's April. Hello? Can you hear me there? You're not very clear…'

'It's not April until Monday, Madam. This is the police station.'

'No. You're misunderestimating me, you cheeky man. You know what I mean. Are you a policeman?'

'I am a policeman, madam. You've called the police station. My name is Constable Elland.'

'Leyland you say? Ugh, horrid cars. Anyway – good – I'm sure you're a wonderful young man. We'd like four, certainly three of you at least, because there's a lot of them. Maybe five, in a van. I want to report a fracas. Some people are having a fracas down below. It's not Spanish.'

'I'm sorry, I'm not sure I understood you correctly, madam. You'd like to report a what?'

'It's not like tapas. It's a fracas, half of them are sailor boys and the others are wearing these skimpy vests and tiny tight little shorts, indecent – is what it is, they're taking it all out in public, Leyland. Are you listening?'

'Madam, my name is Elland…'

'Elland? Where's Leyland? It was him I was speaking to, why can't I speak to him? Are you listening? They're giving it to each other in public, whipping each other with cables and chains. My friend's been filming it. It can't be legal, doing what they're doing on the street. And they're smeared in yoghurt. Everyone's been drinking.'

'Am I to understand you're at an orgy of some sort, madam.'

'It's an orgy all right. A disgrace. You'd better get some

of your men down before it's over. Or you'll miss it. Hello? Hello! He's hung it up on me, Phyllis…'

'Try again, dear. Did you ring 999?'

'No, I rang the reception desk at the station, it's the number on the card by the phone.'

'Oh I wouldn't bother with them. Waste of time, ring 999. Do you want me to speak to them?'

'You call them dear, I might make a bit of a hash of it again. I'll put it back on the cradle.'

'Spink here, Captain. Territorials. Got a message to contact your inspector – something urgent?'

'Hold the line, sir. Putting you through now.'

'Inspector Marshall?'

'Captain.'

'I received your message, Inspector. How can I help?'

'I'll come straight to the point, Captain Sink.'

'It's Spink…'

'Yes of course, Captain – I'm sorry, my apologies – I was thinking of something else. We've got a number of major incidents that we're going to be hard pressed to deal with, at least until my request for more officers is granted. In the circumstances I need as many men as you can muster to help fill a few gaps in the line, if you'll pardon the expression. We're short of manpower, because too many of our officers are tied up guarding the approach roads to Valley Bridge and the bridge itself for the Royal Engineers, so they can defuse an old German bomb a tourist stumbled on today – and that was before the terrorist attack at Carr Wold Parkway and the ship…'

'Terrorist attacks!'

'You're aware the navy have two ships in the bay?'

'Yes, Heddon and Brazen. My son's in the Sea Scouts.'

'One of our officers witnessed a large explosion on HMS Heddon. Their helicopter was destroyed in the blast – the Mayoress and the Town Clerk were on board. The ship is on fire along a third of its length…'

'My God! I had no idea. I…'

'If you please, Captain – there is more.'

'I'm sorry. My nephew's in the Sea Cadets. He's…'

'Two of our patrol cars at the Parkway were attacked by terrorists using automatic weapons before the ship was fired upon, the exit to our garage and car pound has been booby trapped, and I have reports of sabotage by persons unknown on the signalling tower at the railway station and the coastguard Station at Filey. Frankly, we don't have the capacity to cope at the moment. Any men you can provide will be under our jurisdiction of course. If you could bring with you any small arms you may have, they might be needed. My officers will oversee your men until we have more support from our own firearms units. Captain?'

'I'll have to clear it with Northallerton. I don't know who I can get at short notice – we're fourteen short and two on the sick. Half the men are in Germany on a big NATO exercise with the Green Howards.'

'Just do the best you can.'

'Yes, yes of course, until later then…'

'Elland!'

'Inspector?'

'Elland, I want to know straight away when Captain Spink calls back. And your brother, good lad.'

'Yes, sir. I have a Mr Jenkin waiting on the line from

the Council Depot reporting a vehicle theft. We don't have anyone available to send to take a statement. Shall I ask him to come to the station?'

'No. Not now. There may be some soldiers arriving in the next hour or so from the Territorial unit. And they may be armed. Call me the moment they arrive. Who's this Jenkin?'

'The foreman. He's quite agitated.'

'Put the call through.'

'Yes, sir.'

'Hello, this is Inspector Marshall, to whom am I speaking?'

'Charlie Jenkin, I'm duty foreman at the transport depot. I'm calling to report a missing snowplough, a post-hole borer and a stonecutter. Not that this seems to be important to your receptionist right now.'

'Mr Jenkin, may I express my regret that we cannot send you one of our officers to take your statement, but I have several very serious emergency situations to deal with this afternoon and we cannot send anyone to investigate.'

'Them's expensive vehicles – snowploughs, not to mention the power tools, thousands they are. What kind of fool steals a bloody snowplough in April? I reckon it's an inside job – there weren't even a battery in the plough. How'd they know where they were kept, eh? Cos we mothball 'em in the spring – well there's no call… is there… are you there?'

'Mr Jenkin. We will send an officer to you as soon as we can. Now could you please secure your other vehicles for the time being. Goodbye.'

'Suspend the buses as well! Are you pulling me leg? Hello?' But Inspector Marshall had already hung up.

'Elland! Priority calls only to me until further notice.

251

Understood? Your brother's got his hands full at the moment son, although he's not called in. But a pursuit car from Humberside near Grizano's is in sight of him.'

'Yes sir! Priority calls only, sir. Thank you, sir.'

'Don't worry about Sean lad, he's as hard as a kerb. Tell me the minute the army arrive.'

For young people of a certain age, Friday and Saturday nights in Whitborough were always the same and followed a set pattern. Bikers hit the seafront from seven pm sharp, putting in two or three sighting laps of the foreshore to gather together their strays, each gang using the last lap to practice the fine arts of brutal acceleration, braking and wheelies once the immediate area had been checked for the forces of law and order.

After coming together and parking up in front of the beach railings, they swarmed into the arcades to sharpen their reflexes on the banks of interactive games consoles and booths, murdering thousands of aliens, Nazis, Viet cong or killer sharks served up into their gun sights before the change booth ran out of ammunition. An hour or so later a ceasefire was usually agreed, to allow time for the first main event of the evening, a full throttle charge through the town and its outskirts for the Leverly Inn and the Shirestones at the edge of the moors.

Stuffed with cod and chips and adrenalin from their bloodthirsty killing frenzies, swarms of modern day fighter pilots climbed aboard throaty Japanese four strokes or screaming two strokes and took off at speed, leaving a smog of exhaust fumes and the smoky perfume of Castrol R to choke the throats of terrified car drivers pushed into the kerbs in their wake.

At around the same time, in the town centre streets, the punk gangs who had waited for early doors stormed into their local pubs to seize territory around the jukeboxes and pool tables, piling stacks of coins onto the wood veneer sides of the tables above the coin trays, then throwing their jackets over the furniture as a mark of occupation, returning from the bars minutes later with trays of cider.

By nine o'clock the oases of alternative culture were close to capacity. Inside the Stage Door, the Salvation, the Jack of both Sides, or the JennyComeQuick on Long Acre, all the tribes of the music scene were coming out to play. Bikers, rockers, glam rockers, sleaze rockers and moshers partied and intermingled with punks, goths, psychobillies, greebos, skinheads, stoners and rude boys in the bars.

Danny drew up slowly onto the thin kerb of Rope Walk, opposite the fire escape at the back of Mystery City, one of Whitborough's busiest rock clubs, then checked the mirrors of his Ford Capri before getting out and cautiously opening the rear hatch. He lifted out Brian's red tool box, taking care not to make any noise, and set it down close to the rear skirt then locked the car. Another glance up and down the old warehouse fronts reassured him he was still the only visitor on the lane, so he grasped the toolbox and crossed the old flags to the bottom of the fire escape. The emergency exit doors above onto the second landing had been left ajar by the cleaners, to let the warm evening air inside to freshen the club and dry the floors, so taking advantage of his good luck he crept inside and made his way warily past the leather benches, to the hidden access panel at the side of the stage beside the DJ's island.

'What's that hissing noise?' asked Brian, whispering.

'I don't know,' answered Dave, looking over the floor anxiously in the gloom of Edith's pen, searching for a punctured inner tube or a deflating toy which might explain the source of the noise.

The hiss suddenly changed pitch to a faltering squeak, as if the portal through which the air was escaping had suddenly constricted. It changed again as quickly to a deep bass rumble, followed by a series of pops and flatulent blasts of the kind one would expect to hear from a hunting horn made from damp cardboard.

'Oh God, I think I'm going to be sick,' muttered Dave quietly, using all his self control to keep from retching. 'I can't breathe,' he moaned, hurrying to the door and holding it ajar to get some relief' greedily sucking in great gulps of clean air. 'It stinks like a shithouse in a heat wave.'

'Put your mask on,' exclaimed Brian through two centimetres of wadding doused in generous splashes of Ocean Breeze car air freshener concentrate. 'I'm going to the grooming box – keep an eye on sleeping beauty,' he said, walking flush against the wall to the timber store on the adjoining wall over the carpet of wood chippings.'

Dave, feeling guilty, pulled his inadequate decorator's mask back over his nose and chin, then closed up the door, being very careful to push it quietly back into its casing. Satisfied it was secure, he relaxed and turned around, took a deep breath and stepped forwards onto a squeaky football.

The great rhino grunted and half rolled, trying to right herself, looking for the source of the noise – her eyes were now fully opened, though they were next to useless in the gloom. But the scent of strangers and another strong artificial perfume registered instantaneously in the damp recesses of her enormous nostrils. Edith snorted and charged.

Outside the pen shook once, then twice as the panic-stricken interlopers tried to avoid being impaled on Edith's horn or crushed like flies by her rampaging bulk. A rent appeared in the feeding hatch at the side of the hut, splitting the wood and jamming the lid in its seat. Then the side door flew open and the Drake brothers fled for their lives. All the grunts, cries and blows on the baby monitor inside Edith's quarters woke Damien and Mitsu, the waking night staff, who were slumped in their chairs dozing at the desk in the park's office. Scrambling to their feet half awake, they grabbed their rifles, tranquilliser darts and spotlights, forced their eyes to focus momentarily on the monitor receiver board, then ran gracelessly towards the door.

'Crispybatters… dipcurrants, strokyme me.' Lord William Henry Warner Woollens had gone to bed early and was dreaming, talking in his sleep as Edith began cleaning out her shed. As dreams went, it was one of the best he'd had. He was smiling broadly but dribbling, laid on his back in the warm sunshine of a tropical island on a hot bed of smoked salmon, having his skin skimmed with long ostrich feathers held by beaming Polynesian women. The bright Gauguinesque paradise then began to dim as an urgent voice in his head broke forth and tore down the backdrop to his imaginary paradise. It was the voice of an actor recreating the terrible scene when Edmond Dantes was cast into his cell in the Chateau d'If. His audiobook version of The Count of Monte Cristo was still running. Awake now but not in full control of his faculties, his eyes were drawn to a flashing red light within a cluster of two marked 'RHINO', on the bespoke status alert box made from several salvaged Rolls Royce dashboards and instrument lights. Lord Warner Woollens sat up and slid his toes into his Tiger Feet slippers, pulled on his dressing gown then went to his wardrobe for his miner's hard hat and lamp, and opened a case marked 'Speargun'.

www.alistairlavers.co.uk

Whitborough on Sea

Principal street index

261

Bibliography

Bishop, Patrick, *'Fighter Boys': Saving Britain 1940*, HarperCollins, 2003.

Mee, Arthur, *'The King's England, Devon.'* Hodder & Stoughton, 1965.

Cooke, David, *'Yorkshire Sieges of the Civil Wars.'* Pen and Sword Books Ltd, 2011.

Shakespeare, William, *'A Midsummer Night's Dream.'* Penguin Books, 1994.

Hardy, Thomas, *'Far from the Madding Crowd.'* Planet Three Publishing Network Ltd, 2003.

Conway, David, *'Magic: An Occult Primer.'* Aquarian Press, 1988.

www.warbirdsresourcegroup.org, *'Luftwaffe Resource Centre.'*

the lydianmode.com *'The Trial of King Charles I.'*

Principal Characters.

Brian Drake - Proprietor of Clash City Records. Smuggler.

Dave Drake - Brother of Brian and co - owner of Clash City Records.

Dean Beadle - Senior Sales Assistant at Clash City Records.

Michael Oak - Assistant Manager at Clash City Records.

Fenella Parrish - Proprietor of The Owl and Pussycat Interior Design Emporium. Michael's girlfriend

Amie van der Kop - Sales Assistant at Clash City Records. Dog trainer and former S.A Police Dog Handler.

Derek Beautimann - Partner at Beautimann Buerk and Trippe Solicitors. Master of Ceremonies and Grand Wizard of the Black Hand Coven.

Maureen Moment - Derek's Legal Secretary. Deputy Master of Ceremonies for the Black Hand Coven.

Neil Rudding - First Cousin of the Drake Bothers. Trawlerman and Coal Hump Champion 1978-82.

Robert Rudding - Second Cousin of the Drake Brothers. Apprentice machine minder at offset lithography printers Bon Scott & Sons. Guitarist in local rock covers band Dick Armpit.

Inspector Ray Marshall

Detective Sergeant George Broadhead

Constables Andrew Elland, Sean Elland.

Constable Justin Deighton

Constable Clifford Dodds

Lindsay Boldwood - Landlord of The Shirestones Hotel, Cloughton. Ex R.N, Werewolf.

Lord William Henry Warner Woollens. Head of the Warner Woollens family. Owner of Charlwood Zoo and the Charlwood Estate, Cloughton.

Lawrence Baston Demarque. Numismatist and Archaeological Metallurgist. Based in York.

Alan Chipping. Local Historian based in Whitborough.

Albert 'Incapability' Barnes. Semi retired Gardener at Charlwood Manor.

Ludwig Kalbach. Dean's Grandfather. Retired surveyor and former P.O.W.

Elsie Cakebread. Retired District Nurse and Medium. Co-owner of Valhalla Retirement Home.

Anthony Binnie. Owner of Movie Street video hire.

Isla Binnie. Manageress of Isla's Fashions.